Patricia Brown

# A RECIPE FOR DYING

*GladEye Press*
*Springfield, OR*

Interior Design: J.V. Bolkan
Cover Design: Sharleen Nelson
Copyediting: GladEye Press
*Special thanks to Colin Miller & Laura Potter for preproduction reviews and assistance.*

ISBN: 978-0-9911931-8-9

The body text is presented in Garamond, an old style typeface inspired by the famed French printer Claude Garamond in the 16th century. Special sections were set in Candara, a humanist sans-serif typeface designed by Gary Munch.

# A Recipe
## for Dying

PATRICIA BROWN

*For Karly,*
*Happy reading!*
*Patricia Brown*

Dedicated to old friends.

T uesday, May 16: Eleanor Penrose opened one eye and began her daily inventory; Walter isn't here, no one is here, dinner with Angus, must bake a pie. She looked out the floor-to-ceiling window at the Pacific Ocean gleaming in the bright sunlit day. It was time to get her achy old bones up and get busy. Busy kept the blues away.

As she lifted the cover from the birdcage, Feathers greeted her with his normal, "Good morning, Ellie". He was such a polite bird and so affectionate. She welcomed his sweet parrot kisses and gave him a treat. Feathers was Walter's pet. He had learned everything he knew from Walter. Eleanor stroked his sleek, gray feathers and left him to fly freely about the house while she went to the kitchen to start her baking.

Once the apple pie was in the oven, she took off her apron, put on one of Walter's old sweaters, and left the house for a quick morning walk. Even though the sun was shining, the ocean air was always cool. She would take the path to the east through the woods and circle back in time to take the pie out of the oven. Walter would have cautioned her not to leave the house with something in the oven, but Walter wasn't here.

What a grand and glorious day! She breathed in the clean, fresh ocean air and felt like skipping down the path. Too old to skip, she thought sadly. What if you fall? There would be no one to miss you for hours. Your pie would burn and maybe the house too. She walked quickly, now anxious to return before anything bad could happen to an old woman alone. Lost in thoughts of the past she made a mental list of what she would cook for dinner with Angus, oblivious to the lush green of the grass and the fragrant pines that surrounded her until suddenly, there was motion ahead. Startled out of her reverie, Eleanor saw a young girl sitting on the steep side trail clutching one knee to her chest, twigs were in her hair and dirt streaked across her tearful face.

"Oh my, I see you've had a tumble. Are you hurt?" asked Eleanor.

"Well, there is blood," the girl replied.

"I'm a nurse. Let me help." Eleanor did not know why she would tell a lie to a child. It really wasn't like her one bit.

"I think I can walk, but my mom will be really mad if she sees how dirty I am."

"You could come to my house. It isn't far away, and I could clean you up and you'd be right as rain."

"I'm in a foul mood," she sighed.

"Perfect! You can meet my late husband's parrot, Feathers. He's always fowl." Nothing. Maybe this girl had no sense of humor.

Bootsy gave Eleanor a look of skepticism. "My mother told me not to speak to strangers."

"Child, however do you make friends with that attitude?"

"Hmm, I guess my mother is stranger than you!" It was the first smile Eleanor had seen from her. It lit up her face and made her dark, brown eyes sparkle with mischief.

"So, who are you?" Eleanor asked. "I'm Eleanor Penrose."

"My name is Bootsy Greenwood," she said. "I'm staying with my Grandmother, Granny Scattergoods."

"Oh, I know her! Glad to meet you, Bootsy Greenwood, now we aren't strangers anymore!" Eleanor reached out her hand and helped Bootsy to her feet. A small drop of blood rolled down her bare leg from what looked like a minor scrape. Eleanor knew she could deliver on her promise to patch it up, despite her little fib.

As they walked back to Eleanor's house, Bootsy said, "Granny had a stroke. We were afraid she would die. She is in the hospital."

"I know. It's scary when things happen you can't control."

"How did your husband die?"

"My husband . . . dead? I didn't say he was dead . . ."

"You said your late husband had a bird."

"Well yes, he's just late. He's late for everything—appointments, dinner, everything. He went fishing and he hasn't returned."

"How long has he been gone?"

"Three years."

They made it to Eleanor's house. Bootsy paused on the doorstep as Eleanor unlocked the door. The porch was recently swept and had large ceramic pots filled with fragrant flowers of pink and purple, and she noticed the way the beautiful stained-glass window sparkled as it caught the sun's light. Everything looked clean and new, yet Bootsy braced herself for what she knew would meet her on the other side of an old person's door. The blast of old everything—old furniture, old carpet, dust, mold, whatever the awful odor was that clung to old people in their old houses. It was the smell of Granny Scattergoods' house. She hated it as much as she loved Granny. She really hoped Eleanor did not own a cat. But when Eleanor opened the polished oak door, the aroma of freshly baked apple pie flew up Bootsy's nose and tickled the pleasure center of her brain. As she stepped inside she was surprised at the wide bank of windows that looked out at the ocean and lit every corner of the open space. Airy and light, the total opposite of Granny's dark, cluttered space.

"Please excuse me, Bootsy, I'll be right back." Eleanor quickly navigated to the kitchen to rescue her pie. Bootsy walked slowly around the space and took in the contents of the room.

"Beautiful," she thought. Everything in this room is beautiful. From the tasteful art on the walls to the plush carpet on the spotless floor, everything sparkled and shone. Even the books on the bookshelves were richly bound in leather and artfully arranged in a way that pleased the eye. She ran her finger along the shelf and found not a speck of dust. Who lived like this? What kind of old lady was Eleanor?

Eleanor returned and led Bootsy down the hall and into the bathroom.

"Let's get you cleaned up," she said.

As Eleanor worked on cleaning and bandaging Bootsy's wounds, Bootsy continued to take in all the clues she could to learn about Eleanor. The bathroom was free of mildew. There was no ring around the tub or hair in the sink. There were no dirty clothes on the floor or wet towels hanging over the door. Finally, her curiosity got the better of her and she began to give Eleanor the third degree.

"Do you live here alone?"

"No."

"Who else lives here?"

"I'll introduce you later."

"You said you were a nurse. Do you still work?"

"No, I was never really a nurse. I'm a retired teacher."

"Oh, what did you teach?"

"English."

"Why did you say you were a nurse?"

"Forgive me, Bootsy, I just wanted to help you. Sometimes I feel like I could have been a nurse."

"How old are you?"

"Seventy-two."

"How long have you lived in Sand Beach?"

"My husband and I retired and moved here 10 years ago." Eleanor applied the band-aid with a flourish and asked, "How does that feel?"

"Good, thank you, I guess you could have been a nurse."

Eleanor smiled and asked, "Would you like a piece of pie? I like to think I could have been a pastry chef."

"It really does smell delicious," Bootsy replied, licking her lips.

"Well then, let's go into the kitchen."

As they left the bathroom there was a flurry of wings and loud screeching. Bootsy ducked down quickly and screamed, startling even Eleanor who knew it was Feathers.

"Let me introduce you to my roommate, Feathers. He is an African Grey Parrot."

Feathers landed gracefully on Eleanor's shoulder, and said in a low masculine voice, "Well, hello there!"

Bootsy and Eleanor simultaneously broke into hysterical laughter.

As Bootsy ate her delicious piece of apple pie, she gave up looking for clues or signs of old lady flaws and just enjoyed herself. She delighted in the interest Eleanor showed in her and began to talk about herself without caution.

"I'm 10, but my mother says I'm precocious. That means I act older than 10, maybe 12, although my mother says I'm 10 going on 20. Most of my friends can't read as well as I can. I absolutely love to read. My favorite book is *Anne of Green Gables*. Have you read it? I think you might be a kindred spirit." Bootsy paused to take another bite of pie.

Eleanor sipped her coffee and nodded politely. She could not respond before Bootsy began again.

"My family and I live in Portland. We haven't visited Granny as often as we should because my mother and father both work and I mean they work a lot. Sometimes I visited here when school was out for summer vacation, but lately Granny hasn't been well enough to take me. She has something called osteoporosis which makes her bones weak and arthritis too which makes her joints ache. It must be really awful to be old." Eleanor was amused and a little amazed that the words seemed to keep coming without a pause for breath. "We are staying at her house and visiting her in the hospital since she had a stroke, which is caused by a blockage in the blood vessels to her brain. My mother is cleaning her house right now. I just had to get out because Granny hasn't been able to clean very much and her house is a mess."

Bootsy finally paused to take a breath, "My mom is really upset about the house because it reeks. She is trying to get it cleaned up so we can stay there until we know that Granny will be okay. I'm missing school right now but that's fine because school is almost over for the year and I'm sort of bored anyway."

Bootsy took a moment to look around the bright, cheerful kitchen. Everything was white except for the stainless-steel appliances and the dark wooden floor. Sunlight seemed to stream in from every possible opening.

"We have a very nice house in Portland, but it doesn't feel like this. Your house feels . . . comfortable." Bootsy spoke candidly. "It just feels good being here."

"It's not the house," said Eleanor softly. "I feel it too. It must be because we are kindred spirits."

Ding-Dong, Ding-Dong! The sound of a doorbell startled Bootsy. "Oh, you've got company," Bootsy said, clearly disappointed. "I should be getting home. My mom is always warning me about becoming a nuisance—that is a pest. I wouldn't want to overstay my welcome." She wiped her mouth on a napkin and stood to go.

Eleanor chuckled, "No, no, that's Feathers. He's quite a character and often imitates the doorbell. I really never know what's going on around here. Sometimes he imitates the telephone, or the timer on the oven. It keeps me on my toes."

"Well I should be going anyway. Mom will be worried or mad or both. I really enjoyed meeting you and eating your apple pie." Bootsy was a very polite young lady.

"Please come visit me again," Eleanor said. "Feathers and I get lonely, and I enjoyed your company very much." Eleanor walked Bootsy to the door and Feathers flew to her shoulder.

After Eleanor closed the door behind her, Bootsy paused looking around the wide porch. Just as she was about to leave, behind the door, she heard a man's deep voice say, "I love you, Ellie."

Bootsy was happy. She skipped along the path that led downhill to Granny Scattergoods' house. Every now and then she could see the ocean through the pines that lined the lane, and she could definitely hear the rhythmic crashing of the waves on the beach below. She loved Sand Beach. The air was different here—cooler, cleaner, fresher with a hint of seasoning in it. Time was different here. There seemed to be more of it. When they went to the post office to gather Granny's mail, there were no lines of impatient people waiting. Driving to Waterton was just driving—no stop and go—no traffic really. In the grocery store there were fewer choices, but Mrs. Kelly, the owner, called her by name.

Granny's house came into view and Bootsy did a quick assessment, comparing the small beach bungalow to Eleanor's grand, polished house. The gray weathered shingles had seen better days and the orange trim needed painting, but it was truly a beach house with its life preserver decorating the front door like a Christmas wreath and the fake seagulls that sat on their pilings guarding the entryway. Glad to be there, yet reluctant to open the door to the disaster that awaited, Bootsy quietly went inside.

"Mom, I'm home. Where are you?" she called.

"I'm in the kitchen. Come in here. I could really use your help." Judy Greenwood was certainly a force of nature. Maybe even a tornado because when it came to committing to a cause, she was all in. Granny's house was in total disarray, but it was clean. Most of the furniture in the small, cozy living area was on the deck. The carpets had been vacuumed and shampooed. There was no sign of clutter. Bootsy wondered where it had all gone. Even the bowl of fruit that had been on the dining room table had been thrown away. She followed her mother's voice into the kitchen and was shocked to see that every cupboard was open and dishes, pots, pans and miscellaneous items were spread on every surface.

"I've always wanted to clean this place and get rid of all the stuff Granny's collected. It could really be a nice little get-away with some proper attention." Judy was into the transformation.

"What about Granny? Isn't she coming home? What will she say if we get rid of her things?" Bootsy could feel her throat tighten and her eyes began to burn with unshed tears.

"I don't know, Bootsy, I just don't know. We must prepare for the worst and hope it doesn't happen, but I don't think Granny can live here alone anymore. You need to trust me on this." Judy gave Bootsy a hug and as she did she noticed the bandage on her knee.

"What happened to you?" she asked.

Bootsy recounted her mishap on the trail and her meeting with Eleanor.

"Do you know her, Mom? I think she is very mysterious. She lives at the top of the point in a beautiful house all by herself. Well, there is a parrot who talks like a man, and she said her husband has gone fishing, but he's been gone for three years. She also makes a wonderful apple pie. I really like her. Do you know her?"

"Bootsy Greenwood! What have I repeatedly told you about talking to strangers? She could be predator who lures young girls into her home and locks them in the basement. Maybe she sells them into slavery. What were you thinking? You ate her pie? What if it was drugged?"

"No Mom, I have a really good feeling about her. You need to trust me on this. She is a kindred spirit for sure."

"Oh Bootsy," it was a sigh of resignation. "Help me with some of these pans. The neighbors must have been bringing Mom food. There are several dishes that have names on the bottom. We'll have to return as many as we can. Here is one from Mrs. Kelly from down at the store, and this one is from Nancy Wilson. She just lives next door."

Judy lifted a pretty ceramic pie plate with a lid covered with blueberries. She held it in her hands as if to measure its worth before she turned it over. On the bottom of the dish was the name, Penrose.

"That belongs to Eleanor," cried Bootsy. "She told me she knew Granny. I'll return it to her."

"Wait, Bootsy. Let's take a few of these to the closest neighbors and then go down to the Anchor for burgers. I'm starved. You can see your friend another day. We need to visit Granny and take her a few things."

Later, Bootsy and Judy drove to the hospital without any traffic or stopping at lights.

"I had forgotten how simple life can be here," Judy spoke more to herself than to Bootsy. "I might even have time to finish moving the furniture back into the house. Let's hope it doesn't rain."

Granny was sleeping when they entered her hospital room. She looked old and frail. Bootsy was surprised to see Eleanor sitting in a chair by the bed. She rose to her feet and extended her hand to Judy, "I'm Eleanor Penrose, a friend of your mother."

Judy shook Eleanor's hand and introduced herself. Bootsy was beyond pleased to see Eleanor again.

"She just dozed off a few minutes ago. I'm surprised at her resilience." Eleanor whispered.

"The doctor says it was a mild stroke so we are grateful for that, but he said sometimes more damaging ones can follow, so of course we are concerned." Judy eyed Eleanor with just a little suspicion.

"Well I'll be off and let you have some alone time with her. It was nice to finally meet you both. Jean spoke so fondly of you." Eleanor quietly took her leave with a wink in Bootsy's direction.

Bootsy leaned over Granny to see her better. She wished she had remembered to bring a mirror to check for breathing but knew her mother would think it ghoulish. She gently rubbed the gnarled fingers that lay above the covers and Granny stirred. Slowly her eyes opened and focused on the beloved face that hovered over her. She tried to speak but the words that came out of her mouth were not the words she had in her head, "Help me, please help me."

It came out sounding more like, "Goat poop."

Eleanor set the table. She enjoyed putting out her fine linens, lovely china, and crystal stemware even more than she loved to cook. Feeding friends and family was a labor of love and had been for as long as Eleanor had been able to crack an egg into her Grandmother's cookie dough. She knew her friends enjoyed coming to the dinner parties she and Walter had hosted, her children and grandchildren loved the holidays spent together. As Eleanor fussed with the centerpiece of roses, she counted the many blessings that made up her life like a nun counted the beads on her rosary. She was lucky. Her life had been full and rich. She was old but healthy, had enough money to be comfortable, had children who were successful and independent, had friends in abundance, yet she was lonely. "Damn you, Walter!"

Ding Dong.

Was that the doorbell or Feathers? Eleanor checked the clock. It was exactly 6:00, so she knew Angus, who was nothing if not punctual, would be at the door ready to eat.

"Hello, Angus, do come in." Eleanor did not find it difficult to be gracious, especially to an old friend.

"Good evening, young lady, I brought some libations. I hope it goes with whatever you're cooking up tonight."

"A lovely pinot, it will go perfectly with the pork tenderloin, thank you. Would you open it please? I'll get you a whiskey." Eleanor led Angus into the kitchen where she dished up the pork with roasted apple sauce, quinoa, and green beans. She knew Angus preferred red meat and potatoes, but she didn't want to please him too much.

As they sat down to eat, Feathers began to chant from his perch, "Intruder, intruder, get your gun, Ellie!"

"So rude, Feathers. I apologize, Angus. He's a one-man kind of bird." Eleanor removed Feathers from the room as he continued his tirade, "Danger, danger, intruder, intruder!"

"So, what's on your mind, Angus?" Eleanor asked as she sat down to eat.

"Murder," he answered after swallowing a bite of green bean.

"Not Feathers I hope."

"No, no, there was a homicide yesterday. You remember Henry Ott? There's talk that his son did him in to get some inheritance. Henry was up in years and in failing health. It's hard to imagine killing your own father." Angus was a retired police detective who knew everybody in the county, as well as most of their secrets.

"What makes you think it was murder? Henry didn't seem the type to have money." Eleanor was interested but didn't want to appear so. Murder was a grisly business.

"There are a lot of people with money in this town. They just don't flaunt it. You know `Live Simply so Others Can Simply Live' sort of thing. Henry was like that. Lived and worked hard his whole life as a jeweler. He sure didn't deserve to die that way."

"What way was that?" Eleanor inquired.

Angus looked at her under his graying bushy eyebrows, smiled and simply said, "Murder."

After dinner Eleanor dished up the apple pie she had baked that morning and topped it with a big scoop of salted caramel ice cream.

Angus leaned back in his chair and almost moaned with delight, "That was a most delicious meal. I miss Margo's company, but I sure don't miss her cooking. Thank you, Ellie."

No one called her Ellie except Walter. It was time for Angus to go.

Wednesday, May 17. Walter wasn't here, the cleaning lady came today. Eleanor had slept fitfully, dreaming about murder, Angus, and Feathers in a struggle to eat the apple pie. Crazy. She looked at the clock. It was late. Fog had moved in and surrounded her house like a blanket, making it dim and quiet. No wonder she had slept so late. Even Feathers was still asleep. She stretched and got out of the warm bed. She had things to do and places to go.

Bootsy had slept in, too. Granny's house was much improved with a good cleaning. Even the bedding smelled fresh and clean. Bootsy planned to visit Eleanor today to return the pie plate, and maybe see Feathers. She might find more clues about the mysterious Eleanor, and there might be another piece of that pie.

As Bootsy walked to the kitchen she noticed the fog that blocked the view from the windows.

"Awww, that doesn't look good," she muttered to her mother who sat at the kitchen table sipping tea.

"Good morning to you too. That's just fog. It will burn off by noon. Here, have some cereal," she said. "We have more work to do today. I'm hoping you can help me clean out the kitchen. Later we can make a trip to Goodwill and then visit Granny. Are you up for it?"

"Sure thing, Mom, I'll get dressed and take the pie plate over to Eleanor's house."

"I found several of her dishes here. Some are quite beautiful. Look at this casserole dish, and here is the most colorful plate." She held them up for Bootsy to admire. Ceramic dishware of deep greens and blues that were like nothing either had ever seen. "They must be hand thrown and painted by an artist. Be very careful not to break them."

"Okie dokie, artichokie!" Bootsy was in a good mood.

Walking up the hill to Eleanor's house laden with valuable glassware was exercise that made Bootsy feel like a beast of burden.

She imagined herself a donkey struggling up the incline until her arms began to ache with the weight of her load. Then she imagined herself an Egyptian slave on a special mission for her master, all the time considering the reward of something grand at the end of her journey. Eleanor would be so happy to see her dishes returned that she would welcome Bootsy into her home and lavish her with gifts of chocolate and attention. Maybe she would even let her borrow a beautiful book from her collection.

As she came into view of Eleanor's house, she saw a green car outside. Maybe Eleanor had company. She boldly walked to the door, put her burden on a small bench, and rang the bell. Waiting there she worried that Eleanor might think it was Feathers imitating the sound and ignore her, but after a short time, she heard footsteps. A stranger opened the door. She was a short, round woman with curly brown hair and a friendly smile.

"Yes, may I help you?" she asked.

"I'm here to see Eleanor and return some of her dishes," Bootsy explained.

"I'm sorry, Mrs. Penrose is not at home today, but you may leave the dishes."

Bootsy did not want to leave the dishes. They were her reason for visiting Eleanor. Things were not working out the way she had planned. Eleanor was supposed to be home. Now, Bootsy would have to go home, help her mother, and think of another excuse to come back without being a nuisance. But Bootsy reluctantly handed over the dishes to the lady at the door and began the trek down the hill. This time she imagined the strange lady had done something evil to Eleanor and was now chasing her. She made the return trip very fast indeed.

It was late when Eleanor walked into her house that evening. She was tired and sad. Wednesday is a day of woe she thought. The only good thing about Wednesday is that Nora came to clean the house. It was spotless. Eleanor noticed the dishes on the counter with a note from Nora explaining Bootsy's visit. Eleanor sighed and peeled a banana. It would be dinner tonight. She just didn't feel like eating much. She thought about Walter; the young handsome Walter, tall and slender, with those brown eyes that sparkled with mischief and a lust for life. She remembered an ardent lover, a soulmate and friend who could tell a funny story to cheer her when she was down.

She pushed the silverware drawer shut and was reminded of the day after he left, when she entered the kitchen to find all the cupboards ajar and the drawers open. Was someone in the house? She had searched each room checking for other forms of disarray. In the bathroom, the same thing—drawers open. She had just left this room. How puzzled she was until she realized *she* had left the rooms that way and Walter must have followed behind her closing drawers and cupboards for almost 50 years, never criticizing, just making things right. It took her three weeks to break that habit. How long would it take to let him go? Eleanor cried herself to sleep Wednesday night.

Thursday, May 18, nothing, nothing, maybe work in the office, Walter is not here. The morning came with dark gray skies and drizzle. Eleanor had woken to find herself still dressed in yesterday's clothes and lying on top of the covers. It was early still. Eleanor headed for Feathers' cage.

"Top of the morning, Lassie," he squawked.

"Good morning, Feathers," she replied without much thought as she headed for the shower.

When all the things that must be done had been done, Eleanor took her coffee into the office. She lit a fire in the gas fireplace hoping to dispel the gloom she perceived in the space. The fire added a warm glow that reflected off the polished wood lining the walls. Eleanor sat down at her desk just as Feathers decided to join her. He enjoyed her company and sat comfortably on his perch by the window.

"It was a dark and stormy night," he plagiarized in his deep Walter voice.

Eleanor ignored him as she always did when she sat down to write. She was a published poet after all and did not listen to illiterate critics.

> Dull and dreary days
> Broken by sorrow and distress
> Woe and bitterness.
> On life's silver string I thread
> My pearls of happiness.
> Instants only, flashes of delight:
> First kiss, wedding day,
> Golden sun of morning's light,
> Enchantment in God's garden,
> Breathless evening under moon
> Joyous sharing at childbirth
> Pleasures past, gone too soon
> Happiness elusive and unsought
> Jewels my silken web captures.

I roll my beads as I recite
My rosary of remembered raptures.

Eleanor's stomach rumbled. Where had the morning gone? She picked up the phone and called Nancy Wilson. She didn't feel like eating alone.

As she entered The Anchor, she spotted Nancy sitting at a table by the window. Nancy was bubbling over with gossip.
"Did you hear about Henry Ott?" she asked as soon as Eleanor sat down.

"Only that he died. Is there more?"

"Well, there are rumors about poison."

"Hmmmm, that sounds strange. Who would want to poison Henry?"

"His son is the number one suspect. Evidently there is a large inheritance." Nancy whispered and looked around cautiously. You never knew who could be listening in a small town.

Eleanor remembered the conversation with Angus but didn't say anything about it.

"Poison is usually the choice of women. Agatha Christie had a lot of that in her mysteries. Who else stands to gain from Henry's death?"

"I don't really know. Henry kept to himself. Who would have thought he had much money anyway? His wife died years ago. Maybe it's the real estate. His house isn't much, but the view is absolutely gorgeous." Nancy didn't have the greatest view.

"Was there interest in his property?"

The waitress appeared to take their order and the thought of the vegetarian bean burger with kettle chips made the mysterious death of Henry Ott secondary. The two friends chatted away happily and enjoyed their lunch.

"Have you heard any more about Jean?" asked Eleanor.

"Nothing, her daughter is making quick work of her things. I saw her hauling several boxes out to her car. I guess she doesn't expect Jean to come home . . . not sentimental that one." Nancy confided. "Oh, and did you know Gertie Frank has cancer? Just diagnosed last week and already on chemo."

"It must be our age, Nancy. It seems as though everyone we know is sick, dying, or dead." Eleanor sighed.

The drizzle had stopped and the sun shone through a few stubborn clouds as Eleanor and Nancy made their way up the winding road to their homes. Nancy could almost reach out and touch Jean Scattergoods' deck as both houses perched on the steep hillside. Eleanor waved goodbye to her friend and noticed Bootsy peering out the window. Suddenly she was out on the deck with a friendly smile and a big hello.

"What are you up to today?" Eleanor asked.

"Cleaning, helping Mom clean and more cleaning. I'm tired of cleaning." Bootsy dramatically raised her arm to her forehead in despair.

"Would you like to help me bake some cookies? It might be a break from cleaning. Go ask your mother. I'm sure she won't mind now that we're no longer strangers." Eleanor needed the antidote to death and dying that only youth could give.

Bootsy bolted inside and returned before Eleanor could make a mental list of the ingredients needed to bake cookies. Evidently Bootsy and her mother had had enough of each other in close quarters on a rainy day.

Bootsy liked to bake, and better still, enjoyed eating the results. As they worked together they chattered about a list of topics— from school and friends to mysteries and murders. They shared their dreams and some of their nightmares. To Eleanor, it was refreshing, and to Bootsy it was a chance to shine as Eleanor complimented her and lavished attention on her. As an only child, she should have been the center of her parents' world, but in truth they had little time for her. Even when they were with her, they were not present for her. Their work and their devices took them away from her.

Bootsy studied the books on Eleanor's shelves; *Shakespeare, Pride and Prejudice, Tales of Edgar Allan Poe, The Mill on the Floss, The Odyssey, Robinson Crusoe, Paradise Lost, Canterbury Tales.* Books she had never heard of and didn't want to read. She wondered if Eleanor would think she was stupid if she knew this. Eleanor watched Bootsy pore over her collection of classics and smiled. She too was drawn to the beauty of books. She selected a book from a lower shelf and offered it to Bootsy. The title was *To Kill a_ Mockingbird.* She knew it would be a stretch, but she thought Bootsy could handle it.

When it was time to leave, Bootsy surprised Eleanor with a tight hug, and skipped out the door with her book and a bag of cookies.

Eleanor felt suddenly lost. She wandered into her office and glanced at the papers strewn across her desk. She wasn't very tidy when it came to paper. Walter hated that about her. She picked up a poem she had written long ago and snorted. Feathers startled her by snorting too.

"Gee, Walter, it's as if you never left."

Friday; coffee group, Walter isn't here, hair appointment in the afternoon, maybe a visit to Gertie.

Friday morning was bright and clear. The rain had washed all negative ions away so Eleanor woke feeling refreshed and clear-headed.

She greeted Feathers, set him free, and padded into the bathroom to get her tweezers. She rubbed her chin feeling for the whisker she knew was there. How weird was it that her eyebrows were fleeing their home above her eyes only to relocate on her chin! If young people only knew the horrors that awaited them, they would surely be more daring and not choose to live to old age.

Ready at last, Eleanor drove the 10 miles to her coffee group's meeting place of choice. The Boat House offered simple home cooking, great bacon, and privacy. She entered and saw Josephine sitting in her usual spot by the window.

"Good morning, Josephine, I love your green sweater. Is it new?" Eleanor loved Josephine and the color green.

"You look lovely too, Eleanor. I ordered this online. It's a site that supports the neutering of feral cats."

"Is that a new hairdo?" Eleanor noticed Josephine had recently stopped coloring her thick curly locks.

"Yes, I went to Henry Wadsworth's and they did this marvelous technique to blend my gray. Do you like it?"

"I do," Eleanor nodded, "but what I really like is the way you have it styled."

Josephine was proud of her crowning glory and had twisted it into two plaits and piled it on top of her head giving her the look of sophistication she deserved.

"Oh, I just did this because it was wet after swimming," she replied modestly. Josephine was almost as old as Eleanor and had the streamlined body of a swimmer. Swimming contributed to the image she had of herself as a Pisces, or water baby, as well as keeping her fit.

It wasn't long before Pearl and Cleo joined them. As they walked in together, it was easy to compare them. Pearl with her long legs and straight blonde hair looked even taller next to Cleo, who was only a little over five feet. Both sat down and immediately admired Josephine's new do.

They eagerly shared the books they had read, movies they had seen, and stories of grandchildren. Dede entered late as usual. She was the mayor of Waterton and a very busy woman, but one who knew the importance of friendships. Dede knew what was happening in town, just about everyone who ever lived there as well as their children and their grandchildren.

"So, did you hear that Gertie Frank died last night?" asked Dede.

"No, I just heard about her illness yesterday and was planning to visit her this afternoon," lamented Eleanor.

"Who was Gertie Frank?" asked Cleo. She never knew anyone.

"You remember her," scolded Pearl, "She was the one that made a big stink when we had our students keeping journals. It was that whole Phyllis Schafly thing." Cleo and Pearl had taught at Joseph Champion Elementary School together along with Dede before their retirement afforded them the luxury of late coffee meetings and a life devoted to art and leisure.

"Yes, I do remember. How old was she?" Cleo asked.

"She must have been at least 80," Dede said.

"That makes three," added Josephine thoughtfully. "They say bad things come in threes."

"Oh, who died besides Henry Ott and Gertie?" Cleo asked, her green eyes lighting up with curiosity.

"Lidia Garfield was found in her home last week . . . dead as a doornail in her favorite chair. I'm sure she was in her eighties as well," reported Josephine. No one else seemed to know Lidia except Dede, who knew everyone, of course.

"Well, old people die. No one lives forever except for Cleo's mother-in-law," said Pearl. She was pushing 100 and had been the bane of Cleo's married life as well as the topic of many coffee group discussions over the years.

"That's true," Eleanor said, beginning to feel uncomfortable. She remembered Angus mentioning the possibility of murder and Nancy gossiping about poison. She could not hold back her suspicions.

"What if someone is killing off all the old people?" Eleanor asked. "No one would question it since everyone expects old people to die."

"What would be the motive?" asked Cleo.

"Are you suggesting a serial killer perhaps?" Josephine would be the one to go to the shadows, being a retired therapist.

"How creepy," complained Pearl, "Let's talk about something else."

"How did they do it? How would someone go about murdering people without making it look like murder?" Cleo totally ignored Pearl. "This is completely unacceptable, not to mention scary."

"Why? Why would someone want old people dead?" Dede asked.

"You mean other than the obvious reasons of being a burden or inheritances?" asked Cleo.

"Serial killers don't need a motive exactly. "Josephine always spoke with authority. "They have triggers that prompt them to kill, along with personality disorders or mental illnesses of various kinds."

The conversation that followed consisted of each member's own personal definition of 'old'.

"You are not old as long as you are healthy," offered Pearl. She practiced yoga daily and was thin and limber.

"I believe you are old when you stop learning and trying new things," added Cleo, who often tried a new diet or color for her hair.

"When you can no longer take care of your own needs, you are old," said Eleanor.

"Babies and the disabled would be considered old under that definition," argued Cleo.

"Eighty is definitely old. Your body is in decline and most people of that age begin to lose their cognitive abilities," Josephine stated.

"We have nothing to worry about," said Dede. "None of us are over 80."

On the drive to the hair salon, Eleanor played back the conversation about murder in her mind. It might be time to pump Angus for what he knew. She would invite him for dinner tonight.

Eleanor walked into Curl Up and Dye salon that afternoon to get her usual haircut. She didn't believe in dying her hair and rather liked the silvery color of her natural locks. Actually, Eleanor thought she was attractive for an older woman. She wasn't vain, just honest.

"Well, how are you today, Eleanor?" Jessica Honeycutt was a sweet, middle-aged woman who knew how to cut hair. She always greeted her clients with a lovely smile and never talked much about herself.

"I'm good," she said quietly. "You look different. Have you done something new to your hair?"

"Well, I've lost 50 pounds." Jessica answered as she made sure Eleanor was comfortably seated.

"You look great," Eleanor didn't like to comment on people's weight, but Jessica did look good.

"I know, yesterday a young man at the grocery store looked at me," she confided. "I just couldn't believe it. Usually I'm invisible."

Rita Early was getting a pedicure nearby and overhearing the conversation joined in, "Older women are often invisible. I think it's the gray hair."

"Hi, Rita," Eleanor said, "I see you are treating yourself to a pedicure. How lovely."

"I can't reach my toes anymore," Rita complained. "I don't see anything wrong with treating myself every month."

"I just took my rabbit in to get his toenails trimmed," contributed Jessica as she began to wash Eleanor's hair.

"Where do you take the rabbit?" Eleanor quizzed.

"I take him to the vet. He's an indoor rabbit you know and so his nails just grow," Jessica said it so matter of fact that Eleanor began to giggle. She imagined a large bunny getting his nails done at a spa.

"Is he potty-trained?" asked Rita.

"He goes on a pee pad," answered Jessica. It was all too much for Eleanor and she began to laugh and laugh, and soon Jessica was laughing and then Rita joined in and they couldn't stop. When they finally composed themselves, Eleanor just relaxed and listened to the gossip that surrounded her.

Eleanor could hear Rita talking about her grandchildren and how smart they were.

Allison Rood, another stylist, went on and on about her own children and how terrible the education system was. She complained about every teacher in the system.

"There has certainly been a rash of old people dying lately."

Eleanor's ears perked up. Who was talking? Rita Early had stopped bragging about her grandchildren and described the latest funeral she had attended.

"It was so beautiful," she continued, "but unfortunately there were few attending. I guess when you get to be a certain age most of your friends are dead. The other two funerals were just graveside services. I suppose that's best when you are that old." She mentioned the names of three people Eleanor did not know: Howard Welk, Edith Allen, and Edward Eberlee. Maybe Dede knew them. Eleanor was suddenly in a hurry to get out of the salon. She planned to stop at the local Food Mart on her way home. Angus would get his red meat and potatoes tonight.

As Eleanor prepared her dinner of New York strip steaks with chipotle marinade and red wine butter sauce, she hummed a little tune and realized she was happy. Feathers noticed her good mood and joined in with his version while bobbing up and down to her beat. Soon Eleanor danced into the living room to find some real music. She hadn't felt like this in a long while. Music was good for the soul she thought. It always cheered her up, but for some reason she had forgotten about it. While the steaks sat in their marinade, Eleanor poured herself a big glass of Cabernet and sat looking at the ocean. Life was good.

DING DONG DING! Eleanor awoke with a start. She had nodded off! This never happened. For heaven sakes, what time was it? She was totally discombobulated, and half asleep. Was Angus here already? She hadn't set the table or put the potatoes in the oven to roast. Eleanor made her way to the front door, opened it and looked left and right.

No one.

Feathers! As she closed the door she could hear him laughing maniacally, "Gotchya."

Eleanor would have laughed too if she wasn't suddenly in a rush to get ready for her guest.

By the time Angus arrived, the house smelled of roasted potatoes, garlic, thyme, and grilled meat. Angus was in heaven. Eleanor served him his preferred Crown Royal on the rocks and sat down with the rest of her Cabernet to feast on another delicious meal.

"What's the occasion?" he asked after running the napkin over his thick, graying mustache. "Do you need some handiwork done? I don't usually get invited to dinner twice in one week. Not that I'm complaining, you see."

Eleanor decided to be bluntly honest about her intentions, "I've invited you here to pump you for information," she said. "I've noticed a troubling trend of old people dying lately and it made me think there might be something sinister to it. You mentioned murder when you told me about Henry Ott, and now I've learned that five more people over the age of 80 have died in a matter of weeks!" She leaned back in her chair and crossed her arms. "So, what do you know?"

Angus smiled his Tom Selleck smile full of dimples and shook his head. It was all he could do to keep from laughing out loud, but he knew that would offend Eleanor. He wasn't born yesterday.

"Interesting," he said. Then filled his mouth with a big bite of steak and chewed very slowly while he thought of something to say that would get him invited back for more dinners at this table.

Eleanor nibbled on a piece of salad and worried that Angus might think she was like those other bored ladies on the mystery channel who pried into investigations and made pests of themselves. She never really worried about what Angus thought of her before, but for some reason she did tonight.

"That is an idea I hadn't thought of until you mentioned it," he began. "People over 80 often die of natural causes. I suppose if six people in their twenties were found dead in their homes in the course of two weeks in a small town, it would seem suspicious. I'll bring it up to some of the guys on the force and see what they think." There, he thought he had handled that rather well and was patting himself on the back when Eleanor continued with her questions.

"What you know about these deaths? Are they all considered natural causes? You said there was the possibility of poison with Henry. Do you know any of these other people? Should my friends and I be worried about a possible serial killer?"

Angus took another bite of meat. A serial killer who focused on people over 80 . . . not unheard of. There were cases he read about that were like that. Not likely but . . .

"I can't really discuss an ongoing case and I'm not privy to what goes on anymore. Sometimes I play poker with the guys and sometimes they ask me about cases I've worked in the past, but I've been retired a long time, Eleanor."

"So, Henry wasn't poisoned?" she persisted.

"Well he was, oops. I didn't mean to tell you that. Eleanor, this is not something I want you speculating about with your friends. Let me talk to some people and I'll get back to you with more information later."

That meant the subject was closed for further discussion. Eleanor politely excused herself to go for ice cream.

When Angus left that night, he warned her to be careful. She was getting close to eighty.

Saturday, May 20, walk on the beach, work in the office, Walter isn't here, Gertie was dead, visit Frieda. Saturday meant nothing to

Eleanor. She was retired, so every day was Saturday. She woke as usual and checked off her mental list. She thought of Bootsy and wondered if she and her mother were still in town. She would like to spend time with her.

Feathers squawked in an irritated voice and seemed uncommonly out of sorts. Eleanor knew he didn't like Angus and figured he was pouting about his visit. She readied herself for a beach walk and left her house. The air was cool and filled with the cries of seagulls. As she passed Jean Scattergoods' home she saw Bootsy outside sorting rocks near the road.

"I'm going for a walk on the beach. Do you want to come with me?" Eleanor called.

"Sure," it was hard not to notice her excitement. Bootsy ran inside and returned in a jiffy. She carried a pail.

"Do you collect rocks?" asked Eleanor.

"Oh yes. I especially like agates." Bootsy had energy beyond that of a 72-year-old woman, but Eleanor was determined to keep up with her young friend.

Down the hill they hurried under a brilliant sunny sky. Several people and their dogs were already on the beach. That's the way it always was, much to Eleanor's dismay. She spent every rainy, windy day at the Oregon coast looking out at the desolate shore, but the first sunny day brought a host of visitors to her beach. Today she felt glad to share. Bootsy skipped ahead in search of the perfect agate or unbroken shell. The ocean waves broke noisily, but there was no wind. It was a perfect day for beachcombing.

After a lengthy walk they headed back toward a large piece of driftwood to share their treasures. Bootsy had by far collected many more than Eleanor who had no pail and used only her pockets. Bootsy excitedly laid each of her pieces out on the sand. Smooth gray stones, clear orange-tinged agates, a few pieces of broken green glass polished by waves and sand as well as various bits of

28

shells. Eleanor admired them all calling them Bootsy's Booty. Then it was Bootsy's turn to ooh over Eleanor's clear agates and green jade.

"Let's go to the café and have some hot chocolate," suggested Eleanor.

"With whipped cream?" asked Bootsy.

"Absolutely!" Eleanor was already on her feet putting the treasure in the pail.

They entered Brewing in the Wind and found a small table by the window and ordered their hot chocolate and a couple of snickerdoodles. Eleanor remembered these were Walter's favorites, but quickly brushed that thought away. She would stay present for Bootsy. Conversation came easily to them.

"How is your Granny doing?" Eleanor was curious about her neighbor.

"Much better, I think. The doctor says she will need to go to rehab." Bootsy didn't know much more about it because her mother was being mysterious and wouldn't give her any details.

"I'm almost finished with *To Kill a Mockingbird*," Bootsy boasted. "I hope you don't mind if I take it back to Portland with me. We're leaving tomorrow, and I really want to see how it ends."

"Of course, keep it as long as you need to finish it. I know it's a challenging book for you to read."

"The best part is Boo. I like to be a little scared sometimes, but not really scared." Bootsy confided.

"Well in that case you must read the tale of Bandage Man. When you finish *To Kill a Mockingbird* come over and you can borrow *Oregon's Ghosts and Monsters*. It's just the right amount of scary." Eleanor liked to be scared now and again too.

"Oh, that sounds great. Who is Bandage Man?" Bootsy wondered.

Now she had done it. Eleanor proceeded to raise the hair on Bootsy's head as well as a million goosebumps by telling the tale of a giant logger wrapped in bandages who roamed Highway 101 on dark and stormy nights. He was known to jump into the back of people's trucks, eat dogs, and leave disgusting bits of his bandages behind. Eleanor used her deep scary voice and Bootsy was riveted.

"Of course, there is more to the story," Eleanor teased, "but you will have to read it for yourself."

"Do you believe in ghosts?" asked Bootsy.

"I'm not sure. I've never seen one. Do you believe in ghosts?" Eleanor hadn't thought about what she really believed in for a long while. After many years of seeking the truth about spiritual things and religion, she had decided it didn't matter what she believed, because she couldn't possibly know for sure. As she got older she thought more about dying but chose to live a good life and let the chips fall where they may.

Bootsy was quick to answer, "Yes, and I also believe in fairies, goblins, and angels, God, unicorns, miracles, magic, and elves, but not Santa Claus or the tooth fairy." Bootsy rattled on about the Harry Potter books she had read and the difference between fantasy and reality. Eleanor puzzled over her ability to hold on to some of the unbelievable when she seemed so mature. Maybe growing up was just letting go of myths a little at a time.

"Oh my, look at the time," Eleanor said, glancing at the clock. "I should be on my way. Are you finished with that chocolate?"

Bootsy did not want the adventure with Eleanor to end, but she didn't want to be a nuisance either, so she smiled and politely thanked Eleanor for the treats as they left; Eleanor to work in her office and Bootsy to prepare for her return to Portland.

It was almost a crime to hang out in her office on such a beautiful day, but Eleanor was inspired by her conversation with Bootsy and her ridiculous list of beliefs. She sat at her desk and pondered while Feathers quietly watched from his perch. Picking up her pen she wrote:

Avalon
What doors are closed to our humanity?
Caused by indifference or apathy.
Taught by others how to see
What we're told is reality.

What lands exist beyond the mists?
What creatures dwell beyond the stars?
While we make lists of those we've kissed,
And pride ourselves on our cars.

What magic swells in hell's expanse,
Where rite is made and debits paid.
Who even asks if fairies dance
In the wooded glade?

We only give truth to what we perceive,
And that is limited to what we believe.

Eleanor put down her pen and stretched her cramping fingers. She leaned back in her chair and looked into the yellow eyes of the gray parrot.

"It was a dark and stormy night," he spoke in Walter's deep voice.

"You are getting boring," she chided. At this obvious insult, the wounded Feathers flew off showing her his red tail feathers.

Still time to visit Frieda she thought as she picked up the phone to see if her delightful old friend was home. Eleanor knew she would be since she was pretty much a shut-in. But Frieda didn't like unexpected visitors.

Eleanor drove to Frieda's little cottage on the outskirts of town. She and Frieda had met 10 years ago when she and Walter had first moved to the area. Eleanor taught a writing workshop and Frieda took the class to help her write her memoirs. They had been friends ever since, although Frieda never finished her story. It was an interesting life and a tale that needed to be told, but she procrastinated. Eleanor enjoyed listening to Frieda tell about life growing up in Singapore, being captured by the Japanese, and put in a concentration camp on Java. Better still, the two would go for lunch at the local Chinese restaurant, drink tea and eat chow mein, noodles, and shrimp, all the things Walter hated. They would share their daily trials and giggle. Frieda's laugh was musical, and her pale blue eyes twinkled with light.

Those eyes smiled at Eleanor when she entered Frieda's house, but behind the smile, there was pain. Eleanor could see it in her face. Frieda was 87 and had worked hard her whole life as a nurse and then on a dairy farm with her husband, who had died two years ago. Frieda didn't like to complain, but an accident that broke her back left her in almost constant discomfort.

The two friends hugged and sat down for a friendly visit and hot tea.

"I do so love your hugs," Frieda admitted. "No one here to touch me anymore and it feels so nice."

Elsie, Frieda's tabby cat took exception to this by jumping onto Frieda's lap for some heavy petting.

"How are you feeling?" asked Eleanor.

"You know I'm just the same. Sometimes I think I'm ready to go, but who would take care of my cat?" she sighed, "If old age were a person, I'd want to do something mean to them." Frieda laughed, and the musical notes rose like bubbles in champagne.

"So, what's new?" Frieda wanted to be entertained and enlightened.

Eleanor filled her in on the latest gossip and the status of her grandchildren. Frieda's family lived far away and didn't visit often so Frieda adopted the neighborhood children. She loved them as if they were her own and liked to brag about their accomplishments.

"How's your book coming along?" Eleanor prodded even though she knew the answer.

"I have so much to do. I just haven't been able to get to it, girl. You can't believe all the papers I need to go through. Just look at this mess." She pointed to boxes of envelopes, loose papers, and files that were stacked near the dining table. Then she began a filibuster about illegal aliens that lasted seven minutes.

Eleanor let her go on without interruption because she understood the need for those who live alone to talk to others.

It wasn't long before there was a knock on the door and Jessica Honeycutt appeared with a box of hair supplies.

"Oh my gracious me, I totally forgot you were coming today," Frieda apologized first to Jessica and then to her friend Eleanor.

"I didn't know you made house calls." Eleanor was just a little surprised to see Jessica out of her natural habitat.

"Well Frieda is a special customer," Jessica winked at Eleanor like they were sharing some secret.

"Okay, old friend, I'll be off then so Jessica can work her magic on you. Shave or hair cut?" she joked and they all laughed. Eleanor gave Frieda one last hug and heard her offer tea to the hairdresser as she closed the door.

Driving home, Eleanor had a strange feeling that there was something she was supposed to do but couldn't remember what it was. Something left undone, something that nibbled just on the edges of her memory but then was gone. She turned the radio up and knew it would come to her sooner or later.

Sunday, May 21: the Sunday paper, Walter wasn't here, Gertie was dead. After her busy day yesterday, she needed a nice lazy day. Maybe she would just read the paper in bed. Eleanor rose, snuggled into her robe, greeted and freed Feathers, put on the coffee, and walked outside to get the morning paper. Fog lay thickly over the ocean blocking most of her view, but she could still hear the comforting break of the waves. It will burn off before noon she thought.

She found the crossword puzzle, poured a cup of dark, rich coffee, added lots of cream and went back to her bed. Feathers flew into the bedroom and landed on the headboard looking down on the paper as if he could solve the word puzzle himself.

"What is a six-letter word for toxin?" she asked out loud.

Feathers jumped down to get a closer look and Eleanor stroked his gray feathers.

"Pretty sad when you have to resort to conversing with a bird. Not that you aren't a very intelligent pet, but even so, your topics are somewhat limited." Eleanor sipped her coffee and gazed out the window.

Feathers rolled his eyes and squawked, "Get to work, Ellie. Get to work." Then immediately took flight in case she decided to swat his red rear with her paper.

"P-o-i-s-o-n - that was the word." Suddenly Eleanor remembered what she was supposed to do. She needed to find out more about the three elderly people who had died before Henry and Gertie. She could call Dede to see what she knew. She also wanted to share the fact that Angus had admitted Henry was poisoned. What she needed was an emergency meeting of the coffee group. She picked up her phone and made a few calls. Then she finished the crossword puzzle, read the funnies, and got dressed for the day.

She went into the office sat at her desk and picked up her pen.

### Carousel

I choose my horse, the one with sparking eye.
The riders mount their own and we begin.
I blink my eyes and all my life spins by.

I grasp my reins as round and round we fly.
The platform dips and rises as we spin,
Up we rise elated we're so high,

Down to hell we fall and yet don't die
Racing, whirling faster we can't win.
I blink my eyes and all my life spins by.

I want to make it stop and so I cry,
"Slow down," my voice unnatural, shrill and thin.
Up we rise, elated we're so high.

My hair turns gray and I forget to try.
Laughter, fear and pain cut in my skin.
I blink my eyes and all my life spins by.

The carousel speeds madly while I die.
I no longer know which world I'm in.
Up we rise, elated we're so high.
I blink my eyes and all my life spins by.

When Eleanor looked up from her work, hours had passed. She had not eaten breakfast or lunch. Feathers had deserted her in favor of an ocean view and the sun was shining. It was time for some food and a walk. There was nothing better for her mental health than getting out into nature. As she passed Jean Scattergoods' house she thought of Bootsy and her fascination with Boo Radley. An idea began to form in her mind that had to do with a hole in a tree and a secret hiding place for someone special. After a brisk walk on the beach and a short visit with Mrs. Kelly at the local grocery, Eleanor returned via the Scattergoods' house. She stopped near an old alder tree and inspected the hole she noticed earlier. It was perfect. After cleaning out some old leaves and twigs, she deposited two clear agates and a perfect sand dollar. She left wondering how long it would be before Bootsy discovered her hidey-hole.

Monday, May 22, emergency coffee meeting this morning, Walter wasn't here, dentist appointment this afternoon. Eleanor slept hard and woke feeling refreshed. She needed to make something for the potluck breakfast the coffee group had planned yesterday. Josephine would bring muffins. Dede would bring a fruit platter, Pearl always brought her famous walnut walk-a-ways, and Cleo contributed orange juice and a bottle of Prosecco for mimosas.

Eleanor would make a breakfast casserole without eggs since Josephine refused to eat them.

Eleanor hurried through her morning tasks, got the casserole in the oven, and put on a big pot of coffee.

Feathers flew through the house in an excited state sensing a disturbance in the force, "Avast, Ellie, someone's coming!"

When the doorbell rang, Ellie welcomed her friends who had carpooled to her house.

"Something smells delicious. Where is your corkscrew? Never mind, I brought my own." Cleo walked into the kitchen eager to mix the drinks. Pearl and Josephine followed. Everyone was hungry and more than ready to discover the purpose of this emergency meeting.

Sitting at the dining table the talk turned to all things personal.

Josephine began, "I'm fostering another cat. Her name is Minnie and she is so sweet, but I not keeping her. I'm not getting another cat." The announcement was followed by a knowing silence and eye-rolling. Dede made a crazy sign behind her hand, and there was an explosion of laughter from those who knew better.

"I am not a crazy cat lady!" Josephine protested, while Cleo held up her two hands in peace signs and quoted, "I am not a crook!"

"So much denial," Pearl pointed out, "but it's perfectly fine to be a crazy cat lady."

They all had their pets: Feathers of course for Eleanor and dogs for Pearl, Dede, and Cleo. Josephine had five cats.

When things had calmed down, Eleanor broached the subject of murder by poison.

"What do you know about the deaths of Howard Welk, Edith Allen, and Edward Eberlee? Did any of you know them?"

Dede spoke first, "Howard Welk went to my church. I read scripture for his funeral, but there weren't many people there. He must have been ill for a while because I don't remember seeing him at church for some time."

"When did he die?" asked Cleo.

"Maybe two weeks ago," Dede responded thoughtfully. "He was definitely over eighty."

"Oh," Pearl just understood where this discussion was going. "Wasn't Edith Allen that tall, white-haired lady that still drove around town in her pink Cadillac even though she was in her nineties?"

"I remember reading an article about her in the *Fish Wrapper*." Cleo was excited that she actually knew something about someone. "We were on the same schedule at Curl Up and Dye. I used to see her there and admired her thick and beautiful white hair. She was very hard of hearing. Some of the conversations I heard were so funny. You know the ones like, 'Today's Thursday' 'I'm thirsty too' 'Would you like a Margarita?' 'I never learned that dance.' I didn't know she was dead. Eleanor, do you still have last week's *Fish Wrapper*? She might be in the obituaries."

Eleanor went to look for the paper hoping she hadn't used it to line Feathers' cage.

When she returned with the paper, they were pleased to discover that Edward Eberlee's obituary was right next to Edith Allen's. Both had died in their homes of "natural causes" and both requested no funeral. Graveside services were held for family only.

"Rita Early attended all three services. Do you think she was family?" questioned Eleanor.

"Do you think she could be the murderer?" Cleo was suspicious. "You know how murderers sometimes return to the scene of the crime."

"Rita goes to every funeral. She likes the food, she's a busybody, not a killer," snorted Dede.

"What do you think, Josephine?" asked Pearl.

"Let's review the facts. Six people have died in the last two weeks. They were all over eighty. They all died at home of natural causes. It sounds normal to me." Josephine stated logically.

"Oh, I forgot to tell you," added Eleanor. "When I had Angus over for dinner the other night he let it slip that Henry Ott had been poisoned."

It was suddenly very quiet.

"What kind of poison?" Josephine broke the silence.

"I don't know. Angus was very stingy with the details." Eleanor said.

"We definitely don't have enough information to cry murder. Yet it is very odd that so many older people have died recently." Pearl spoke thoughtfully.

"Old people die, that's not odd," Josephine remarked, "but it would be sad if someone could get away with murder because we all accept that old people die."

Eleanor drove home from the dentist and her mind kept returning to the morning's conversation with her friends. They had no proof of foul play and no real means of finding out if the victims were really victims. It was a helpless feeling. Maybe she should just let it go.

When she got home, she kicked off her shoes and made herself a cup of tea. The best thing about being old was being able to do nothing if you felt like it. She turned on the television and spent the rest of the day watching Hallmark channel mystery movies.

The telephone woke her from a deep sleep. It was late, and Eleanor realized she had nodded off despite the interesting movie. Stranger still, it was the second time this week it had happened.

"Hello," her voice was thin and full of sleep.

"Eleanor, this is Angus. I need to see you right away. Can I come over?"

"Sure. What is it?" Eleanor was mildly surprised and somewhat frightened by his tone.

"I'm outside your door. Will you let me in?"

Eleanor went immediately to the door. Angus entered and bowed his head in a sorry gesture of sadness.

"You're scaring me, Angus."

"I know how fond you were of Frieda VanHorn, so I wanted to tell you in person. The people she hired to do her yard work found her dead this afternoon. I'm really sorry to tell you this. It seems as though she had been dead a while."

Eleanor sat down. She couldn't take it in right away. Didn't she just see Frieda? Oh, how sad to live and die alone. Poor sweet Frieda.

"I just saw her on Saturday afternoon." She said sadly.

"The coroner estimated her death to be Saturday evening. It must have happened right after you left her." Angus said gently.

"What happened? Was it her heart?" Eleanor wanted to know that she had gone peacefully without pain.

"Well, I really don't want to tell you, but we think she was poisoned. You may have stumbled onto something, Eleanor. There are more deaths than you know. The police have been suspicious for some time. It's been happening all over the county. It may be a serial killer and that makes it very difficult to solve because there seems to be no motive other than killing people who are old." It was more words than Eleanor ever heard from Angus at one time and it chilled her to her soul.

"I brought her cat instead of taking it to a shelter. It's in my car, but I figured you might want it, knowing how Frieda loved it. I'll bring it in if that's all right." His face was filled with concern.

Eleanor nodded. She watched Angus go outside.

For the first time since she and Walter had moved into this house, Eleanor was afraid to be alone and she had been alone often. Angus returned with the cat carrier and a bag of kitty belongings. Eleanor bent down and opened the carrier. Elsie came to her immediately as if they were old friends. Eleanor stroked her fur and did her best to welcome the kitty.

"I need a drink," she said as she shook off her discomfort and rose to go to the kitchen. "Do you want one?"

"Absolutely," Angus followed her and watched carefully for signs of weakness or fainting.

Eleanor poured whiskey into two glasses. She didn't bother with ice or soda, just drank it straight. Angus had never seen her drink anything but wine. Then she put out some food and water for the cat.

"Everything I told you has to be kept between us. The police don't want to tip their hand and let the killer know they are onto them. I hope you understand that I told you because I knew about your suspicions and the friendship you had with Frieda." And the friendship I have with you. Angus didn't say the last part out loud.

"I appreciate that, Angus. Thank you. I feel suddenly uneasy and creeped out that there is a murderer out there." Eleanor moved into the living room and sat on the sofa.

"Do you want me to stay with you for a while?" Angus was being more than kind as he settled his large frame in next to Eleanor. Just then, Feathers flew into the room in a flurry of wings crying, "Murderer, murder, murder."

"Yikes, who is going to keep the bird quiet?" Angus joked, but neither of them laughed.

41

Tuesday, May 23: Gertie Frank's funeral was this afternoon, Frieda was dead, Walter wasn't here, a serial killer was on the loose, Angus was on the sofa and a cat was asleep on her bed. Eleanor woke in a mental fog. She got up, washed her face and dressed herself. She wasn't sure if Angus was still out there, so she quietly peeked into the living room. He had made coffee and was sitting in the kitchen reading the morning paper. How odd it felt yet comforting somehow to have someone there.

"Good morning," she chirped trying to sound normal. It wasn't every day she had someone sleep over.

"Morning." Angus acted as though it was an everyday occurrence. "Want some coffee?"

"Yes, thank you. Did you sleep?" Eleanor wanted to know.

"Yeah, after all that whiskey I was more than comfortable on the sofa." Angus smiled revealing two deep dimples.

"How about some breakfast?" Eleanor offered.

"No, I'd better be on my way. My car is parked out front. Don't want to ruin your reputation. I just didn't want to leave without saying goodbye." Angus was old fashioned.

"Thanks again, Angus. Are you going to Gertie Frank's funeral this afternoon?" Eleanor didn't want him to leave but didn't want him to stay either.

"Yep, I'll see you there. Just so you know, the police will want to question you about your visit with Frieda. It's just routine since you may have been one of the last to see her alive. Are you okay?" he asked, looking a little too closely at her old face. She hoped his eyesight was as bad as hers, so he wouldn't see any whiskers.

"Yes, I'm fine. Thanks again, Angus." Eleanor spoke as they walked to the door. She watched him through the window as he drove away. What would the neighbors think? What would Walter say? Who cares? She thought about the information she had learned last night. A serial killer was poisoning old people. How long had this been going on and how many victims could there be?

She was suddenly distracted by the cat meowing at the door. Afraid to let Elsie outside, Eleanor looked through the bag of kitty things. She found a small bag of litter and put some in a plastic tub from under the sink. Elsie knew exactly what to do and did it. Much relieved, she proceeded to her bowl and mewed again. Eleanor studied this new addition as she ate, cleaned herself, and settled comfortably in a patch of morning sun. Something seemed strange to Eleanor. Inspired by the cat she stepped into her office and picked up her pen.

Elsie

Elsie, now it's plain to me
You're not what you seem to be.
It took so long for me to see
(Plus a course in sexuality)
What was there so obviously
Beneath your tail hanging free
In a furry clump of secrecy...
Hidden masculinity!
I love you just the same L.C.

Eleanor chuckled to herself. Everything is fodder for my pen she noted.

Later that day, Eleanor slipped into the back pew of the Methodist church beside her friends Josephine and Dede. She noticed several people she knew who had come to honor Gertie Frank. It seemed that the entire church had turned out, plus Gertie had a huge family that included numerous nieces and nephews as well as the entire dairy community. She looked around but didn't see Angus.

Three hours later, she and Josephine emerged into the daylight. Dede had left an hour ago to attend an important meeting. Who knew people had so much to say about a little old lady who spent most of her life opening her home to family, friends, and neighbors. So many pictures and such funny stories they told about her too. It made Eleanor want to be a better person. Maybe she should start going to church. She'd had these feelings before and knew they would pass in time.

"Josephine, I need to tell you something about Frieda," Eleanor began but stopped when she saw Angus approaching.

"Good afternoon, ladies." If Angus had a cowboy hat he would have tipped it, but he merely nodded to them both and walked away.

Eleanor remembered the gag order and wondered if Josephine was the serial killer. Ridiculous! Nevertheless, she decided to keep her silence.

"I heard about Frieda." Josephine picked up where Eleanor stopped. "I'm sorry. She was very dear to you."

"Yes, did you know she had a cat?" Eleanor was testing the waters.

"Oh!" Josephine was quick on the uptake. "What kind of cat? Does it need a home?"

"Come over to my house and I'll introduce you." Eleanor invited.

As soon as they opened the door, Eleanor knew something was amiss. Chairs were toppled, a favorite lamp lay on the floor, next to the broken remnants of a crystal vase and worse . . . gray and red feathers. Eleanor ran through the house looking for Feathers and found the cat on her bed licking his paws. He looked up at her sweetly as if to say, "No worries, I've taken care of everything."

She discovered Feathers hiding in the office on his perch by the window. He was visibly shaken and flew from one side of the room to the other crying, "Murderer, murder, murder!"

Josephine had chosen to comfort the cat, but after one look at Eleanor's stricken face, she plucked L.C. up and deposited him in the laundry room and closed the door.

It took 10 minutes of cooing softly to coax the disgruntled bird onto her arm where she stroked him until he felt safe.

"I shouldn't have left him out of his cage. I just wasn't thinking." Eleanor felt horrible. "I've never had a cat."

"Jaws and claws, jaws and claws!" Feathers wasn't finished with his story.

"I don't see any blood," observed Josephine. "Let's put Feathers in his cage where he will feel safe and I'll help you clean up this mess."

While they worked to set things right, Feathers could be heard growling, "Beware the Jabberwock, jaws that bite, claws that catch. Murder, murder."

An hour later Josephine left with the cat.

Feathers chortled, "Callooh! Callay!"

Eleanor would never call him illiterate again.

Wednesday, May 24. Eleanor did not want to get out of her cozy bed. She stared at the ceiling while she recounted the things that needed to be remembered: Wednesday is full of woe, Frieda is dead, Gertie is buried, Walter isn't here, Josephine took the cat. She would not leave Feathers at home today, a serial killer was poisoning old people, Nora would be here to clean the house.

She dragged herself into the bathroom to complete her morning ritual. She felt a little better. Feathers did not greet her when she lifted the cover from his cage. He merely peered at her with one eye and then closed it again. He must have been exhausted after yesterday. Eleanor dressed and ate a small bowl of cereal. She loaded Feathers, cage and all, into her car, tucked the morning paper under her arm and drove away.

When she returned later that evening, the sun was setting over the ocean in a glorious display of color. Gold and crimson faded to deep purple and the darkness that was night.

Eleanor heard the phone ringing. She dreamt of Walter. He just called to say he loved her. Reality seeped in and Eleanor fumbled for the phone, knocking over a glass of water.

"Hello," she managed in her morning voice.

"Eleanor? Is that you?" It was Angus. "Did I wake you?"

"No, oh no," she lied. She glanced at the time. It was early for a call from Angus. "What's up?"

"I was thinking you and I might go out to dinner tonight. I figure it's my turn to feed you. What do you say?" Angus didn't mince words.

"Okay." Eleanor shook her head hoping that would clear the sleep out.

"I'll pick you up at six." Angus hung up.

Eleanor hung up too and thought about Thursday, May 25. She needed to mail a birthday card to her daughter, a sympathy card to Frieda's family, walk, Walter wasn't here, serial killer still on the loose, now dinner with Angus.

Eleanor got up to check on Feathers. As she walked to his cage she felt an ache in her feet that she hadn't felt before. Feathers seemed his old self. Yesterday had been good for him after the scary cat caper the day before. She wondered how L.C. fared at Josephine's cat house and then laughed out loud at her own cleverness.

"Talking to yourself, Ellie?" She could hear Walter tease her as he often did when he caught her having an animated conversation. He would mimic her facial expressions and laugh. She didn't miss his spying, but she missed his laughter.

"Okay, Feathers, what will it be today?" she asked as she put fresh pellets in his dish.

"Apple please," he answered.

Eleanor left the cage door open and went to the kitchen for fresh water and fruit. Feathers followed her all the while chatting companionably. She stroked his feathers tenderly and fed him a bit of apple.

"Thank you, Ellie, I love you, Ellie," he imitated Walter's voice.

"I think I love you too," she admitted reluctantly.

On her way to the beach, Eleanor remembered the hidey-hole near Bootsy's house. How strange that she thought of it no longer as Jean's house. So quickly we adapt to change. She wondered where Jean was recuperating and how she might be getting along. She wondered about the poisonings and it occurred to her that Jean could easily become a victim of the killer. She was over eighty. Who else did she know that might be at risk? Shouldn't the police be alerting people so that they could protect themselves? So many questions. Eleanor had no answers and no idea where to get them. She didn't know how to reach Jean's family, or Frieda's family. These women had been her friends, but she didn't really know their children. Eleanor had left a card for Gertie's family at the funeral. She wouldn't know how to contact them either. Was that normal? Even her closest friends from the coffee group didn't share their children's addresses or phone numbers. Eleanor had never had any reason to contact them. She knew where they lived generally and the names of their grandchildren and accomplishments, but they were basically out of reach.

Just out of curiosity, Eleanor checked the hidey-hole. The treasures were still there. She passed Bootsy's empty house and continued on her way.

The weather looked promising. It was too early for wind and except for numerous sea gulls, Eleanor had the beach to herself. She walked briskly along the water line where the sand was wet and firm. She felt the breeze lift her hair and allowed her thoughts to flow. Further down the shoreline she saw the body of a seagull and watched as it was washed away by an outgoing wave. How simple nature was! Birth, life and death were all taken in stride. The clean up so easy . . . dead body washed away without a trace. Humans were so dramatic with their rituals and so tiresome with their grief. She thought more and more about dying and wondered what her death would be like. She hoped for what she called the "Cadillac of Death," which would be living until she died in her sleep or just dropped dead with no lead-in that consisted of a painful dying process. No long goodbyes for her. When she was no longer useful but before she became a burden on those she loved, she would just die. Wasn't that everyone's wish? And when it was over, well who cared? Who spent hours planning their own funerals, choosing the songs, food, passages, and final resting place? Some people did, but that wasn't what she wanted. What was a celebration of life? Why celebrate it after death? She would have an enormous party while she was still living and then nothing. Fine, but how does one get the Cadillac of Death? Sometimes you just have to take what you get and for many it was awful and prolonged.

Old age was filled with pitfalls and losses. Eleanor realized she was in a period of loss. What if she was the last of her friends to die? No one would remember the young, vital Eleanor. Who would come to visit? Who would reminisce about sock hops, skinny dipping, or transistor radios? What would she do when she could no longer figure out how to manage the new technology? She might not be able to use the phone or turn on the television. If she lost the ability to drive, she would have to leave her home by the ocean and move to the city. Eleanor shook her head. She could control her thoughts. There was nothing to be gained by this line of thinking except anxiety.

Just then, something glimmering in the sunlight caught her eye. As she reached down for it, a sneaker wave rolled in soaking her to her knees. Now she was angry with herself as well as wet. She knew better than to take her eyes off that beautiful but treacherous ocean. At least no one was on the beach to witness her distress. She decided to head home knowing it would be a miserable walk with shoes full of sand and sea water, but the shiny thing lay revealed on the sand at her feet. Checking the waves, she stooped once more and picked up a ring. It looked like gold with a large clear blue stone cut like a square. Eleanor slipped it on her finger and began the hike home. When she reached Bootsy's tree, she took off the ring and put it inside the hidey-hole.

As she approached her house, Eleanor noticed the police car parked outside. She remembered Angus telling her they might want to talk to her about the day Frieda died. Seeing her, the officer got out of the car and walked toward her. She recognized him immediately as a young man who took her writing class a few years ago at the community college.

"Hello, Mrs. Penrose." He smiled showing off a spectacular set of white teeth.

"Andrew McGraw, how lovely to see you again." Eleanor didn't always remember names but felt pleased with herself today at getting this one right. "Sorry, I'm soaked and really need to get out of these wet things. Please come inside." Eleanor kicked off her soggy shoes and socks and left them on the porch.

Officer McGraw entered the house and waited while Eleanor changed into dry pants.

"Thank you for waiting," offered Eleanor as she returned. "Please sit down. Could I get you something to drink?"

"No thank you, Mrs. Penrose. I just have a few questions for you about Frieda VanHorn and then I'll be on my way." He flashed that dazzling smile again, and Eleanor caught herself wishing she was just a little younger and mentally slapped herself for being so foolish.

"What do you need to know?" she asked.

"Tell me about the last time you saw her. When was it?" Officer McGraw took out a little notebook and began to write.

"I went over to her house Saturday afternoon about 3:00. We chatted, and I left about 4:00." Eleanor remembered Frieda's blue eyes and began to tear up.

"What was the reason for your visit?" he continued.

"We were friends. I just wanted to see her. There wasn't really a reason other than that."

"How did she seem to you? Was she ill or depressed? Did you notice anything off or unusual?" he seemed to be writing down a great deal more than Eleanor was saying.

"No, there was nothing unusual. Frieda was old and often in pain from her arthritis, but she seemed upbeat that day."

"Did you drink anything while you were there?" he asked casually.

"We both had tea, I believe. Frieda only drank Lipton's green tea." Eleanor suddenly remembered the unexpected visitor. "I almost forgot Jessica Honeycutt came just before I left. I was surprised to know that Frieda's hairdresser made house calls."

The officer looked up briefly and continued writing as he spoke, "Is that the Honeycutt that works at 'Curl Up and Dye'?"

"Yes, she does my hair too." Eleanor added.

"I think that's all I need right now. Please call me if you remember anything else." He spoke as he moved to the door and was gone.

He didn't even say I had been a great help, Eleanor thought. Maybe she hadn't been. Was there a clue there somewhere? He did ask if she had something to drink. Was the poison in Frieda's tea? Did Jessica Honeycutt have any reason to poison Frieda? Maybe she poisoned the shampoo. Eleanor remembered reading a mystery about nicotine poison in a victim's shampoo.

Eleanor needed a shower. She would inspect the shampoo carefully.

Eleanor spent the rest of the day putzing around the house doing laundry, tidying up, catching up on correspondences, and taking a much-needed nap. She rarely slept during the day, but lately she found herself dozing off while reading or watching television. Maybe this was normal for someone her age. She hoped she wasn't coming down with something.

When 6:00 rolled around, Eleanor found herself looking forward to Angus's arrival. She chose to wear black slacks and a new pink sweater that put a glow in her cheeks. After primping in the mirror, she even put on a bit of mascara and applied a tint of lipstick. Absolutely unheard of, she thought. What was happening to her?

The door bell sounded, and she hurried to answer it.

Angus did not ask her where she wanted to go but had already decided on the Galley. It was near the water, decorated like the inside of a vessel, and had delicious seafood. They sat in a corner by the window and ordered Crown Royal for him and white wine for her. The sun had not set yet and its rays sparkled as they hit the water.

"It's beautiful here," Eleanor sighed. Suddenly she felt happy to be alive in this moment.

Angus tilted his head and smiled in agreement. "It never gets old: sun on the water, good whiskey, and pleasant company to enjoy it."

They sat and sipped their drinks talking about trivial things, remembering old times and lost friends. Time passed quickly. Their waitress brought their dinners. Eleanor ordered grilled halibut with tomato vinaigrette and was surprised when Angus opted for grilled salmon with red beet and orange relish and coarse-grain mustard beurre blanc.

"I didn't know you were such an adventurous eater." She said between bites.

"You only live once. I'm not who you think. Sometimes I like something different." Angus was just a little defensive.

"Do you like it?" she quizzed.

"Can't go wrong with salmon," he filled his mouth with a big bite and smiled. Eleanor had no idea if he really liked it or not. She silently thought he looked handsome in his jeans and sports jacket.

"How's Frieda's cat?"

Eleanor related the sad story of Feathers and the cat who everyone thought was a female but turned out to be a male. She recited her poem in the most theatrical way and they both laughed until tears ran down their cheeks. Then they ordered more drinks and watched the sun set.

"So beautiful and yet so dangerous," Angus looked at the ocean and then at Eleanor.

"I got slammed by a sneaker wave this morning, so I know exactly what you mean. Then Andrew McGraw showed up to inquire about Frieda's death. Why do they think it was poison?" Eleanor had been patiently waiting for this opportunity to question Angus.

Angus had hoped to avoid any talk about the case. He really didn't know all that much anyway but he threw out the only clue they had, "Henry Ott had a dog, Spike. Whoever poisoned Henry also poisoned Spike. It was weird, so they did an autopsy and found pentobarbital in his blood and in the dog too. During that investigation, they learned that there were similar deaths attributed to pentobarbital around the county. Some were thought to be suicides. Now they are treating every death as a possible homicide."

"Frieda? For sure?"

"Uncertain, once they know what to look for, a simple blood test can tell. We may never know about all of them because pentobarbital can't be detected after two days. A lot of those older people who died might have been poisoned, or they might have had heart attacks. Frieda didn't have pentobarbital in her system. She had stopped taking her prescription medications. All of her pill vials were empty, but she was found sitting in her chair like the others." Angus was ready to change the subject. He didn't want to upset Eleanor and end up sleeping on her sofa again, so he pointed to the ever-growing beauty that was unfolding as the sky turned blood red.

Eleanor woke from a delightful dream starring Tom Selleck. She felt all warm and tingly as she went through her mental list: Friday, May 26, coffee group, walk, work in her office, Walter wasn't here. She really needed to call her daughter, Erin. "Get out of bed, old lady." Sometimes her body responded to an authoritarian voice.

The Boat House smelled like bacon and strong coffee when Eleanor opened the door and found her seat among her favorite people.

Cleo and Pearl both sported wounds on their faces as though they had been in a bar room brawl.

"What happened to you two?" she asked.

"Skin cancer," they answered in unison.

"Was it a two-for-one sale?" Eleanor kidded, knowing it wasn't really funny. What can one say under the circumstances? The C word always conjured thoughts of suffering and death, yet her friends didn't seem concerned.

"We never used sunscreen when we were young and now we're paying for it." Pearl said.

"It won't kill us," added Cleo, "at least not until after breakfast."

"How strange that both of you have it at the same time!" Josephine hinted that it might be contagious and made a mental note to contact her dermatologist as soon as possible.

Pearl took the opportunity to share the interesting patchwork quality of skin on her arm, "My grandmother had this pattern on her arms and I always thought it was so beautiful, and now I have it."

Cleo squinted and studied it closely while Josephine reached over the table to feel it.

Just then Dede joined them, "Did you two have a knock-down-drag-out?" and the entire conversation was repeated for her benefit.

"My neighbor had the same thing last month. She looks much better now. I'm sure you two will survive." Dede reassured them, and they believed her because she was Dede.

"Did you see this article from the *Oregonian* about the early signs of Alzheimer's disease?" she asked as she whipped out a section of the morning newspaper.

"No, what does it say?" Josephine was piqued because no one would deliver the daily paper to her house because she lived up the river.

"Let's see, memory loss that disrupts daily life, like forgetting something you just learned, asking the same questions repeatedly and relying on lists." Dede looked at the others with one eyebrow raised.

Silence, even though they all knew they relied heavily on their calendars and made copious lists.

She continued, "Difficulty planning or solving problems; such as paying monthly bills or following a recipe, and difficulty completing familiar tasks; like losing your way to a friend's house." Here they all looked at Cleo.

"It was dark and pouring down rain. Plus, I wasn't wearing my glasses." Cleo defended herself because she took the wrong turn on her way to book club when it was at Pearl's house. No one would have known about it if she hadn't blabbed, but it frightened her when the road narrowed and turned to gravel.

"Moving on," Dede continued, "Time or place confusion; not knowing the month or season or forgetting where they are or how they got there."

"Annie Dodd," they said together remembering their concern about her when she told them about driving down a familiar road and not knowing where she was.

Strange movements from Josephine caused the others to stop and look her way. She had both arms inside her top and was twisting it around her body in the most awkward way revealing her bare midriff.

"Was it on backwards?" asked Dede?

"Yes, the tag was in the front," she said as she struggled to get her arms into the proper holes while her friends began to titter. Soon the tittering turned into laughter and they couldn't stop.

The waitress came to take their orders. By now she knew each by name and their usual breakfast preferences.

"Do you remember that old cult movie *Harold and Maude?*" Cleo began digging in her bag.

"Is that the one about the old woman who has an affair with a young man?" asked Pearl.

"Yes," Cleo pulled her iPad out and began tapping. "I was thinking about how Maude killed herself when she hit 80 and all the people who have been dying lately have been over 80. You've got to see this."

She directed their attention to a page on the internet titled "Maude Squad".

"What's the Maude Squad?" Josephine asked.

"Just tell us," Pearl ordered. She didn't want to listen to any more readings.

"It's very mysterious, but it's an organization that puts people out of their misery after they reach 80." Cleo explained.

"Like the Hemlock Society." Dede added knowingly.

"It doesn't say exactly how they do it, but maybe they are responsible for the deaths here. I got the impression they don't follow all the rules set out by the Death with Dignity Act." Cleo said.

"If they don't follow the law, that's murder," said Josephine, ready for an indictment.

"What if the victim asks for it somehow?" Eleanor asked thoughtfully. "What if they are suffering and want to die?"

"Still murder." Josephine persisted.

"But if that's what is happening here, we can stop worrying about a serial killer." Dede reassured them.

"Let's just go with that then." Cleo put her iPad back in her purse just in time to get a refill of coffee.

Eleanor waited for the waitress to leave then lowered her voice, "Angus told me that Henry and some others were poisoned with pentobarbital. Isn't that the drug used by the Death with Dignity people?"

"I'm sure that's it. Remember when my mother saved all her pills so if she needed to die, she could do herself in and then got Alzheimer's and forgot where she put them?" Cleo laughed. "There is just no winning!"

"That's why they say old age is not for sissies." Dede quoted. "We have to take care of each other. We're in this together. If one of us begins to fail in some way we must take action."

They looked at each other knowing none of them would ever say a word if one of the others began to "fail" as Dede put it. They loved each other too much.

Eleanor was on a mission. A thought had occurred to her on the drive home, and as soon as she entered her house she rushed to her office to work on it. Bootsy would never find the hidey-hole without some clue to point her in that direction. She needed to set the stage for mystery and Eleanor decided a secret code would do the trick. There was a simple one she had used before where each letter of the alphabet corresponded to a number. A B C 1 2 3. She quickly wrote a little poem to lead Bootsy to the tree. She wanted to have it all in place before her family came for the weekend—if they came for the weekend.

Eleanor found herself hoping that was the case as she printed out the code:

23-8-1-20 2-15-15 18-1-4-12-25 4-9-4 6-15-18 19-3-15-21-20

9-12-12 4-15 6-15-18 25-15-21 19-15 3-8-5-3-11 9-20 15-21-20

9-14 20-8-5 20-18-5-5 1-3-18-15-19-19 20-8-5 19-20-18-5-5-20

20-18-5-1-19-21-5 23-1-9-20-19 19-15 21-19-5 25-15-21-18 6-5-5-20

She cut the bottom out of a small plastic bottle, inserted the note, and put the bottom back. Perfect.

Eleanor changed her clothes and left the house. As she walked down the hill she remembered the conversation during coffee. What a lovely diversion Bootsy gave her from the topics of dementia, cancer, and death. It was much better to think about secret codes and treasures hidden in old trees. She felt revitalized as she put her plan into action. She left the bottle on Bootsy's deck near one of the guardian seagulls where it could not be missed and continued on her way to the beach.

Her mind wandered to her own grandchildren who had grown past the age for such games. There was a time when they visited often, but school, friends, and sports had taken them out of her everyday world. Now they were traveling with their parents on a year-long tour. How selfish of them! How wonderful for them! She would manage. Walter always said they were successful parents because their children grew up and left the nest. He quoted some nonsense about bows and arrows. A metaphor that meant they never really belonged to us. No one ever really belongs to another. Eleanor often thought Walter belonged to her, but time had proven her wrong on that score too.

Weekenders who arrived early paraded on the beach with their dogs and children. Eleanor lifted her face to the breeze and felt it lift her hair. Too much beauty to feel sad, she thought as she picked up the pace and searched for treasures along the shore.

On her way home, she picked up her mail and delighted in a colorful postcard from Amy. They were in Paris. How lovely to spend spring in a French villa. She could go there. What kept her here? She knew.

When she got back to her house she kicked off her shoes and took the mail into the office where she added the postcard to a drawer filled with others like it. She sorted the mail, paid the bills and picked up her pen:

> I walk alone,
> The night is cold but I feel
> Neither chill nor warmth.
> A hundred tiny lanterns twinkle
> In the grass,
> While millions flicker up above.
> The night is here
> The cold is real
> There are a thousand sights and smells
> As sharp as broken glass
> But my eyes are dimmed by foggy membranes.
> My senses dulled by the armor I inhabit.
> Locked in tight
> My mind
> Like fine gold dust
> Escapes and scatters into night.

Feathers looked down from his perch, strangely silent. His yellow eyes seemed to judge her, for what she didn't know. Neglect maybe.

Eleanor stretched her weary body and went to Feathers to stroke his smooth feathers and coo sweet nothings to him.

Eleanor accomplished everything on her to-do list, bathed, washed her hair, and brushed her teeth. There was nothing on television she wanted to watch. She wandered aimlessly around the house making sure the doors were locked, the windows closed, and Feathers tucked in his cage for the night. In the kitchen, every dish had been washed and put away.

What would she be doing if Walter were here? Most of the time they were in separate rooms working on their own projects or reading companionably; she on the sofa and he in his chair. Sometimes they watched a movie together. He always made the popcorn. It was his thing. What was so different now? She could just pretend he was in another room, yet she could not. She had tried that. There is something about being alone, really alone, that feels palpable, as if emptiness is like a being who sucks all the air out of the room, and the only sound is the constant ticking of the clock, just to remind you that there is only time and no one to share it. Eleanor lamented that there was no Walter to tell about the pelicans she had seen on the beach today. He loved wildlife. She regretted that there was no Walter to tell her there was a full moon tonight and it would be the flower moon. He would tell her to put on her shoes and lead her out on the deck to watch it rise over the hills, drape his jacket over her shoulders, and he would be there when it set over the ocean; only he wasn't. Eleanor was alone.

"Enough," she spoke to her sad and sorry self. Not wanting to wallow, Eleanor went in search of something to distract her. In the living room she searched through her CDs, put on *Meet the Beatles* and sang along to "I Want to Hold Your Hand." The soundtrack of her youth was just the ticket.

She woke a few hours later and wandered toward her bedroom. The full moon hovered over the ocean like a torch lighting the white foam of the waves below. It was beautiful. She stood transfixed. If she was an artist she would paint that moon against a dark indigo sky, but really nothing humans could do would ever match it. She put on her shoes, threw an afghan over her shoulders, and stepped out onto the deck. The breaking of the waves was louder and pleasantly soothing. She looked to the sky and sang a song from her childhood:

> I see the moon
> The moon sees me
> The moon sees the one I want to see
> So God bless the moon and God bless me
> And God bless the one I want to see

Eleanor watched until the moon disappeared into the sea.

Saturday dawned and Eleanor woke with the sun shining through her windows. Saturday, May 27, no Walter, but maybe Bootsy would return for the weekend. Such unexpected delight caused Eleanor to sit up and almost jump out of bed. She could hardly wait to see if Bootsy could figure out the note and find the treasure.

Feathers greeted her loudly, whistling a happy tune. It was going to be a great day. Eleanor readied herself for a brisk walk on the beach, hoping she could beat most of the weekenders and not have to share her stretch of sand. As she passed Bootsy's house, she noticed their car parked along the lane and saw that the bottle with the note was gone. How long would it take for her to unlock the code? She hurried on her way feeling somewhat young and vibrant. Nothing could make a person happier than fresh air and sunshine.

On Eleanor's return, Bootsy jumped out of the bushes, "Boogity Boogity!" she squealed. It startled Eleanor only for a moment. Then her surprise turned to delight, and relief turned to laughter. In her hand, Bootsy held the treasures from the hidey-hole and her face was bright with excitement and joy.

"How exquisite to be young and fresh and so full of life," thought Eleanor. She wanted to catch some of it. "Hooray, you're back!" she exclaimed.

"This was the best," Bootsy chirped. "I loved the clue and the treasures." She held up her finger with the blue ring on it and chanted;

"What Boo Radley did for Scout

I'll do for you so check it out

In the tree across the street

Treasure waits, so use your feet."

It pleased Eleanor that Bootsy found it all exciting. Everything old is new again through the eyes of children.

"Is it okay if I come over to your house?" Bootsy asked shyly.

"I would love your company today." Eleanor meant it. "You better check with your mother." She knew from experience that this was a step never left to chance.

They climbed the hill together sharing their favorite parts of *To Kill a Mockingbird*. Bootsy held Eleanor's book, which she hoped to trade in for the one about monsters Eleanor told her about earlier. Kicking off their shoes at the door, they entered the house and went immediately to the bookshelf where Eleanor found *Oregon's Ghosts and Monsters* and put it in Bootsy's eager grasp. Bootsy wanted to read about Bandage Man as soon as possible but didn't want to give up one minute of time spent in the company of her new friend.

"Let's bake brownies," suggested Eleanor.

"I love brownies!" Bootsy was all in.

As they worked in the kitchen Bootsy filled Eleanor in on her week at school. She had had a falling out with her good friend, but they had made up just in time for Bootsy to leave for the weekend. There had been several very important tests and assignments that Bootsy had accomplished with little effort, and there was an annoying boy who followed her around on the playground for no good reason.

"So how is Granny Scattergoods?" Eleanor asked.

"We visited her on our way here yesterday. She is still in rehab at a place called Twin Oaks, but Mom says they will put her in a home like my Dad's mom. I don't like the rehab center. It is full of old people and it smells like pee. I'm sure Granny hates it there too even though she can't say so. She shakes her head and says something that sounds like 'goat poop'. She has to be in a wheelchair because her left leg is paralyzed, and her left arm doesn't work either. Even her left face is pulled into a frown that makes her look like someone else. Mom says her tongue is paralyzed and that is why she can't talk. I want her to go back to her house. I think she would like that best." Bootsy ended on a sigh. "Do you think she will get better?"

"She might," Eleanor's tone was guarded. She didn't know how serious Jean's stroke had been or how strong she was and certainly didn't want to give Bootsy false hope.

"Mom says Granny might have another stroke and could die at any time. What do you think will happen to Granny if she dies?" Bootsy asked.

Eleanor didn't know how to respond because she didn't want to step over any line Bootsy's family may have drawn concerning life after death. "I don't know for sure. What do you think?" she asked.

"Mom says they will cremate her and throw her ashes in the ocean, but she will be an angel in heaven. I don't think Granny would like to be an angel because she was afraid of high places. That is called acrophobia. Do you believe in heaven, Eleanor?" Bootsy continued.

"I don't think I do. If I did I might have to believe in hell too and I just don't think a God I could believe in would ever send anyone to a place like that." Eleanor had stopped researching things she couldn't find answers to long ago.

"What if God is just the good in people?" Eleanor was surprised Bootsy would think such a thing.

"Then we would all be gods," she responded.

After deep consideration Bootsy spoke, "Granny would like that. I think she would rather be a goddess than an angel."

Eleanor remembered something she had that might make Bootsy feel better. "Come with me," she ordered.

Bootsy followed Eleanor into a room she didn't know existed. It might have been a bedroom. Shelves lining one wall were filled with beautifully decorated boxes. Eleanor searched through one or two until she found a necklace of some sort. It took Bootsy's breath away just looking at it. From a thin, silver chain hung an iridescent stone trapped by ornate filigree work. When Bootsy touched it, the stone turned a pale yellow and she felt a strange tingling in her fingers.

"Is it magic?" she asked.

"Not magic, but it is supposed to have healing powers. It's called Moonstone and is connected to the divine feminine. It can provide health and protection to your granny. You can take it to her when you visit her." Eleanor didn't remember where or why

64

she had it. It was most likely a gift from Josephine who enjoyed the studying of all things goddess.

"It looks like the moon," Bootsy said, studying it closely. "Will you help me put it on? If I wear it, I won't forget to take it to her."

"Excellent idea," Eleanor agreed as she assisted with the clasp.

Bootsy looked at the blue ring on her finger, "Now I have something special for each of my grannies. This blue ring is the color of my Nana's eyes. She will love it."

They could hear the oven timer go off in the kitchen and rushed off to take out the brownies.

Feathers followed them into the kitchen and did a little dance as he watched their every move.

Spying the moonstone around Bootsy's neck, he invited himself down for further investigation, startling her by landing on her shoulder. Spontaneous giggles erupted with lots of stroking and sweet high pitched nonwords that sounded to Eleanor like baby talk.

"Feathers is a sophisticated gentleman of mature age," chided Eleanor. "He responds to adult language."

As if to dispute Eleanor, Feathers rubbed his feathery face against Bootsy's smooth cheek and gave her a bird kiss on the lips. This caused even more giggling, which ended with Feathers flying off in a fit of parrot like humiliation.

"Well, I guess you never really know someone," quipped Eleanor.

Bootsy studied Eleanor closely, "Your eyes are blue too just like my Nana's. I don't remember her before she got sick and now she doesn't know me. I wish you were my Nana."

Eleanor smiled sadly. Bootsy didn't know just how well she understood.

While they waited for the brownies to cool, they returned to what Bootsy now thought of as the treasure room. Eleanor said she had seen something there that needed more attention. Much to Bootsy's delight, Eleanor brought out a brightly colored kite in the shape of a fish with long purple tails streaming behind.

"Let's go fly a kite." Eleanor began to sing and was pleasantly surprised when Bootsy joined in with a sweet clear voice,

"Up to the highest height!
Let's go fly a kite and send it soaring
Up through the atmosphere
Up where the air is clear
Oh, let's go fly a kite!"
And the day was perfect.

Later that evening, after her bath, Eleanor massaged cream on her tired old feet. She felt new calluses and wondered how long she could keep up with Bootsy. She remembered another night when Walter had caught her rubbing lotion on those same feet.

"Give up on your face?" he teased. She missed his humor and the clever things he said that for some reason surprised her. Eleanor never thought of him as clever or funny, but he was. After their honeymoon one morning as they lay in bed she asked him what he wanted for breakfast.

"Sheepherder's Delight," he answered.

"What's that?" She figured it was something his mom made for him. She had never heard of it.

"A little piece of you," he laughed as he reached for her.

Those days were gone, but at least she had her memories.

"Memories don't keep you warm at night." She told herself as she pulled the comforter over herself.

Sunday, May 28, Eleanor woke well rested. Today she would walk, read the Sunday *Oregonian*, Walter wasn't here, and she needed to read the book for book club. If her hips didn't ache she would just lie in bed a little longer, but they did so she sat up and stretched every achy joint. Bootsy would be busy today doing "family stuff". She and her mother planned to take a picnic to Granny Scattergoods. It made Eleanor happy to think of them together. Who knew where the father was? Busy professionals didn't always find time for their families. Jean Scattergoods would be thrilled. Eleanor planned to visit her sometime later in the week, but not today. Today Eleanor rested.

The crossword puzzle was easy this morning and she zipped through the Sudoku and jumble too. Eleanor poured herself a second cup of coffee and distractedly perused the personal ads until one caught her eye:

Maude, I'm ready for you. Meet me at 301 Water St, Silverton, OR.

Strange, Eleanor never read the personals, but today the words jumped off the page at her. Could this be the Maude Squad? The seeds of an idea began to form in her mind. Maybe this explained how they knew when to go and where to bring their form of mercy to those over eighty. It didn't answer all the questions she had but it was a start. Should she call Angus? Should she go to 301 Water Street to see if the person who lived there was over 80 and wanting to die? If she called Angus, she could definitely not go to Silverton, but it might be a pleasant road trip for her coffee friends. Of course, it might be the silly idea of a lonely old woman with too much time on her hands and nothing more. She decided to call Cleo to check her own reality.

Her conversation with Cleo was brief and that in itself was unusual considering how much Cleo liked to talk, but as it turned out Cleo reminded Eleanor that it was Memorial Day weekend and her family had gathered to celebrate with a cookout. Although she was in the middle of something and children were heard in the background, Eleanor could tell how excited Cleo was when she related news about the personal ad. Cleo was totally in for the trip to Silverton. They would call the others and go on Tuesday.

Tuesday morning dawned gray and foggy, but as Eleanor woke and recited her litany of daily dos: Tuesday, May 30, the real Memorial Day, go to Silverton, Walter isn't here; she knew it would be warm and sunny in the valley. She dressed accordingly, fed Feathers and herself then jumped in her car to pick up her fellow investigators.

The ladies of the coffee group decided to meet at Dede's house because she lived in town. Cleo insisted on driving, "You know I get car sick unless I can hang on to the steering wheel."

The others relented even though they knew Cleo never knew how to get anywhere. The two hours would fly while they talked about everything except their surgeries or illnesses. These topics were forbidden because they made Cleo squeamish.

"So, what do you think will happen when we get there?" asked Cleo. "Do we have a plan?"

"I will go to the door and ring the bell," Eleanor began.

"Should we stay in the car?" asked Pearl.

"Maybe you could say you are collecting data for the census," Josephine added. "Then you could ask how old they are and if they live alone."

"That's a great idea," chimed in Dede. "But don't they take the census every 10 years? We are only in the middle of a decade."

"Maybe I could be taking a survey." Eleanor regrouped. She really liked the census idea.

"You will need a clipboard, paper, and pen if you want to look official," Josephine said.

"We can stop at the Office Depot in Salem. I know exactly where it is," Cleo crowed.

The others simply rolled their eyes and kept quiet. Maybe she did know.

After a quick stop at Office Depot, which turned out to take an hour and a half, the ladies returned to the car, loaded their purchases in the trunk, and decided they needed lunch. So far everyone was having a great time. While Josephine and Cleo had checked out office chairs, Eleanor found her survey supplies and Dede and Pearl wandered into a resale shop. Eleanor spotted a diner on the same street, so in they went.

"I'd really like a martini," Cleo informed everyone.

"I could drive your car since it is just like mine," offered Josephine.

"Better keep our heads clear. We don't know what we will find on Water Street," cautioned Dede.

They all ordered sandwiches and iced tea then continued on their quest.

As they drove down Water Street they noticed several emergency vehicles near their destination.

"Cleo, pull off to the side," ordered Eleanor as she rolled down the window. A young woman with a baby on her hip stood on the sidewalk staring down the street.

"What's happened?" asked Eleanor.

The woman tore her eyes away and gave Eleanor a vacant look before answering, "Mrs. Ragsdale died."

"Oh, I'm so sorry. Was she a friend of yours?" Eleanor continued.

"Well, she was my neighbor and the sweetest person." The woman was obviously in a state of shock and continued to watch as two men wheeled a gurney with a body bag out of the house and put it in one of the vehicles.

"Was it an accident?" Eleanor was desperate to learn Mrs. Ragsdale's age.

"I don't really know how she died. She was very old and lived alone. I usually bring her mail to her door and ring her bell. Today she didn't answer. Her little dog didn't even bark, so I knew something was wrong. When I went inside she was just sitting in her chair as if she were sleeping, but I could tell she wasn't there really." Her voice faded to a whisper. "I called the police. I didn't know what else to do."

"Ask her about the dog," whispered Pearl.

"Did you find her dog? Can we help in any way?" Eleanor's voice conveyed her deep concern.

"That's the strangest thing. Her little dog was sleeping on her lap." She stepped away from the car as a man approached and began talking to her. A big boat of a car pulled up behind them and Cleo slowly drove down the street while everyone else craned their necks to see the address on the house.

"There it is," pointed Dede, "That is 301 Water Street. We need to get out of here before someone starts questioning us as suspects."

"They all think she died of natural causes because she was old," Cleo reminded them as she sped down the street and headed for home.

"We don't know that for sure." Eleanor was thinking of Angus and the facts he knew but didn't share.

For a long time, no one spoke. It was eerily quiet.

"I wonder if the dog was really sleeping," Pearl said breaking the silence.

"Henry Ott's dog was poisoned along with Henry. Angus told me that," Eleanor said thoughtfully. They were all trying to come to some conclusion that made sense.

"So this is what we think we know: some group known as the Maude Squad is killing people at their request," Josephine began.

"Yes, and they are all over 80 and sometimes they also kill their pets," Pearl said seemingly more concerned about the pets than the people.

"Maybe they ask to have their pets put down too so they won't worry about what happens to them after they're gone," Cleo speculated.

"The personal ads are their way of communicating with the Maude Squad when they are ready to die," Josephine said as she continued her train of thought. "I wonder how they find out about this squad."

"Cleo found out about it on the internet," answered Pearl.

"I wonder who belongs to this squad. Do you think these are people of compassion, or just people who get off on killing?" Cleo was going to a dark place.

"Well, what are we going to do with this information?" asked Dede.

"I'm going to tell Angus about what we learned today. He'll know what to do." Eleanor felt better about that decision.

"I think we all need to read the personal ads in the newspaper. Maybe we can stop whoever is doing this before it happens again," Pearl added. "I'm thirsty. Let's get milkshakes at the Dairy Queen."

Even milkshakes could not lighten the mood in the car on the way home. Questions about morality divided the group.

"I think suicide is wrong," Dede stated.

"It's so hard to know if you haven't walked in that person's shoes. Some people suffer horribly from physical and mental illnesses. I don't blame them for wanting to end it," declared Cleo.

"There is much to be learned through suffering. Despair is not an option. Things can always get better. There are new medicines and cures being discovered all the time," Dede argued.

"I think what we have here is just plain murder," Josephine said, reiterating her opinion from earlier. "If it was assisted suicide, they would go through the proper channels and not this cloak-and-dagger nonsense."

"I'm not sure what requirements a person must meet to be eligible for an assisted suicide, but I'll bet it doesn't include just being over eighty," Eleanor added.

"Don't you have to be terminal?" asked Pearl. "I'm sure you have to have two doctors agree that you're terminal."

"Aren't we all terminal?" asked Cleo.

"I'll google it," offered Dede.

"It won't make any difference. These people are servicing old people who for one reason or another want to die. They probably don't qualify for a legally assisted suicide or their families wouldn't allow it," Eleanor added.

Dede continued her search and reported, "Here are the eligibility requirements: a resident of California, Oregon, Vermont, or Washington, 18 years of age or older, mentally competent (capable of making and communicating your health care decisions, and diagnosed with a terminal illness that will, within reasonable medical judgment, lead to death within six months."

"There's the catch," Dede countered, "Who really knows if death will come within six months. Lots of people surpass their doctor's best guess about that."

"We don't know everything," Pearl interjected. "The Maude Squad might have their own requirements and these old people might meet them."

"Fortunately, we won't be in the position to judge. The law will take care of it and our opinions won't matter in the least." Josephine clearly was not in favor of what she considered murder.

"I can't help but wonder how to contact this Maude Squad in the first place." Cleo pondered. "There is no contact information on the internet."

As Cleo lost herself in thought, she lingered too long, and the red light turned green, causing the impatient driver behind her to lay on the horn.

"What's the hurry?" she muttered as she stepped on the gas. As the young man in the car came from behind, he revved his motor, passed her, and gave her the finger. "No respect anymore for little old ladies," Cleo complained. Dede gave him the finger back and they continued on their way home.

Wednesday, May 31, the last day of May, Nora would come to clean, day of woe, Walter wasn't here, but he was there. Eleanor ate her meager breakfast of yogurt and cereal, drank her coffee, got in her car and drove away.

Rosewood Manor sat on a lush green hillside surrounded by stately oak trees and flanked by rose gardens and a pond. Eleanor was always impressed by its lovely façade. It could have been someone's private home once, but now it was a facility that expanded in the back to house its many patients. Unlike other nursing homes with their glass and metal entryways, Rosewood's solid oak doors welcomed her warmly as its guest. As she entered the foyer, she could smell the scent of lemon furniture polish and flowers. The carpet cushioned her every step and the walls were covered with happy landscapes. None of it made Eleanor happy.

She signed the visitor's log and walked the long hall to Walter's wing. Here she punched in the security code that allowed her in and kept the patients from exiting. A young woman with a bright smile and blue scrubs welcomed her with a nod, "Walter is in his room". Eleanor walked slowly, taking in the condition of the common rooms and the other patients. Everything looked neat and clean. The patients were dressed. Several of them shuffled toward the dining area, their eyes vacant. An energetic woman with gray hair approached Eleanor and grabbed her hand.

"I'm so glad to see you, dear!" Her voice was full of joy, but Eleanor knew the joy was misplaced and Marietta thought she was someone else. Eleanor always played along.

"Marietta, you look fabulous." Eleanor forced a smile. She could not get her hand free.

"I'm wearing my new red shoes," she carried on as she led Eleanor closer to the dining area. "The ones you brought me last week." Eleanor had never seen the red shoes before, but she nodded and patted Marietta's hand.

"I'm off to visit Walter." She slipped her hand away and continued to room 113.

Marietta waved wildly and spoke in a girlish high-pitched voice, "I'll save a place for you at lunch."

Walter sat in his chair looking out the window. He was dressed in jeans and a freshly pressed shirt. He wore a new pair of Nikes. Eleanor studied his clean-shaven face and wondered if he always looked this good, or if it was just every Wednesday when they knew she would visit. She thought about coming unexpectedly on some other day, but never did.

"Good morning, Sweetheart." Eleanor approached him cautiously. She never knew from one visit to the next how he would respond.

He slowly raised his eyes to her face. A glimmer of recognition came and went. He furrowed his brow as if trying to get it back, but it was gone.

Eleanor bent to brush her lips on his upturned cheek, sat on his bed, and began what was her weekly litany, filling him in on all that had happened during their time apart. Walter continued to look out the window, interrupting her only once when he spied a red-winged blackbird sitting in a shrub outside. "Nest," he said, pointing with a well-manicured finger. It wasn't much, but it was moments like this that made Eleanor feel Walter might still be in there somewhere.

"Let's go outside, Walter." Eleanor rose and took Walter's hand as he obediently got up from his chair.

They left Walter's cozy little room and walked slowly down the hall to a door that opened to an enclosed garden area. Several other patients sat on benches enjoying the sunshine, but no one spoke. Walter ambled over to a tree and studied a leaf closely. Eleanor watched and waited. It was her Wednesday ritual. A day with Walter and nothing else, and it was often a day of nothing. Even as she knew it was so, she hoped for something more.

Lunch was served in the dining room at noon. It was turkey on toast with gravy and green beans and chocolate cake. Eleanor ate with little appetite as she made small talk with Marietta and one of the aides who hand-fed another patient at their table. Walter remained quiet and was able to feed himself with shaky hands. Eleanor watched and wondered how long before he needed help.

After lunch some residents retired to their rooms to nap while Eleanor and Walter found seats in the theater to watch an old movie. It helped the time go by. Eleanor could pretend for a short while that Walter was still hers as she held his hand and watched

Jimmy Stewart save Dean Martin from the gallows. She knew when
he nodded off by the change in his breathing, but she enjoyed the
warmth of his skin and the intimacy of his touch.

As they left the theater, Eleanor spotted Alice in one of the
living areas. A guest musician sat at the piano playing show tunes.
Several residents sat while others stood around tapping their feet
to the beat of "Singing in the Rain". Marietta danced around the
room delighted by the whole affair. Walter saw Alice sitting on
a loveseat across the room and moved to sit beside her, leaving
Eleanor standing by herself. It was the hateful part of every visit
that Eleanor dreaded . . . Alice. She watched as Walter smiled
sweetly at this other woman and seemed to whisper in her ear.
What did he say to her? Who did he think she was? Alice was
old with short white hair and big blue eyes. Eleanor had never
heard her speak, but knew she had a past as a barmaid and who
knew what else. She definitely had something that pleased Walter.
Eleanor felt her eyes fill as Walter reached for Alice's hand. She
quickly walked to a nearby restroom and locked the door. She knew
Walter couldn't help it and neither could Alice, but that didn't take
the sting out of it. Eleanor washed her face, composed herself, and
decided to go home.

It was a long drive and Eleanor was always exhausted and sad
when she arrived back in Sand Beach. All she wanted was a bath to
wash away the stink of the day and then bed.

Thursday, June 1, sunny and bright to follow woeful Wednesday,
Eleanor thought as she woke. Nora had cleaned the house. She
desperately needed to talk to Angus about the Maude Squad,

maybe dinner. Did she feel like baking? No, but a walk for sure, and something for Bootsy in the hidey-hole. Walter wasn't here. Get up!

Eleanor had neglected Feathers and felt guilty. She knew how much Walter enjoyed it when she brought him to Rosewood Manor and felt guilty again because she hadn't done it yesterday.

"Hello, my pretty." Feathers didn't seem to hold a grudge. He seemed to like Nora and had spent the day with her as she cleaned.

"No harm, no fowl," Eleanor joked, laughing at her own wit.

Eleanor readied herself for a long walk through the trees on the path behind her house. Just recently she read about the benefits of trees on your mental and physical well-being. She knew from her own experience that sunlight and fresh air could heal a weary soul. She moved dynamically down the path determined to put thoughts of Walter and Alice out of her mind. Sometimes as she walked and emptied her mind solutions to bothersome problems and creative ideas came unbidden. It was as if a muse waited for an opening in her otherwise busy brain and unexpectedly flooded her mind with marvelous ideas.

Eleanor pondered the puzzle of the Maude Squad. Who would you contact if you wanted to die? Who would do it? How would you let them know? Was it murder or kindness? Was a life full of pain and misery a life worth living? Did people have the right to die when they had reached their limit? Did other people have the right to keep them alive once they had decided enough was enough? Was there something to be learned through suffering? She couldn't imagine allowing a pet to suffer. How could it be different for a person? All these questions passed through her mind, but she had no answers.

Her thoughts turned to Walter. She knew he would hate the thought of losing his mind and the memories of a lifetime, yet she witnessed first-hand the joy in his eyes as he watched a bird build a nest and felt the warmth of the sun on his face. Reluctantly she admitted to herself that Walter enjoyed the part of his life now that he shared with Alice. Maybe in his mind, he felt the sweetness of a new love. The thought brought a pain so real she almost doubled over with grief and tears spilled down her cheeks. These were tears of pity for her, not for Walter. She felt the release of emotions long held in check but understood she could not go to this place too often or stay there too long. Eleanor could control her thoughts, had to control her thoughts, because to do otherwise was to invite in the demons of depression and anxiety.

She wiped away the tears and forced herself to plan a dinner party. Who would she invite? What would she serve? She would invite Angus and the coffee ladies. Should she include their husbands? Yes, the more the merrier. She would host a murder mystery dinner party! It was the perfect solution to lift her spirits. She knew reaching out to others would take her mind off her own troubles. Eleanor's mind wandered to thoughts of Bootsy and her granny. She wondered how Jean was doing and felt negligent for not visiting her. When she returned to her house she decided today would be the day to do it. She showered, dressed quickly, and drove to Twin Oaks.

It had been a long time since Eleanor had visited anyone here. As she pulled into the parking lot she noticed the crumbling stonework on the exterior of the building and thought the two oaks that flanked the entryway had seen better days. Dead Oaks would be a better name she muttered to herself. She grabbed the bouquet of yellow daisies she bought at the Safeway store and headed inside.

Bootsy had it right. The overwhelming stench of urine hit her like a slap in the face as she opened the door. The lobby was filled with shabby, faded furniture. Eleanor watched as several older residents shuffled down the long sterile hallway and others sat in wheelchairs. She asked the receptionist for Jean's room number and followed them. Her heels clicked on the cold, vinyl floor and with each step she gave thanks that Walter did not reside here, that she had two good legs to carry her where she wanted to go with little or no effort on her part, and a heart that could still be broken.

Jean Scattergoods lay in her bed in room 109. She looked pale and terribly thin under the yellowed sheet. Her gray hair was tangled, and her eyes were crusted with sleep. She reminded Eleanor of an old, abandoned cat that wandered into her yard once. Eleanor wanted to wash her face, comb her hair, and hold her. Instead, she smiled warmly as Jean's eyes opened and met hers. There was a hint of the old Jean as she recognized Eleanor and for a moment the right side of her lips turned up.

"Jean, I'm so glad to see you." Eleanor struggled to keep the concern out of her voice. "I brought you some daisies. I know yellow is your favorite color."

Jean tried to sit up but could not. She seemed agitated and pointed with her right hand to a pad that lay on the bedside table. Eleanor elevated the bed and put the paper in her hand along with a stubby pencil.

Jean began to scribble words on the pad while Eleanor watched the drool run down her chin. Eleanor smiled to see the moonstone necklace peeking out of Jean's gown. Bootsy had been here.

Suddenly the door flew open and a large woman in blue scrubs entered the room. She looked at Eleanor in surprise and then smiled at Jean.

"I see you have a visitor, Jean." Then she directed her flat, brown eyes to Eleanor. "I didn't know anyone was coming today or I would have cleaned her up earlier. She was sleeping and I didn't want to wake her. I see you brought some flowers. Daisies are such a happy flower. I'll put them in some water."

Jean wadded her note into a ball and Eleanor took it without reading it. There were no words to describe the desperate look that went with it.

"I'm sorry you can't stay, but Jean needs to go to physical therapy and I need to get her dressed," Blue Scrubs apologized when she returned with the daisies in a vase.

"I understand." Eleanor smiled. "I'll come back another time. You can count on it, Jean." Eleanor squeezed her friend's hand.

Jean's lips twisted and her jaw moved as she tried to speak, "Goat poop," was all Eleanor could understand.

As soon as she got in her car she opened her fist and read Jean's note. "I want to die" was all it said.

Eleanor was troubled by Jean's condition and her situation. Why would her daughter leave her in such a terrible place? She certainly understood Jean's wish and wondered if there was hope for her recovery.

As she drove down the lane that ran by her house, Eleanor noticed Angus's car and saw him appear from the deck.

"There you are," he said, his face breaking into a smile when he saw her.

"What brings you out here? Did you hear me thinking of you?" Eleanor smiled in return.

"Just in the neighborhood and thought I'd stop by," Angus said.

"Well come in. I'll make some fresh coffee. I have something I'd like to discuss." Eleanor led Angus into the house and busied herself in the kitchen while Angus tried to make nice with Feathers who refused to give him the time of day.

Eleanor put out some chocolate chip cookies. She knew Angus had a sweet tooth. The two chatted about ordinary things while they sipped their coffee until there was a natural pause in the conversation and Angus asked, "What's on your mind that needs discussing?"

For some odd reason what came out of her mouth surprised her. "I'm thinking of selling Walter's boat. He won't be using it anymore and I know that you like fishing. Do you want it?"

Angus's eyebrows shot up, but he maintained his cool. Eleanor never discussed anything to do with Walter. After several early attempts, Angus had given up. He wondered what had changed and if this signaled a breakthrough for Eleanor. Maybe she was finally facing the fact that Walter would never come home. He visited his old friend at Rosewood Manor occasionally and knew the disease had progressed. Selling the fishing boat was a good sign in Angus's eyes. "I'll have to look at it. What shape is it in?"

"Don't know and don't care. It's stored at the marina in Garibaldi and I haven't seen it in three years. You can have it if you want it. If not, I'll sell it on the internet." Eleanor hadn't given that boat much thought over the years but had simply paid the moorage fees. She would not miss it.

"I'll take a look at it this afternoon and give you a call later." Angus finished his coffee and stood to go.

Eleanor walked him to the door and realized she had not told him about the Maude Squad, the personal ad, or the trip to Silverton. She didn't know why, but she knew from now on, Angus would be left in the dark.

Friday, June 2, Eleanor woke to a view socked in with fog, coffee group, plan a dinner party, Walter wasn't here but he had been in her dreams. It came back to her slowly. Walter was with Alice in his room at Rosewood Manor when she walked through the door. The smug smile on Alice's face said it all while Walter looked dazed and confused. Remembering the betrayal caused Eleanor to burn with an anger she had never felt before. How dare this happen to her! She could still see Alice with her arms wrapped around Walter as if he belonged to her. Eleanor's Walter was now lost to her and without a word Alice told her, "He is not yours, he is mine."

The dream played before her eyes, more real than if it had happened, more painful because she believed it to be true and knew there was no coming back. There would be no, "I'm sorry, Ellie." No, "Please forgive me, Ellie." No, "Take me back, Ellie."

Eleanor took her anger to the bathroom, scrubbed her face, dressed and drove to the Boat House, all the while rewinding the nightmare and muttering nasty words to Alice that only she could hear. She created an entire movie around the scene that included dialogue, costumes, and actors who might play the parts of the hideous triangle. By the time she sat down with her friends she was in a dark and ugly funk.

Josephine was the first to sense a disturbance in the usual calm that surrounded her.

"Are you alright?" she asked cautiously.

Cleo and Pearl studied her quietly as she slammed her menu on the table.

"It's that sleazy barroom skank!" Eleanor erupted. "She's got her claws into Walter and I'm just beside myself."

The ladies gave each other knowing glances. Eleanor seldom shared her Wednesday visits with them and usually kept her feelings under wraps. They knew the score and never brought up Walter's name unless Eleanor did it first.

"What happened?" prodded Cleo.

"It was just a dream, but I can't shake the feelings that came with it." Eleanor admitted.

"Get it out and then maybe you will have some peace," prompted Josephine, who put great stock in dreams.

"Walter was cheating on me with Alice and I walked in on them. It was so real and awful. Alice looked me right in the eye and smiled while Walter acted like a mindless idiot. She had her arms wrapped around him like an octopus. I hate that whore!" And then the poised and always perfect Eleanor began to sob. It was a very quiet, ladylike sob, but sob she did. Great fat tears rolled down her aging cheeks and plopped silently on the menu in front of her.

Her friends sat stunned until Pearl said, "I hate her too!"

Josephine patted her lovingly on the shoulder while Cleo handed her a tissue.

"Let it all out," Josephine cooed. "You know Walter would never betray you. He loves you very much."

"He just doesn't remember. Maybe he thinks Alice is you," Cleo added as she began to rapidly fan herself with the menu.

"She doesn't resemble me in the slightest," protested Eleanor. "She is an uneducated barroom hussy."

"We all hate her," Pearl repeated.

"Maybe we could contact the Maude Squad and have her taken out," suggested Dede. "Cleo, take off your shoes. That always helps me with hot flashes."

Cleo kicked off her shoes and continued to fan herself.

Eleanor wiped her eyes and smiled. She did feel better. Friends could help. She felt a little foolish but much loved.

The reference to the Maude Squad prompted Cleo to put down the menu and pull the personal ads from her purse. "You must see this," she said excitedly.

Eleanor was grateful to have the attention drawn away from her emotional outburst, but was shocked to read the ad that read: Dear Maude, meet me in Waterton at Twin Oaks, room 109, Jean

"Oh no," gasped Eleanor.

"Is it Jean Scattergoods?" asked Cleo.

"I visited her yesterday. She was in terrible shape and Twin Oaks did not impress me. Honestly, I don't blame Jean for wanting out of this life," Eleanor said sadly. "She gave me a note before I left that simply said, 'I want to die'."

"How could she contact the Maude Squad?" Dede wondered.

"I wonder how she even knew about them," added Pearl.

"What are we going to do about it?" Cleo demanded. "Eleanor, did you tell Angus about the Silverton connection?"

"No, and I'm not going to tell him. If Jean wants to die, I think it is her right." Eleanor spoke with a conviction she didn't know she had.

Josephine raised her eyebrows, "I think it's time we made a visit to the Death Café."

For some time, Josephine had been contemplating her own death. Being a therapist gave her insights into the entire dying process. She knew someone her age must face the truth that death was part of the cycle of life and needed to be accepted as such. Considering health issues, accidents, and age, Josephine knew death could come at any time and she wanted to be mentally prepared, so she read, researched, and meditated on the subject. She knew a little about the Death Café where people went to openly talk about death but had never gone there. It was a rare thing in a society that feared death so much it hid from it by numbing its truth with drugs and alcohol. The Death Café was the perfect place for those looking to embrace death to find something like the Maude Squad. Josephine found one online and made arrangements to visit the Death Café the following day after some serious shopping.

Eleanor woke on Saturday, June 3, excited to start on an adventure with her friends. She did not think about Walter. After spending some quality time with Feathers, she drove to Dede's house where she met with Pearl and Cleo. They piled into Eleanor's car and drove up the Wilson River to pick up Josephine.

It was almost a two-hour drive into Portland, but time flew as they chatted about current events, family drama, and Cleo's new kitchen design.

"The grandchildren are coming to visit tomorrow," reported Cleo. "I love it when they come and also when they leave."

"Isn't that true?" Dede agreed.

"Steve is always the first to complain about their visits and yet he doesn't spend any time with them. He often disappears and takes a nap," continued Cleo. "Men are so strange."

"Yes, and then they give the grandchildren a pair of scissors and your most expensive roll of ribbon and let them cut it into one-foot pieces!" Dede was obviously reliving a very painful experience.

The others in the car checked Dede out and immediately broke into giggles that escalated into hysterics.

"Have you been to that new little shop on the corner of Third and Main?" Cleo inquired after gaining control of herself. "I'm looking for some new barstools for my kitchen."

"I've been in there once," answered Pearl. "I didn't see barstools there."

"They have lots of cute things," Josephine added. "They take old stuff and fix it up."

"When I was there, they had this awful music blaring. I kept moving around the store trying to get away from it and then discovered it was my phone." Pearl laughed at herself and the others joined her.

"Let's stop at the Crap Warehouse," suggested Dede. "I need some new ribbon."

"You mean the Craft Warehouse?" asked Eleanor.

"Isn't that what I said?" Dede responded.

"Yes, I'd like to get some new brushes and I can't find purple acrylic paint in town." Cleo liked to dabble in the fine arts.

Eleanor took the turnoff to the craft store and the shopping began.

It wasn't long before they tired of shopping, loaded their prizes in the back of the car, and set off to find the Death Café.

"My feet hurt," complained Cleo. "I hope you can find a parking place close to the café."

"Don't worry," Eleanor reassured her. "I Googled this place and there is a parking structure nearby." Recently, Eleanor had noticed that her feet ached more than usual too, and she knew Josephine would never complain but had knee replacement surgery and was often stiff and slow, especially after sitting for a while.

The Death Café was being hosted in a funky little café on Burnside. As they entered, people turned around to give them a look, and then returned to their conversations. The lighting was dim and the walls were filled with colorful abstract paintings. Eleanor expected a gypsy palm reader to appear at any moment. The ladies sat down at a table decorated with flowers and skulls. There were only two men and five other women making a total of 12 sitting like knights at the round table.

Soon after they were seated a thin, white-haired woman in a red suit appeared and introduced herself.

"Welcome to the Death Café. I'm Wilma Black and I am your hostess for this evening. To those of you new to this experience I'd like to reassure you that it will be a casual meeting to discuss the many aspects of death that our society does not discuss openly. It is a forum for voicing your beliefs, your fears, and maybe sharing your experiences. Let's start by writing why you want to talk about death." Here she passed out little squares of paper and pencils.

Everyone quickly wrote and then put their papers in a bowl that Wilma collected. She pulled one out at a time and read:

We are all dying.

Death is part of life.

Someone I love has died. I want to reach him.

I want to face my fear of death.

I just came for the cake. (here everyone laughed)

I'm old and know death is coming.

I want to know what other people think about death and the afterlife.

People around me are dying.

I want to know how to die with dignity.

Is there a group that will facilitate my death when the time comes?

Everyone dies.

Is there an alternative?

"So, this is why we talk about death," Wilma continued. "Hopefully, discussing death will allow us to live our lives more fully. Shining a light on the things we fear relieves that fear and the anxiety that goes with it, and of course there will be cake and tea.

If we take these talking points one at a time, we will hopefully touch on everyone's concern. We are all dying, and death is part of the life cycle. These are definitive. Does anyone have something to offer about reaching out to a loved one who has died?"

One of the older ladies spoke out, "My husband was sick for a long time. We knew he was dying and we often talked about what might be on the other side of this life. He assured me that he would give me a sign to let me know that he had passed over and was all right. After he died, I must admit, I did not actively look for a sign, but later I found that if I opened myself to them, they were all around me. The first one came with the porch light. It hasn't worked for years. He was sick and I didn't care about fixing it, but one night the dog began to bark as though someone was at the door. When I went to look, no one was there, but the light was on. It's happened several times since and now I know it's his way of visiting me."

"Do you feel his presence?" Josephine asked.

"Yes, but it's different and very hard to describe, yet comforting. One night I dreamed that he called me on the telephone and we shared a very interesting and intimate conversation. He told me how much he loved me." She couldn't continue as tears ran down her face.

Josephine picked up the conversation without missing a beat. "I had a similar experience with my father who was very reluctant to display emotion, yet after he died I also received a telephone call from him in a dream. He was very loving and kind. He told me things I had always wanted to hear: how much he loved me and how proud I had made him. He even apologized for not telling me while he was alive. It gave me great comfort also."

Several others had stories too. The transition from one concern to another happened automatically until everyone was suddenly quiet. That was when Wilma offered cake and tea.

As they sat enjoying their refreshments, Eleanor decided to go for broke, "Has anyone here ever heard of a group called the Maude Squad?"

"Wasn't that a television program about young police officers?" inquired one of the men.

"M-a-u-d-e, not M-o-d," Eleanor clarified.

"Remember the cult movie, *Harold and Maude*? Where a young man obsessed with death, hooks up with an old lady high on life?" Cleo added. "It was an inspiring film in the seventies with some catchy tunes all by Cat Stevens."

Suddenly the other man began to sing in a beautiful tenor voice, "If You Want to Sing Out, Sing Out"

At some point they all joined in on the parts that they knew. Eleanor felt as though she was in a musical. When it ended they all clapped and laughed. It was the perfect way to end an interesting evening, yet they had learned nothing about the Maude Squad.

The ladies walked back to the car and settled in for the long drive home. As soon as they were on the road, Cleo mentioned the fact that the man with the lovely singing voice had pressed a note into her hand before leaving. They turned on the overhead light and giggled like school girls until they saw what it said: *Check the dark web.*

Sunday, June 4, Eleanor lay in bed thinking about the previous evening. Death seemed to consume her every thought lately, but the visit to the Death Café had been light and uplifting. Today, she would lounge, read the Sunday paper, complete the crossword, oh . . . she almost forgot about finishing that book for book club. Bootsy must be here. Maybe she would see her when she walked. She couldn't remember if she had left anything in the hidey-hole. Amy would want to Skype tonight as she did the first Sunday of every month. Too much to think about. She slowly rolled out of bed to begin her day.

By noon, Eleanor was ready for an outdoor adventure. She passed slowly by Bootsy's house, but it appeared dark and empty. Perhaps they were too busy to visit this weekend, or maybe they were with Jean now. She checked the hidey-hole, empty. Eleanor continued on her way but without the usual spring in her step.

Her mind wandered to thoughts of the dark web. Even the notion of accessing the underbelly of the internet appalled and frightened her. Cleo knew someone who knew someone who had extensive tech skills and might help her research it. No one in the coffee group wanted this content listed on their browser's history. Eleanor wasn't sure how these things worked but was sure that opening the dark web would be like unlocking the gates of hell and letting the demons of evil into their simple lives. How did those old, sick suffering people use the encrypted internet to get to something like the Maude Squad if that is what they did? She knew Frieda didn't possess the skills to do it. She had once asked Eleanor where she could get a ribbon for her typewriter. There must be something they were missing. It had to be something easy, but what. Maybe it was as simple as word of mouth. It seemed to Eleanor that anything they could uncover; the authorities could also find. They were talking about murder after all, but it was murder of the most expendable . . . the least valuable people . . . the old.

Eleanor decided to put these thoughts on hold. It wasn't necessarily her duty to solve this puzzle. She had a book to read, a party to plan, and perhaps a nap.

Dark clouds loomed as Eleanor returned to her house on the hill. An uneasy squall blew in from the west and large raindrops plopped heavily as she stepped onto the porch. It wasn't unusual for unstable spring air to bring a lightning storm to the Oregon coast. Eleanor realized she was out of touch and hadn't watched the news or caught a weather forecast in days. She offered a prayer of gratitude to the universe for her cozy shelter as she kicked off her shoes and went to the window to watch the flashes of lightning over the ocean and listen to the rumble of thunder. She always found these storms exciting and electrifying.

As the lightning moved closer, Eleanor went to the kitchen for a cup of tea. Just as she returned to the living room with the hot drink in hand, the lights flickered, and the power went off. Without a thought, Eleanor reached for her cell phone and called the utility company to report the outage. "Just another day in paradise," she muttered to herself.

Feathers, who had been hiding quietly in his cage, flew to her shoulder when he heard her voice. Together they watched the storm move away to the east. The rumble of thunder growing faint as it marched off in the distance.

Eleanor snuggled under her afghan with a book, a cup of tea and Feathers for company. It would be hours before the power was restored, but it wasn't an unpleasant way to spend the afternoon.

When Eleanor woke, it was dark. Disoriented at first, she reached out for the table lamp and turned on the light. Yes, there was power once again. It was late, but Eleanor had not finished the book before dozing off once again. What was she going to accomplish today? Finish the book, take a nap, and plan a party. Two out of three wasn't bad—no, one out of three. Surely, she could finish the book before she went to bed. What she needed now was dinner and a shower.

Eleanor ran to answer the phone. She remembered Amy would call as soon as she entered the shower. The time difference made it difficult to communicate often and Eleanor didn't want to miss her time with family. She hungered for it. Dripping wet, with a towel wrapped around her she panted the hello that traveled across a continent and an ocean and listened to the response that filled a void in her old- lady heart.

Later, Eleanor finished the book club selection and watched a movie on the cable channel. Still unable to sleep, she wandered into the office and sorted through some old papers. She noticed the box with the murder mystery party materials in it and began to read the instructions. One of the characters was named Jean. Suddenly she remembered that Jean Scattergoods was waiting to die at the hands of the Maude Squad. Why hadn't she thought of this before? Why wasn't she sitting at her bedside waiting to see who it was? Who was coming?

Eleanor thought she would never fall asleep. Tossing and turning and checking the clock to see if it was time to get up was torture, yet when she did open her eyes, the sun was shining and the sky reflected blue in the ever-changing ocean. Eleanor mentally listed what she knew: Monday, June 5, book club tonight at Dede's house, she needed to send out the invitations to the murder mystery party, Walter wasn't here, Jean was waiting to die. She quickly dressed, grabbed a piece of peanut butter toast and drove to Twin Oaks to visit her friend Jean.

As she sat in the parking lot she decided to call Cleo just as a precaution. Someone needed to know what she was doing in case the Maude Squad came and did her in too.

"Cleo, this is Eleanor. I'm at Twin Oaks."

"Really!" exclaimed Cleo. "Pearl and I are here too. I guess great minds think alike."

"Thank heavens!" said Eleanor. "I'm in the parking lot, but I'll be in shortly. Is Jean still alive?"

"Yes," replied Cleo, but there was something in her voice that said otherwise.

That was all Eleanor needed to get her out of the car and into that forsaken place.

Long before Eleanor entered Jean's room, she heard Pearl and Cleo laughing. Certainly, things couldn't be as dire as she thought, yet she knew nothing was too sacred to them when it came to joking around.

Jean was in her bed seemingly asleep.

"We tried torturing the old gal to get the scoop on the Maude Squad, but she wouldn't give up a thing," Cleo spoke out of the side of her mouth as if she were a gangster.

"She's been sleeping the entire time," qualified Pearl. "The nurse on duty thinks she may have had another stroke."

"Can you believe we didn't think of this sooner?" asked Eleanor. "I just thought about her last night. I spent the entire night tossing and turning until this morning."

"Cleo called this morning wondering why we weren't camping out here to see who showed up to do her in," explained Pearl. "We just got here and were planning to call you when you phoned."

"I guess we got caught up with the idea of the Death Café. Did anyone think to call Josephine and Dede?" asked Eleanor.

"There's nothing for them to do here. Jean is still among the living so the Squad hasn't come yet. We may have to take shifts," added Cleo.

"Tonight is book club at Dede's," reminded Pearl. "She will be busy making something delicious for dessert."

They looked at each other and then at Jean, who rested peacefully in her bed.

"We will all be at Dede's tonight." Cleo voiced the thought they all had. None of them were willing to give up Dede's dessert to sit by Jean to catch the death squad.

"Did either of you sign in when you got here?" asked Eleanor.

"No," Pearl answered for both of them.

"I guess reading the guest log won't help us then," Eleanor surmised. "Murderers won't be signing in."

"No," sighed Cleo.

Eleanor walked closer to Jean's bed and took her hand in hers. It felt cool and lifeless. She watched for the rise and fall of her chest. There was no sign of the moonstone necklace to protect her now. They all watched and waited as each breath became shallower and less frequent until there was just one long exhale and then nothing.

"What do we do now?" whispered Cleo.

Pearl was looking around the room as if to see Jean's soul rising.

"We better alert the staff," Eleanor said as she gently stroked Jean's slack cheek. She knew there was no need to whisper. Her neighbor was no longer there.

As Eleanor talked to the aide about Jean's death she noticed the glimmer of a silver chain around her neck.

"I'll be sure and take that moonstone to Jean's family." She pointed to the necklace and announced with authority, "It was a special gift from her granddaughter."

The aide sheepishly took it from around her neck and placed it in Eleanor's hand without a word.

The three friends met for coffee at the Boat House. They needed to debrief.

"Well, that couldn't have been the work of the Maude Squad," said Cleo.

"No, I think Jean just died from her stroke," added Eleanor. "I asked at the desk if she had had any visitors recently and there was no one. Pentobarbital works right away, so that rules them out unless you did it, Cleo."

Cleo acted offended but she wasn't.

"Why didn't they take her to the hospital if they thought she had another stroke?" Pearl wanted to blame someone.

"She had a do not resuscitate order," explained Eleanor. "Jean really wanted to die, so it is better this way. I feel sorry for Bootsy though. She loved her Gramma Scattergoods. It's hard for the young to understand an older person's desire to move on."

"I'm not that old but I can see it coming," said Cleo. "The aches and pains and promise of lingering disease are not something to look forward to."

"Add to that list, becoming a burden on those you love and who once loved you," added Pearl.

"Then there is the guilt your loved ones have about letting you go, so they push all the pills and remedies that keep you alive long after you should go," lamented Eleanor.

"That is the guilt of children who ignore you most of your life and then prolong your suffering in the end. My children have promised to help ease me out because they love me and want my money," Cleo laughed.

They all felt a little better for having a hearty laugh and decided to go their own ways and meet again at Dede's for book club that evening.

Eleanor wondered where Bootsy and her family were and if they knew of Jean's death. As she passed Jean's house she noticed the dark and abandoned look of it and thought they must still be hours away in their Portland home. It would be a sad time for Bootsy—time to spend surrounded by her family. Eleanor knew she would need space to grieve. She stopped her car at the hidey-hole tree and slipped the moonstone necklace inside. Bootsy would know she was thinking of her.

Book club at Dede's was always more about the dessert than the book. No one could match Dede's culinary masterpieces by taste or artful design, but they all tried, which made every meeting one to anticipate.

The group itself had evolved over time to include eight members. They chatted amicably for a few minutes until everyone arrived and then began with a round robin where each member gave their brief opinion of the book. Because Dede had chosen the book, she facilitated the discussion with well-thought-out questions.

"So, what is it that you know for sure?" questioned Dede in an attempt to bring the discussion to a personal level.

"The only thing you can count on in this life is change," contributed Kimberley who had been recently divorced. "You certainly can't count on men to do the right thing."

"Sometimes men can do the right thing, especially if they have good hands," declared Dolly as her eyebrows went up and down meaningfully. "I met a man at the airport once who had very nice hands."

"There is always death and taxes," added Wren. "We all die in the end and must pay our taxes."

"Some are clever enough to weasel out of paying their taxes," countered Josephine, "although the dying part is absolutely true."

"Maybe those are the only certainties in life," Dede remarked.

"What about cycles, such as the seasons, day and night. I'm fairly certain the sun will rise tomorrow," added Mercedes who looked at most things through scientific eyes.

"There should be scientific certainties, but you can't really count on that since science changes as we learn more. You know we are at risk of losing this planet so maybe the sun won't rise in the morning." Kimberley seemed determined to argue her point that change was the only absolute.

"Maybe Kimberley is right and the only certain thing *is* change. Death is just a form of change as are the seasons and day and night." Eleanor could see Kimberley's point.

"If change is the only thing we know for sure, what do we believe to be true?" Dede was determined to delve deeper into the group's personal belief systems.

"I believe that there is a balance in life. There is no joy without sorrow, no love without hate, or peace without war. Life is just like art. It is light bouncing off of dark." Cleo had obviously given this idea much thought.

"That explains why bad things happen to good people," added Pearl. "I can't prove it, but I just know there is an afterlife. Did you know that Jean Scattergoods died this morning? Cleo and Eleanor were there with me at her bedside when she passed over."

"Did you open the window so her soul could escape?" asked Josephine.

"Do you really believe that? Why would a soul need to go through an open window?" scoffed Cleo. "It should be able to pass right through a solid wall."

"Did you feel her spirit in the room?" Josephine continued.

"I did look around, but really there was nothing." Pearl admitted.

"Was she a friend? Did she have a pet?" asked Mercedes. "I didn't know her. Did she suffer much?"

"She was my neighbor, and a friend," Eleanor said, "and I think she did suffer."

"That is tragic," Mercedes frowned. "I just don't understand the necessity for people to suffer. I would never let an animal suffer like that."

Mercedes was the local vet and suffered from extreme compassion.

Dede wanted to ask about the Maude Squad but didn't want to have that discussion during book club, so instead she invited Eleanor into the kitchen to help with the dessert.

"No signs of foul play," whispered Eleanor as she entered the kitchen with Dede. She knew exactly what Dede wanted to know.

Dede served a light, lemony concoction topped with raspberries and a sprig of mint. It was quiet for some time as they consumed the delight, oohing and aahing over its beauty and flavor.

Mercedes announced the title of the next book selection and worried she would miss it because she had to travel to Mexico to pick up some drugs for her clinic. Wren and Pearl forgot the title of the book selection and needed to have it repeated. Cleo asked who would host the next meeting, which was silly because the person who chose the book was always the hostess. They discussed pushing the next meeting back a week due to the holiday weekend in July and accommodating Mercedes' trip. They chatted a little more about community issues and then all left at once, leaving no opportunity to discuss poison or murder.

Tuesday, June 6, Eleanor had slept like a log and woke feeling refreshed and invigorated. Her mind clearly ticked off the tasks to be done: pay bills, get those party invitations out, plan the menu for the party, send a sympathy card to Bootsy and her family, walk, Walter wasn't here. She rolled out of bed with more enthusiasm than she'd had in a long time. She was alive and it felt good.

Returning from her walk on the beach, Eleanor examined the exterior of her house. She checked the siding for signs of wear and tear, living in a coastal climate was hard on homes. The salty air rusted the metal gutters and the high winds tore off shingles. As she inspected things she noticed the pink blossoms on the plant that grew along the side of the house. She immediately thought of Frieda. The memory came clearly of the day Frieda had pulled that plant by the roots from her garden and given it to her.

"Don't worry," she cautioned, "you won't be able to kill it, girl."

Eleanor had planted it on the sheltered side of the house and forgotten about it. Yet every year it returned and thrived, reseeding, spreading, and delighting her with its beautiful trumpet shaped blossoms. Eleanor liked the determined plant and the memory it provided.

She completed her inspection and heard the telephone ringing as she entered the house.

"Hello" she answered a little breathlessly.

"Hello. Is this Eleanor Penrose?" a woman's voice asked.

"Yes, it is." Eleanor tried to place the unfamiliar voice.

"This is Nina VanHorn, Frieda's daughter-in-law. I understand you were a friend of Frieda's."

"Yes, I was very fond of Frieda. I'm so sorry for your loss." Eleanor was suddenly filled with a feeling of sadness. She wondered if Nina felt it too.

"I've been going through some of her things and I found a box with your name on it. I didn't go through it, so I can't tell you what is in it, but it must be something she wanted you to have, or maybe something she needed to return to you. I'd be happy to deliver it," Nina offered.

"I have to come into town later today, so I could stop by and get it and save you a trip out here if that helps." Eleanor needed to pick up a few things at the supermarket.

"That would be great!" Nina was obviously relieved not to have to travel out of her way to Sand Beach.

"I'm only here until the end of the week and there is so much to do. Frieda collected a lot of things and there are so many papers to go through. I'll look forward to seeing you this afternoon." Nina ended the conversation.

Eleanor reevaluated her plans for the day to include a trip to town. If she hurried she could pay her bills and maybe address the invitations to the party before she left. She quickly finished her tasks with such focus and clarity that she astounded even herself. There was no hemming or hawing over who to invite, or what to serve. The decisions were made and that was that. She even had time to shower and change her clothes before she left with her grocery list in hand.

As Eleanor drove up to Frieda's house, she once more felt that feeling of sadness and loss. She thought this surely was the last time she would visit this spot. Eleanor knocked on the door and was greeted by a small dark-haired woman with a warm smile.

"I'm Nina," she said as she extended her hand in friendship. "You must be Eleanor, please come in." Eleanor had never met any of Frieda's family, and was surprised to find Nina so likeable. She had always felt Frieda was mostly abandoned by them. It wasn't for her to judge. They had their lives to live and it seemed they had chosen to live far away.

"Yes, it is a pleasure to meet you," Eleanor said, returning a warm smile.

"Well, I've put the box over here." Nina went to retrieve a box among many and handed it to over to Eleanor. It was clear that she wanted to get back to her tiresome task of clearing out Frieda's mess.

"Will there be a service of any kind?" Eleanor asked.

"No, we didn't think Frieda would want that," Nina responded.

"Okay, well thank you." Eleanor didn't know what to say. The box was heavy and a little awkward. She moved toward the door and Nina rushed to open it for her.

"Thank you for coming for it. I do appreciate that," she repeated as she held the door open.

Eleanor put the box in the trunk next to her groceries and drove away wondering where Frieda's children were and why only one daughter-in-law was clearing out the family memories.

When she got home she carried her groceries into the kitchen forgetting the box that was Frieda's gift as she hurried to put things away.

Wednesday, June 7, Eleanor did not want to open her eyes. She knew it was Wednesday, day of woe, and after the delightful day she had yesterday, she did not want today, but if Cleo was correct in her belief that life is light bouncing off of dark, she knew she had to have her day of woe to balance her delight. She rolled over and looked out at the perfect sky and sparkling ocean. The beauty of it all should make it better. Nora would clean her house. Eleanor would take Feathers to visit Walter. Maybe Alice was dead. The day would fly by. Eleanor rose to face the day.

The week flew by with no one dying, no funerals, and no drama. It was almost a perfectly normal few days. Eleanor woke Friday, morning looking forward to her coffee group. It was the only thing on her schedule. It was the ninth of June.

She entered the Boat House and was surprised to find everyone already there including Dede. They were all a twitter about the invitations they had received to the murder mystery party. Eleanor was elated that her idea had a fan base with such enthusiasm.

"What do you think a character named Captain Underwear should don for this occasion?" asked Josephine mischievously.

"There is no Captain Underwear," corrected Eleanor, "although that would be hilarious. I wish there were. Who would you like to see in their under garments, Josephine?"

A rather serious discussion about men's underwear ensued.

"When I was in high school, Mr. Keaton, the typing teacher had us put a pair of boxers over the keyboard so we couldn't see the keys. Then we put our hand in the leg holes and typed blindly," shared Cleo.

"Is that what you call hunting for a pecker?" asked Pearl with a twinkle in her eye.

It took a beat before they all laughed until tears ran down their faces.

Fortunately, there were few customers on this Friday, but their cackling drew the waitress near to take their orders or get in on the joke. They all ordered their usual and continued the chatter.

"Did anyone see Jackie Ann's obituary," asked Dede as she pulled a copy of the *Fish Wrapper* from her bag.

"I didn't know she died!" exclaimed Eleanor.

"What happened to her?" asked Cleo who was also in the dark.

"It was quite sudden," informed Pearl, "although she never recovered from the death of her husband. I think she just quit wanting to live."

"I read an article about people who die from broken hearts. It's a real thing," added Josephine.

No one disputed it. They remembered Jackie Ann as a prankster who taught at the high school and on occasion shared time with them. Everyone's friend, she seldom had time to be anyone's friend and was joined at the hip with her husband, Jon. They worked together at the school, traveled together, golfed together, literally did everything together until he had a heart attack on the golf course two years ago.

Dede proceeded to read the obituary:

*The world's best teacher passed into legend June 1. Jackie Ann Hinkley Heart was born to teach and shared her gifts with Waterton's children, many who later became doctors, lawyers, teachers, and even presidents of countries. She was born in poverty but rose to great wealth when she married her soulmate, Jon Heart. Together they traveled the world and shared everything, including their unique teaching strategies. Geography was never as interesting anywhere else as it was in her classroom. She was able to bring it to life with her own personal experiences. Jackie never had any children of her own professing to own all of the children. She shared a love of cooking, golfing, and was a talented pianist, once performing at Carnegie Hall. Her passion for jogging was duly noted by her neighbors who regularly witnessed her on the streets in her stylish athletic attire. Everyone admired her physicality and beauty as well as her zest for life and perfect personality. She will certainly be missed by all who truly knew and loved her.*

*No service will be held at her request. Donations can be made in her name to Liars Anonymous.*

When Dede finished, they all just looked at each other in stunned silence and then erupted in more hysterical laughter.

"She was a liar even after death!" snorted Cleo.

"I'm sure she wrote this herself," added Dede.

"It is all a pack of lies," Pearl giggled, "she didn't even teach geography."

"I love it," Josephine chimed in. "We should all write our own obituaries."

"She wasn't old enough to be a victim of the Maude Squad," Eleanor said, changing the subject. "Did the dark web turn up anything, Cleo?"

"Not really. My friend didn't want to go there. Over 80 percent of its content is child pornography. I just don't think any of the people we know would go there." Cleo sighed. It seemed like a dead end.

Talk returned to the murder mystery party and what they would wear and what Eleanor intended to serve for dinner.

Eleanor left the Boat House with a mental list of things to do to get ready for the party. Dede offered to go to Party City with her to buy decorations and possible costumes for a pirate-inspired theme.

Later that day as Eleanor unloaded her purchases from the car, she once again noticed the box from Frieda and packed it into the house. She was exhausted, but in a good way. This was the kind of fun she enjoyed. She ate a simple dinner salad, showered, and went immediately to sleep.

Saturday morning came quickly. Eleanor lay in bed checking off her to do list. It was June 10, one day away from the party. She needed to shop for dinner and drinks, begin the process of decorating, put her costume together, Walter would have loved this, but Walter wasn't here. She almost jumped out of bed and hurried to Feathers to release him from his cage. Little did he know the important role he would play tomorrow night. Maybe she could teach him some pirate talk. He already knew "arrgh". Walter may have taught him some other phrases that he had forgotten. She never really paid much attention to Feathers until Walter left. First things first, Eleanor needed a morning walk to energize her.

Walking by Jean's house, she noticed again the abandoned look of the place. Maybe they were all in mourning in Portland. She hadn't heard anything about a funeral. She needed to send a sympathy card but didn't have their address.

Nancy was out on her deck and waved excitedly. Perhaps she knew something.

"I'm pretty excited about the pirate party." Nancy stepped out to walk along with Eleanor.

"There's a lot to do. I'm excited too," Eleanor responded, picking up the pace. She really did have to hurry this morning.

Nancy continued to walk and talk. "I have the perfect dress for Lady Rachael Hall," she said. "I'm so glad you chose her for my character. Dennis has an old Halloween costume that will work for him. You always have such fun ideas."

Eleanor didn't want to be a spoilsport by changing the subject away from fun to death but she was curious about Jean.

"Have you heard anything about Jean's service? Will there be a funeral?" she asked.

"I haven't heard a thing. My guess is there will be nothing. Knowing Judy Greenwood, she will probably sell the house and never look back," Nancy opined.

"How sad for Bootsy." Eleanor truly felt sorry for her if there was no closure planned. She knew funerals were more for the living than the dead. She couldn't count all the people that had taught her so much she didn't know about people she loved and thought she knew. Old people especially had a lifetime of adventures their children didn't know about. Who would tell the stories when they were gone? Their friends were most likely gone too. Eleanor wondered how many stories went to the grave with the elderly.

She really needed this time to think about the party and shook her head as if she could rid herself of the sad thoughts that way.

Nancy was good company and together they briskly covered two miles as they planned the dinner for the murder mystery. She offered to come early to help Eleanor set things up and Eleanor realized she was grateful for her friendship.

Eleanor hurried to shower, dress, and drive into town to do her shopping. She decided to serve bouillabaisse with a rouille and stopped at the Fish Peddler for fresh seafood. What better to serve a bunch of murderous pirates than fish stew? Then there was another stop at the liquor store for rum. She would make grog. Everything else she needed, she got at the local grocery store. Eleanor could feel her spirits rise in anticipation of a fun night. She turned up the radio and sang along loudly.

The rest of the day was spent prepping for the meal and tidying up the house for guests. Eleanor wanted to be available to her guests and not tied up in the kitchen.

By evening, she was utterly exhausted, but still needed a costume. She poured herself a glass of wine and went into what Bootsy called the treasure room. Inside the closet Eleanor pulled out a trunk filled with old Halloween costumes. She was sure she could find something in here that would work. Her character was Anne Skye, a woman who had killed a servant with a kitchen knife in a fit of rage. She pretended to be a man and along with her brother, Jack Skye, boarded a pirate ship to get away from the law. All Eleanor needed was the costume Walter had worn in the June Dairy Parade years ago. He had been a pirate on a float. It was the only time she could remember Feathers allowed out of the house without his cage. He perched proudly on Walter's shoulder with a thin leather cord tied around his foot. The bird could not be trusted.

It didn't take long to find the outfit. Her grandchildren had raided the trunk years ago, taking most of the good stuff for their own parties and dress-up occasions. She sniffed it. It didn't stink or even smell of Walter. She was glad she didn't have to wear a corset and dress. This was perfect.

Eleanor had slept like a dead person. When she woke on Sunday morning, it took her a few minutes to remember what day it was. Her brain was fuzzy from a hard sleep. Sunday, she thought, Sunday paper, crossword puzzle, walk, long lazy nap, Walter wasn't here . . . oh crap, murder mystery party! She had things to do, so she pulled herself up and out of bed. Maybe there would still be time for the crossword puzzle while she sipped her morning coffee.

Later that day, when most of the preparations were complete, Eleanor gave herself permission to take a short nap so she could enjoy her own party. She just didn't have the stamina that she once enjoyed.

Nancy arrived to help decorate. When they finished, Eleanor was pleased with the result that turned her cozy home into a pirate ship, with fishing nets filled with seashells, an old trunk, and even a very nautical-looking helms wheel she put on the deck. The weather cooperated too. There was no wind, just a gentle breeze that blew in through the open sliders and the pleasant and constant breaking of the surf on the shore.

Nancy left to dress and Eleanor wandered through the house checking on every aspect. When she was satisfied, she eagerly donned the baggy pants, white billowy shirt, and headscarf. She decided to forego the boots for bare feet and added one large, gold earring. As an afterthought she smeared black around her eyes and was quite amused at the effect. Jack Sparrow never looked this good.

Feathers was all atwitter, sensing something outrageous was a foot. He flew through the house shouting, "Avast, Matey! Ho ho ho and a bottle of rum."

Eleanor suspected her costume must have triggered a memory from his past adventures with the dread pirate, Walter. There was a moment of sadness, but it quickly passed as her guests began to arrive in full pirate regalia. Eleanor sighed deeply and greeted them with hugs and cups of grog.

As it turned out Captain Underwear was the murder victim, and everyone had a motive to kill him, either because he was having an affair with their woman, knew their secret, or was in the way of their path to power. Dede and Pearl were pretending to be men also. Pearl had even bound her breasts. Nancy was dressed to the nines as Lady Rachael Hall.

"Aren't you uncomfortable, Pearl?" whispered Eleanor when she finally recognized her.

"Not yet, but don't worry, if I become uncomfortable later, I plan to release the girls and reveal myself as the sex goddess I am." Pearl was in rare form, literally.

Many of her guests brought bottles of booze as hostess gifts, which Eleanor put in the kitchen, knowing they could not possibly drink that much.

They chatted, drank, and gathered on the deck to read their parts. Everyone expressed delight at the way the deck appeared. They marveled at the fishnets draped over the railing, the coils of rope, and the sternwheel. Little twinkle lights would add to the atmosphere as darkness approached. The sound of breaking waves and the salty sea air made it perfect.

"Perfect, this is just the perfect setting for this gathering," gushed Josephine as she stood next to her husband, Richard, taking in every detail. Josephine was a people watcher and never missed a clue. It was her life's work to study the behavior of others and it gave her delight as well as power. While others dulled their senses with alcohol Josephine never touched the stuff and retained her sharp observation skills.

"Don't break character," cautioned Cleo.

"Impossible," thought Josephine who always played herself.

And so the mystery continued until they broke away for dinner. Eleanor's dining room table was expanded to its maximum and everyone sat at their designated place by pirate name. Simple shrimp cocktails were served while Eleanor completed the finishing touches on her bouillabaisse. Nancy was there to lend a hand, warming the crusty rolls and filling the empty grog cups.

"I should have hired a serving wench," laughed Eleanor, who was pleased with the way everything was going.

Angus entered the kitchen just in time to carry the large soup tureen to the table. The smell of saffron, bay leaf, thyme, onions, and fennel wafted from the pot as Eleanor ladled the thick, rich fish stew into the bowls and each diner passed them around the table. Full of rum and good cheer they ate and joked and thoroughly enjoyed themselves. Feathers made a guest appearance as they were sopping the last of the stew with their crusty bread.

"Get back to work, you swine!" he screeched as he flew around the room. For a minute it was as if Walter had joined the party.

No one knew how to respond, but the rum took over and laughter ensued.

Every pirate brought their dirty dishes into the kitchen and soon enough the table was cleared. They began to refill their drinks and ready themselves for the final part of the mystery.

Nancy's husband Dennis opened the bottle of rum he brought and mixed himself a rum and coke.

"One of my clients brought this back from Mexico. I'm eager to try it," he said as he offered to mix one for Eleanor.

"No thanks, Dennis, I've had my quota for tonight and am switching to water." Eleanor knew her limits.

Together they went back on the deck to join the others.

The evening grew darker and the twinkle lights added a special aura to the deck. It was almost romantic instead of mysterious. They sat on benches and played their parts to the hilt. Angus sat close to Eleanor and whispered in her ear that he thought she made a very delicious fish stew. Just as Pearl was about to reveal herself as a woman and release the girls, Dennis slouched over and fell onto Nancy.

"What do you think you're doing?" Nancy pushed him away.

Everyone thought it was part of the game, but Dennis did not respond. They all laughed and rushed to help Nancy out from under Dennis' limp body. He was very good at playing dead. It was Angus who detected the seriousness of the situation. No one else seemed alarmed until they heard the authority in his voice. "Eleanor, call 911!"

There was no 911 on a pirate ship.

The emergency response team arrived in minutes from the fire station in Bayside.

Dennis was not dead but remained unconscious. No one ventured a diagnosis, but Nancy left with him in an ambulance when it arrived and rushed him off to the hospital. Eleanor would have gone too but felt the need to stay with her guests. They lingered for a while, but the party was over, and after making a variety of guesses as to what had happened to Dennis, they left. Angus stayed and loitered in the kitchen. Eleanor didn't know if he was looking for clues or dessert.

"Can I get you anything?" she finally asked.

"What was in the stew?" he questioned.

"Do you think he has food poisoning?" she didn't want to be the cause of his distress.

"No, we would all be sick then. Besides that's not how food poisoning works. You don't pass out. Maybe he's allergic to something you put in the stew." Angus tried to reassure her, but there was something he knew that he wasn't telling.

Eleanor showed him the recipe she used for the bouillabaisse and rouille. He studied it carefully.

"Huh, what was he drinking?" he continued.

"Grog, like everyone else," she answered and then remembered the Mexican rum. "He made himself a rum and coke with this." She found the bottle of rum and gave it to Angus. "He said a client brought it from Mexico."

Angus opened it and sniffed. "I don't like this. There's bootleg liquor made in Mexico that is sometimes infused with grain alcohol or dangerous concentrations of methanol. It can make people sick. I'm taking this to the hospital."

"I'm coming with you." Eleanor grabbed her jacket and they were both out the door.

No one at the hospital seemed concerned that a bevy of pirates had gathered outside Room 103. The entire murder mystery guest list had arrived to check on Dennis. Angus gave the doctor his theory about the rum and they were told to go home and let Dennis sleep it off. They would keep him overnight for observation.

"I'm just glad it wasn't his heart," confessed Nancy, who was reasonably concerned about her husband.

"I'll take you ladies home," offered Angus. "There's no sense staying here all night. Dennis will be rested in the morning, so you should be too." And with warm hugs and reassurances that everything would be fine, Eleanor's murder mystery party came to an abrupt end.

Eleanor woke Monday morning, June 12, she remembered the party and how fabulous it had been, the decorations, costumes, company, food and drinks, and the horrible ending. She had clean-up to do and was terribly worried about Nancy's Dennis, but it was too early to call. She could only go about her business and hope that Nancy would call with good news.

It was later that day after Eleanor had cleared away all traces of the party that Nancy called.

"Oh, Eleanor, I'm so sorry that we spoiled your party. Dennis is fine. He woke up early this morning and remembered absolutely nothing about the entire episode. You might have thought he was drunk and blacked out, but it was the bootleg rum from Mexico. Thank heavens for Angus. The hospital tested a sample from the bottle he brought and found highly toxic substances in it. I've brought Dennis home and he is just fine."

Nancy was obviously relieved. She and Dennis were at that age when they thought every little symptom could mean the end was near.

"Don't worry about the party. It was mostly over. I'm so glad Dennis is all right and that no one else had a drink of that rum," Eleanor said. "On the positive side, I believe Dennis may have saved us from viewing Pearl topless. It's a picture I don't want etched in my mind." Eleanor laughed along with Nancy and after a few more minutes they hung up. Nancy wanted to call and thank all of the other guests for their concern and let them know Dennis was okay.

Eleanor received calls from all of the party-goers thanking her for the mostly delightful evening. They gushed over every detail and offered their own conclusions as to who was the murderer. By dinner time,

Eleanor suffered from a severe case of telephone ear as well as hunger. Surprisingly enough there was little in the house to eat. She had spent so much time on her party meal there was nothing left to feed herself. She looked in the refrigerator and saw the uneaten dessert, rum cake. She decided to take herself out to dinner at the Anchor.

Dining alone wasn't Eleanor's favorite way to enjoy a meal, yet there were a few positives. Sometimes she met interesting people. She decided to eat at the bar. No need to take up a whole table when there is just one. She ordered a glass of wine and leisurely looked around at the occupants. Most seemed to be locals who waved or nodded in recognition when she came in, but there were several vacationers. As she sipped her drink a man approached the bar and attempted to sit next to her. She scooted over to make more room.

"I'm from Texas, and I've got a big spread," he said. His voice was deep, and his eyes were full of mischief.

Eleanor chuckled at his pun. "How does a Texan come to be on the Oregon coast?" she asked.

"Ah, I'm not from Texas. Just trying to make you laugh," he confessed. "I'm from Idaho and just looking around the countryside. It's pretty here."

"Yes, it is," she agreed. The conversation continued until they felt like old friends even though they never introduced themselves. Dinner came, they ate, and then Eleanor walked home and the ersatz Texan returned to his motel. It was a pleasant evening and nothing more. Eleanor knew women who would have gone to the motel with a strange man or invited him home with them. She didn't judge, but she never felt lonely enough to engage in that kind of behavior. Maybe she was just a prude. She didn't mind being alone. It was different from being lonely.

The telephone was ringing when she got to the front door. She rushed to answer it thinking it could be something about Walter or one of the girls.

"Hello," Eleanor gasped, slightly out of breath.

"Are you okay, Mom?" It was Erin, the worrier. "I called earlier and there was no answer."

"Of course, I just stepped in the door. I was down at the Anchor having dinner. Are you all right?" The apple doesn't fall far from the tree, or so Walter would say when he compared Eleanor to her daughters.

"Yes, we're all fine here. I just called because this Sunday is Father's Day and I thought Ben and I would bring the kids to Rosewood to see Dad. With Amy and her family in France, Dad might have a lonely Father's Day. Are you going to be there?" Erin was a planner.

"I hadn't given it much thought." Eleanor told Erin all the details of the murder mystery party from planning, decorating to execution and dismantling. Nothing was left out.

"I can understand why you haven't been thinking about Dad. You've been busy, but it sounds like so much fun and excitement." Erin liked a good time too.

"Well, if you are coming to Rosewood on Sunday, maybe I'll skip my Wednesday visit and meet you there." The idea of a Wednesday of no woe suddenly seemed appealing.

"Will they let us take Dad to lunch or brunch," Erin questioned.

"I don't see why not. He's not a prisoner there." Eleanor thought maybe that wasn't true. He was locked in. Perhaps he thought he was a prisoner, but surely it would be okay to take him out for a while. Would he try to escape? Who knew? It had been months since she had taken him out for a doctor's appointment. His disease had progressed since then. All these thoughts flew through her mind in quick time. She didn't want to bother Erin with them, so she just reassured. They completed their plans and hung up.

Eleanor felt free knowing there would be no Wednesday of woe and then suddenly exhausted thinking about Sunday with Walter and the kids. She took a shower and crawled gratefully into her bed.

"Tuesday, June 13," Eleanor thought as she woke to a foggy day. It was the anniversary of her father's death. She let her mind wander back in time to when she was a little girl sitting on his lap while he watched television, sharing one of those humongous Hershey chocolate bars. Trying to conjure up her father's face after all this time left her curious. She got up and wandered into the office. Frieda's box caught her eye, but she wasn't looking for that and pushed it aside. Eleanor focused on a picture album and began to leaf through it. Here was her father, a handsome man with a thoughtful face and loving smile. That was what she remembered. How appropriate that she should think of him, his death day and Father's Day so close together.

She carried the album to the kitchen to brew some coffee, stopped to greet and release Feathers, and decided to wash her face before returning to the office with her coffee. Her mind wandered again and she picked up her pen:

Daddy's Dipper
Daddy's silver dipper hung
from a nail on the kitchen wall.
To fetch and fill it for him
Was my task when I was small.
I filled that cup with many things
All fresh and clear, the best.
Daddy sipped the water up
And his heart drank all the rest.
What's happened to the dipper
That moistened Daddy's lips?
What's happened to my Daddy
Who no longer water sips?
Time has changed that dipper
And turned it red with rust
While Daddy lies in hallowed ground
With lips of ash and dust.
Or maybe Daddy's dipper hangs
Among stars that burn and glow
While Daddy spills its splendor
To fill me here below.

Eleanor had entered the zone where there was no time. She was surprised to see Feathers in the office and not once had he quoted, "It was a dark and stormy night." She stood and stretched. It felt good, but not as good as bacon and eggs would feel. She quickly dressed and headed off to the store for groceries.

As she passed Bootsy's house, she noticed for the first time the "for sale" sign hanging on the property. There were no cars. Eleanor stopped to check the hidey-hole. It was empty except for a small piece of paper.

*Dear Eleanor,*

*I'm sad we are selling Granny's house. It means I probably won't see you again. Mom wouldn't let me come to say goodbye. She thinks I am a nuisance. Thank you for being my friend and for the gifts in the hidey-hole. I hope your husband comes home soon.*

*Your friend,*

*Bootsy*

Eleanor was sad too. She enjoyed Bootsy's company and looked forward to her visits. How had she missed her? She pushed the note deep into her pocket and continued on her errand.

Eleanor woke to a cool drizzling rain. It was Wednesday, June 14, Flag Day, no Walter, Nora would come to clean, she hadn't thought about that. As she moved to get out of her bed, her back seized in a spasm that made her gasp in pain. She quickly lay back until the pain stopped. She must have pulled something when she carried in the groceries yesterday. Pearl was always telling her she needed to do yoga to strengthen her core. Maybe she was right. It seemed that Wednesday would be a day of woe after all.

Eleanor spent most of the day in her robe, lying on the couch icing her back and eating aspirin. Nora cleaned around her and made sure she ate and rested. She even cleaned Feathers' cage.

There was no way she could have visited Walter. Hopefully she would be recovered by Sunday. She wondered what would happen if she never visited him again. Would she feel guilty or would she feel free? She worried about the visit on Sunday when Erin and the grandchildren might witness Walter with his new love. It shamed her in more ways than one. She didn't want their pity as the woman scorned. She didn't know if they already knew. They never spoke of it. What if the grandchildren asked questions? It would be embarrassing to watch them touching or kissing, but maybe they wouldn't have to if they took Walter out. She would focus on that.

Thursday, June 15, another wet day. Eleanor knew June was often wet on the Oregon coast. The weather was unpredictable. Her back felt better, but she would take it easy today, maybe read a book, or watch a movie. She would call Erin and solidify their plans. Knowing her youngest daughter, she suspected Erin had already made reservations somewhere and called Rosewood to inform them of their plans to spring Walter. Eleanor propped herself up on several pillows and wallowed in her infirmity. "Might as well enjoy myself," she thought.

"Friday, Friday, Friday is my favorite day," sang Eleanor as the day broke with a beautiful sunrise and not a cloud on the horizon. It was coffee day, Eleanor had slept well, and her back felt pretty good. Nothing was on her agenda except coffee with her friends. It was June 16, Friday. "Do not jump ahead to Sunday," she cautioned herself. She eagerly got up, made coffee, got the paper, and busied herself solving the crossword, jumble, and sudoku—and all before her coffee group met. Yes, she was back!

The Boat House was quiet on this beautiful Friday morning. Eleanor eagerly sat down at their usual table and waited patiently for the others. It wasn't usual for her to be early, but this morning was different. Eleanor was in fine fiddle. The waitress brought coffee and warmly welcomed Eleanor as one of the locals.

"Good morning," she chirped.

"What's new?" Eleanor asked casually.

"Did you hear that Claire Dobbs and Adele Grimes both died?" It was obviously big news she was eager to share.

"No." Eleanor was shocked. Both women were acquaintances and Claire had once been a member of her book club. "What happened to them?"

"I don't know any details," she confessed, "just that they died. I heard they were both found in their homes. It was probably heart attack or the like. I think they were both old." She hurried off to get more coffee as Dede and Pearl arrived.

Eleanor felt the hair on the nape of her neck stand on end and a chill went down her spine.

"Did you hear?" Dede and Pearl had been discussing the deaths as they came in from the parking lot.

"I just heard about Claire and Adele if that's what you mean." Eleanor was still in shock. "Tell me what you know."

Dede and Pearl sat down and were just about to tell everything when Cleo and Josephine came in laughing about some foolishness, but they stopped abruptly when they saw the expressions of their friends.

"What's happened?" asked Cleo, "You all look as if someone died."

"You better sit down," warned Pearl.

"I don't like this," moaned Josephine as she obediently took her seat.

"Claire Dobbs and Adele Grimes are both dead," Dede informed them.

"What? Were they in a car accident?" asked Cleo.

"All I know is they were found in their homes. It looks like natural causes. Claire was in her chair and Adele evidently died in her sleep." Dede had told all she knew.

"How old do you think they were?" Cleo asked suspiciously.

"I don't think they were eighty. As far as I know neither was ill either." Dede continued.

"Not to speak ill of the dead, but I never really liked Adele," Josephine confessed. "She had a way of making me feel like shit on a stick."

"Me too," added Pearl. "I always felt totally incompetent when I talked to her."

"She thought I was very intelligent. I didn't have a problem with her, but I didn't know her the way you did," Cleo admitted.

Dede and Eleanor held their peace.

Eleanor finally asked the question they were all thinking, "Do you think it was the Maude Squad?"

"How could it be?" asked Dede, "neither one of them was over eighty."

"Maybe we don't know all the rules," added Cleo. "Maybe there is more to the Maude Squad than we know, or maybe they have gone off the tracks."

"Has anyone been watching the personal ads?" questioned Pearl.

"I haven't seen anything suspicious," said Cleo. "Have you heard anything new from Angus, Eleanor?"

"I have not," Eleanor answered primly. "The last time I spoke with him was at the murder mystery party and we didn't discuss this kind of murder then."

"Maybe you should pursue that avenue," suggested Josephine with a wink.

"Oh, stop it!" Eleanor said, realizing she was blushing.

"I have an idea," Cleo blurted, unaware of the gentle tease that was occurring.

"What is it?" Eleanor was grateful for the distraction.

"I'll put an ad in the personals myself telling Maude I'm ready. Then we will wait to see what happens." Cleo's eyes sparkled with delight.

"That is dangerous!" exclaimed Josephine. "What if someone comes to kill you?"

"I'll give them Pearl's address." Cleo laughed and suddenly everyone was laughing.

"It occurs to me that the last three deaths have something in common." Dede spoke after the giggles had subsided.

"What is that?" asked Josephine, wiping her eyes.

That was when the waitress came to take their orders. Of course, they all had their usual and as soon as she left, Dede picked right up where she had left off.

"Claire Dobbs, Adele Grimes, and Jackie Anne Heart were friends, and all went to the same church," Dede declared.

"So, are you implying the church killed them?" asked Cleo.

Dede arched one brow and gave Cleo the dreaded teacher look. "No, but they would never contact a death squad to do them in, so maybe there is something else at work here."

"Perhaps they knew too much. Maybe they found out about the Maude Squad and who was doing the mercy killing so they had to be silenced," suggested Pearl.

"And maybe they just died a nice peaceful death," Josephine offered sensibly.

"If what you think is true, Pearl, we had better watch ourselves. We are the ones who have been searching for answers and surfing the internet about the Maude Squad. Not being eighty might not save us."

Cleo seemed honestly worried and ready to give up any idea of drawing them out. "Yes, maybe we should just stick to our own business. I think the best resource is for Eleanor to pump Angus."

Josephine was like a dog with a bone.

Eleanor took a long drink of water, hoping her friends would ignore Josephine's remark. It seemed crude and unlike Josephine. Did she know something Eleanor did not? Whatever it was, Eleanor did not want to discuss Angus now. Fortunately, their breakfasts arrived and Eleanor took the interruption to change the topic. "Erin and her family are meeting me this Sunday to visit Walter. It's Father's Day. I hope that brazen hussy doesn't show up and spoil it," she worried.

"Erin's a grown up. I'm sure she understands the illness and can handle whatever happens," Dede offered.

"Maybe, but the children . . ." Eleanor didn't finish her thought before Josephine put in her two cents.

"Eleanor, it must be horrible for you to watch Walter with this woman. Just remember he isn't cheating on you. It's the disease. Don't make it your disease."

Eleanor knew Josephine was right as usual. Maybe she was worried about herself, or at least the perception others might have about Walter and her. She really didn't want to be seen as the woman scorned. It didn't fit with the storyline she had written for her happy everafter life.

"Doesn't Erin visit her Dad without you there?" asked Cleo.

"Yes, of course," answered Eleanor.

"Then she's more than likely seen them together already," responded Cleo.

"We certainly can't protect our children and grandchildren from the unpleasantness of life," Pearl added. "Sometimes we need it to learn the lessons life is supposed to teach us."

These friends are so wise Eleanor thought. They could see into her fear and draw out a truth she knew she needed to hear. No one's life was perfect. You could have the finest home, the best view, the most money, a brilliant education, and successful career, and still not achieve perfection. The love of her life was still the love of her life. She was just no longer the love of his life.

"What do you think the universe is trying to teach me through this experience?" Eleanor pondered aloud.

"What do you think?" Josephine prodded gently. She could see the pain in Eleanor's eyes.

"Maybe I think I'm all that and the universe is trying to tell me I've just been lucky so far. Maybe Cleo is right about light bouncing off of dark and this is my dark." Eleanor sighed. It wasn't often they spoke of Walter and the pain his disease caused her, but when they did it had a healing effect.

"You have lived a charmed life. Really, we all have been very lucky, and I say lucky and not blessed with purpose. Blessed somehow conjures the notion of a god who favors some of us over others. I just can't accept that," Cleo declared.

"I think we are entering a phase of loss," Pearl said. "Our friends are dying, we are losing our strength and stamina and even our ability to remember."

"When our husbands are all dead or in the home, let's get a big house and live together," suggested Cleo.

"Yes, or we could live in one of those tiny house communities. We could each have our own space yet be close enough to do things together." Josephine was all in until she remembered her husband, Richard, was at least 10 years younger than she and genetically predisposed to live well into his nineties. "Maybe Richard could live with me in a not so tiny house," she amended.

"Steve promised me many years ago that he would outlive me," Cleo said, "so I won't have to worry about being alone or having to do yard work."

"Let's wait and see how it plays out," Dede added.

"Cleo, do not put that ad in the personals," ordered Pearl.

"No, I won't," she reassured as they all gathered their things and went off in their own directions.

Eleanor had much to think about as she left the Boat House. She had a craving for something sweet and decided to stop for ice cream at the grocery store. Did she want to have Angus over for dinner? No, she would stop for some special items just for her. She did not want to think about Angus, so she just put him out of her mind, but made a mental list of ingredients she would need to make dinner for him. When she left the store, she had everything she needed for baby back ribs with crispy yams and coleslaw . . . and Waterton ice cream of course.

Later, as she prepared for the meal and sipped her glass of pinot noir, she was happy that Angus was coming for dinner. She enjoyed cooking and looked forward to an evening with someone she considered a good friend. He might even have details about the recent deaths.

Promptly at 6:00 p.m., Angus was at the door. Feathers made his usual fuss and flew about calling, "Lock the door, Ellie. Lock the door!"

Angus looked especially handsome and smelled of Old Spice. His hair was combed and his mustache was neatly trimmed, totally opposite his appearance as a badass pirate.

Eleanor took it all in, including the bouquet of colorful flowers in his hand. "Come in, Angus. What a lovely bouquet. Don't mind Feathers. He hasn't had his nap today."

"That is some delicious aroma I smell." Angus headed into the kitchen following his nose.

Eleanor put the flowers in a vase and poured Crown Royal for Angus. They filled their plates in the kitchen and sat down to eat at the table Eleanor had prepared. There were lots of paper napkins in anticipation of a very messy meal. Angus wasted no time getting right down to business and gnawed his ribs to the bone. Eleanor tried to be neat but it was impossible. They looked at each other and began to laugh. It was a picture right out of the book, *Tom Jones*, without the lusty bits. Eleanor had barbecue sauce on her cheeks and the tip of her nose. Angus' mustache was covered in it and some had dribbled down his chin.

"Eleanor, you are the best cook I know," Angus managed when he had regained his composure.

"And you are the most appreciative eater I know," Eleanor responded.

Feathers flew in to investigate the loud laughter screeching, "Lock up the silver, Ellie!"

For some odd reason this set them off laughing again. It was a wonder neither of them choked.

When they finished their feast and cleaned themselves up, Angus looked at Eleanor very seriously and said, "I know this meal is going to cost me and I'm willing to pay the price. What do you want to know about the recent deaths of Claire and Adele?"

Eleanor would have hung her head in shame if she had any, but instead she simply acknowledged the fact that Angus was on to her and said, "Everything, I want to know everything you know."

Angus nodded his big head and smiled until his dimples appeared while he thought about the facts and where he could begin.

"Well, according to my sources, Claire Dobbs was dying of cancer. As you already know, she had cancer several years ago, went

124

through some horrendous treatments and thought she had it licked. She just discovered it was back and couldn't face it. We believe she committed suicide."

"Did anyone know she was ill? How did she do it?" Eleanor expressed her curiosity openly.

"Her husband died about the same time Jackie Anne Heart lost hers. They developed a close friendship. She didn't have any children, so she was on her own. The thought of going through that again without the support of her husband and best friend was more than she could bear. At least that is what the police have concluded." Angus knew she would want more, but he paused here and waited for her to ask.

"And . . . what method did she use?" Eleanor prompted.

"Don't know for sure yet. We didn't find anything in her house but wine. Two wine glasses and an empty bottle indicate she had company earlier in the evening. She was found fully dressed sitting in her chair by her cleaning lady Thursday morning. There will be an autopsy and we'll know more then," he concluded.

"What about Adele?" Eleanor persisted.

"That's where the story gets interesting." Angus leaned back in his chair, picked up his empty glass and rattled the ice cubes.

Eleanor quickly responded by bringing the bottle of Crown Royal to the table. After Angus refilled his glass, he continued.

"You know Adele never married. She liked women and loved Claire." He paused here to let the full shock soak in. He enjoyed Eleanor's expression of surprise. Her eyes widened and her mouth made a barbecue-stained ohhh.

"I didn't know! How did you determine this?" Eleanor was always in search of the facts and would not tolerate speculation.

"There was a letter—a love letter—sort of poem found at Claire's house. It was written and signed by Adele." Angus tried to remember what the poem said but couldn't.

"How do you know the letter was meant for Claire? Maybe Adele was in love with Claire's husband and Claire found out and confronted Adele. Then Adele killed Claire in a fit of jealousy." Eleanor emoted.

"That would make more sense if Claire's husband wasn't dead." Angus could still use logic even after a second drink. "Let's say Adele loved Claire. Claire confided in Adele about her recurring cancer, so Adele killed Claire to spare her from a long painful death, then she went home and killed herself because she couldn't live without Claire."

"I like it." Eleanor poured herself another glass of wine. "But what if some third party, someone we don't know, knew about Claire and Adele's affair and was blackmailing them. They refused to pay, so the third party offs them both."

"No," Angus said, shaking his head. "Who would care if Claire and Adele had an affair? Neither of them had money, that we know of, so what would be the motive? Maybe if Claire's husband wasn't dead, he might kill them both, but who else?"

"Claire belonged to a very intolerant fundamental church of some sort. Maybe they killed them because they thought they were sinners." Eleanor didn't put a lot of thought in this one.

Angus shook his head again. "No, no, no, religious people don't kill sinners, well, maybe some of them do, but that's highly unlikely."

"Well maybe we don't know the whole story. Maybe Claire had a child we don't know about and that child showed up and killed her because he was mad that she gave him up. Then Adele found her and killed herself out of grief." Eleanor was stretching it now. "You know lots of people keep secrets and take them to their graves."

Angus stared into Eleanor's eyes for a long time. "Do you have secrets, Eleanor?"

126

"Of course, I do. Everyone has secrets and I'm not about to share them with you, Angus McBride!" Eleanor smiled wickedly. "I intend to take my secret barbecue recipe to my grave." Angus burst out laughing.

Saturday morning came and Eleanor woke later than usual embarrassed as she remembered her dream. She opened her eyes and bolted upright to make sure Angus was not in her bed. Finding no evidence of a night spent in drunken lust, she collapsed into her pillows and sighed in relief. Saturday, June 17, nothing, she could think of nothing that she had to do. It was strange. She recounted the previous night and the information Angus revealed. Somehow the facts were tangled with the ridiculous tales they had spun as they drank their way late into the night. It was a wonder she didn't have a hangover. Wait a minute, there was a kiss. Was it in the dream or did it really happen? Eleanor's brain was fuzzy. Maybe she was hungover.

She got up and went to the kitchen in search of clues. On her way she lifted the cover from Feathers' cage and greeted him. He was full of warm words and gentle parrot kisses. "I love you, Ellie." Suddenly it all came flooding back. There *was* a kiss, an almost kiss at the door as Angus prepared to leave. She remembered wanting it. She remembered Angus leaning down into the kiss and Feathers flying onto his head in a flurry of beating wings crying, "Time to go, so long, good-night, adieu, don't let the door hit you on the way out!"

It had startled them both and Angus had left laughing.

Eleanor found the kitchen spotless and remembered Angus helping her clean up. She made coffee and went out to get the morning paper. She decided it would be a laid-back day; coffee, crossword puzzle, walk on the beach, maybe an afternoon nap. Why not? Tomorrow she would miss her lazy Sunday due to visiting Walter.

She had just poured her first cup of coffee and settled down with her crossword puzzle when the doorbell rang. Eleanor wondered who would be visiting on a Saturday morning. Maybe Feathers was at his tricks again, but when she opened the door she was surprised to see Angus. Without a word he simply took her in his arms and kissed her. It was a long, gentle kiss. She was too old to say she felt her knees buckle, or maybe she was old and they did buckle. When the kiss was over, Angus turned around and walked back to his car.

"I needed to do that," he said and then he drove away.

Stunned, Eleanor closed the door. She wasn't dressed, hadn't even washed her face or brushed her teeth. She stood by the door and thought, "What was he thinking? Maybe he dreamed a dream too. What had they drunk last night? She was a married woman. This was wrong on so many levels. Or was it? Walter had a girlfriend. Maybe it was all right for her to have a boyfriend. She always thought of Angus fondly as a friend. Would this spoil it? Could she still invite him to dinner and pump him for information? Did he love her? How did she feel about him?"

Eleanor went back to the kitchen and poured another cup of coffee, then nestled into her spot on the couch to read the paper. She put her cup down next to her other cup and realized this would be a very strange day.

Concentrating on the Sudoku was next to impossible. Eleanor picked up the phone and called Josephine. They made a plan to meet for lunch at the Cow Bell Café.

Eleanor waited anxiously for Josephine. Josephine was never late, but today Eleanor was early, so wait she did. She tried not waiting but watching instead. She looked out the window at the passersby and watched the waitress as she took orders. She made up stories about the customers in the booth across the room and studied all the cow paraphernalia that hung on the walls. She desperately hoped she would see no one she knew.

Josephine slipped into the booth across the table and looked closely at her friend.

"What is it, Eleanor?" Josephine asked.

"How did you know about Angus?" Eleanor demanded, and then in a stream that kept coming and coming, she related the entire evening with Angus, the dream, and the morning kiss.

"I see," Josephine responded.

"But you knew. How did you know?" she asked again.

"I see," she repeated. "I have spent my life watching and listening to people. It wasn't hard to see how much Angus adores you. Even before Walter's illness, it was evident. Even when he dated other women, he had eyes for you. I'm surprised you didn't notice at the mystery party how he never left your side. He was there helping with the heavy lifting, pouring drinks, acting like your partner."

"Oh," Eleanor sighed and put her head in her hands. "What am I going to do? I truly care for Angus, but I'm married to Walter. Everything was so simple before. This has just messed things up."

"How is that?" Josephine prodded.

"I never acknowledged before that he might have those kinds of feelings for me. I just wanted to keep things simple and friendly. I must be blind. Even Feathers knew. Now things will be awkward."

"Are you saying you don't have those same feelings for him? Because your dream says otherwise." Josephine was right, and Eleanor knew it.

"Okay, I'm 72-years old, my husband has dementia, doesn't know me, and has a girlfriend. What would you do?" Eleanor asked.

"That is not important," Josephine continued. "I've been married three times, because I picked some losers. You seem to have lucked into two great relationships with two good men. This is your story, not mine. Look at your options. You decide."

"My options . . ." Eleanor paused to consider what these might be. "I think I have to know more before I can consider my options. Angus may have some say in my options. I guess I need to talk to Angus."

"Yes, but do you know what you want?" Josephine questioned.

"I will never leave Walter. Even though he doesn't know me anymore," she said, "he's still my husband and I love him. I care for Angus and want him in my life. I want him as a friend and companion. The other stuff, kissing and hugging would be nice, but I'm not sure I want to marry him. He may not want to marry me either. Maybe he just wants to eat my cooking." Eleanor was feeling less anxious about the whole affair.

"This could work if Angus doesn't have conditions of his own that might be in conflict with yours." Josephine added. "Do you know how lucky you are Eleanor? I was thinking about what Pearl said about this being a time of loss for us. Look how broken Jackie Ann was when she lost her husband and Claire as well. Women without men become invisible in our society. They don't get invited to parties or dinner, and when they do they often feel like third wheels. It is an entirely new phase of their lives and often a very lonely one, one that most don't look forward to entering. Angus is a gift to you."

"Yes, I realize that." Eleanor was feeling better by the minute. Josephine was helping her put things in perspective. Even though she didn't have Walter, she wasn't a widow. She still had something to cling to even if it was false hope. What if they found a cure for his dementia and she got him back? She could visit him, talk to him, and touch him. Now she had Angus too. No reason to be alarmed.

Eleanor filled Josephine in on the details she learned from Angus as they enjoyed their cowbell burgers. There wasn't much that shocked Josephine, but her eyes did get round when she learned about the affair between Claire and Adele. Wasn't life full of surprises?

That night as Eleanor propped herself up in her king size bed and opened her book, the telephone rang.

"Eleanor, it's Angus. Are you still talking to me?"

Did she detect fear in his voice? "Of course, I'm still talking to you," she reassured.

"I wasn't sure after last night and this morning. I thought you might never want to see me again."

"I always want to see you. You are my dear friend and I need all the friends I can get."

"That's not exactly what I want to be, if you want the truth. I want to be the first thing you think about every morning and the last thing every night." Angus was making a declaration. Eleanor hoped it wasn't an ultimatum.

"When you ring my bell in the morning and call me before I turn out the light at night, it's a sure thing I'm thinking of you," she teased.

"We need to talk. Let's go to the marina tomorrow and take the boat out. I'd like to test drive it before I decide to buy it. We could talk then about you and me." Angus was not wasting any more time.

"I'd like that, but tomorrow is Father's Day," she said. "Erin is meeting me at Rosewood to visit Walter. Let's do it Monday." She wanted Angus to know that Walter was still in the picture.

There was a pause. Maybe he was checking his calendar or maybe not. "Okay, Monday, let's say 9:00. I'll pick you up."

"It's a date," she said, wondering if she should have offered to meet him there. What if things didn't go well? It could be an awkward drive home.

"Good night, Ellie," he said before hanging up.

Sunday, June 18, Father's Day with Erin and her tribe, Walter and Alice, brunch, Paul McCartney's birthday, do not jump ahead to Monday with Angus. Eleanor rose, dressed, and drove to face her fears.

When Eleanor arrived at Rosewood Manor, she saw Erin's car in the lot and knew they were already inside. She entered the foyer through the oak doors, signed her name below Erin's, punched in the entry code, and stepped into Walter's world. There was no sign of Alice. Eleanor let out a sigh, surprised that she had ceased to breath. She spotted Walter immediately. He held Erin's hand while the two teenage children walked on his other side, and Erin's husband, Ben, trailed behind. Walter looked wonderful, handsome even. He was dressed in sharply pressed khakis and a white shirt. His hair neatly combed, face freshly shaven, and a smile that declared him a happy man. Maybe today would be a good day.

Together they walked a short distance to a sweet restaurant where Erin had made reservations. Erin's children were so attentive to their grandfather, it made Eleanor's heart swell. Walter didn't say much but nodded occasionally as if he were interested and could track their conversations. They all enjoyed their brunch of fresh fruit and eggy concoctions.

"Dad's having a good day." Erin smiled as her two teens helped him open his Father's Day gifts and Ben snapped a few pictures to commemorate the day.

"I don't often see this side of him," lamented Eleanor. "It makes me happy and sad at the same time."

"I understand how hard it must be for you, Mom. I've seen Alice," Erin admitted. "He really doesn't know what he's doing anymore, and she seems to be good company for him here."

"I don't blame him, Sweetie, but I still don't like her." Eleanor confessed.

"I think she is deeply into her dementia, more than Dad," Erin added. "She doesn't speak. At least I've never heard her say a word."

"Let's don't talk about her," Eleanor ordered. And the topic was closed.

When they returned to Rosewood Manor, Eleanor spotted Alice immediately. She approached them with a shuffling gait and touched Walter's arm gently. It was then that Eleanor noticed the blue ring on her finger—a blue that matched her eyes. It was exactly like the one she had given Bootsy. She was puzzled. Could there be two such rings?

Erin interrupted her thoughts as they said their goodbyes with hugs and kisses. Standing alone, Eleanor watched as Walter and Alice walked away from her, together, his arm thrown casually over her shoulder. A single tear ran down her cheek. Lost in her own pain she didn't notice the little girl standing beside her until she felt a tug on her sleeve.

Bootsy had watched their return. She read Eleanor's face, noticed the single tear, and guessed that Walter was her missing husband. It took Eleanor a beat longer to realize who Alice might be.

"Oh, Eleanor, is Walter your husband?" asked Bootsy.

"Yes," Eleanor almost whispered her answer. "Is Alice your Nana?"

"Yes, she's my Nana Greenwood. It is just so weird. You lost your husband and I lost my Nana and somehow they found each other."

"Yes, and we found each other too." Eleanor looked away from Walter and Alice as they faded from view and looked down at Bootsy. "I think you should call me Ellie. We are definitely kindred spirits."

Bootsy smiled and Eleanor wiped her tear away.

"Are your parents here?" Eleanor asked as she looked around.

"No, I rode my bike here. We only live a few blocks away. I come here every Sunday, at least whenever I can." Bootsy revealed her loneliness shyly.

"How about I give you a ride home?" Eleanor suggested.

"That would be great!" Bootsy was ready to leave. It made Eleanor curious to know how this family spent a Father's Day and confirmed her suspicions about Bootsy's parents being unavailable to this sweet little girl.

As they drove to Bootsy's house, which turned out to be more than several blocks away, they made plans to meet next Sunday at Rosewood Manor. Maybe they would meet every Sunday at Rosewood Manor. There would be no more Wednesdays of woe.

On the drive home, Eleanor had ample time to make sense of all the events that were happening and the feelings that were swirling through her mind. She began to see the barroom skank that was Walter's lover instead as the sad, lonely woman who was Bootsy's nana. Eleanor could give her Walter because she planned to take Bootsy—light bouncing off of dark.

Monday, June 19, Walter wasn't here, Bootsy's nana and Alice were one and the same, Bootsy would be at Rosewood Manor on Sunday afternoons, no more Wednesdays of woe, Angus was coming at 9:00 to take her to the marina. Eleanor felt light and free. It was a beautiful morning, clear and bright and full of promise. She felt a lightness of spirit she hadn't experienced in a long while. Perhaps it was letting go of the loathing for Alice. Somehow freeing Alice and Walter from the dungeon of blame had set her free as well. She got out of bed with more vitality than usual. She had things to do and places to go.

Promptly at nine o'clock, Angus was at her door.

"Good morning, Ellie." There was no trace of awkwardness around Angus as Eleanor welcomed him inside.

"Would you like a cup of coffee?" she asked.

Suddenly Feathers swooped into the room squawking, "Don't feed the animals, Ellie!" He landed on Eleanor's shoulder and glared at Angus first with his right eye and then with his left. "Three's a crowd," he continued.

"I think I'll skip the coffee," Angus decided. "I packed us a little picnic for the boat ride. Let's head out to the marina. Are you ready?"

"Absolutely, let me get a jacket. Eleanor and Feathers went off in search of the jacket. Feathers turned on Eleanor's shoulder and continued to give Angus the stink eye on his way out of the room.

"I love you, Ellie," Feathers could be heard as Eleanor returned without him.

"Silly bird!" Eleanor exclaimed.

"I think he's a bird who knows what he wants," Angus commented, "I admire that in a parrot."

Eleanor wondered what Angus wanted, and if he would admire her for wanting something altogether different.

The drive to the marina was relatively quiet. Neither wanted to start the discussion they knew was coming, both fearing the loss of a warm and comfortable friendship replaced by something uncertain.

Eleanor had called ahead to have the boat taken out of dry storage and ready it for their day on the water. Walking down the steps to the water flooded her with memories of days spent fishing with Walter. Somehow the marina, the boats with their masts, the smell of fish, and the crying of the gulls all belonged to Walter's world. The walkway was wet, and Angus carefully held Eleanor's elbow as they made their way to Walter's boat.

It looked the same as she remembered, and what she remembered was a pretty boat. She knew nothing about the specifics. It was just a boat Walter used for fishing. A boat he had named Ellie. She wondered if Angus would change that.

They clambered aboard. Angus seemed right at home in the boat, and asked no questions about its size, motor, or history. Then, he had probably been on it more than Eleanor. She wondered if he was thinking of Walter too and remembering the many times the two had gone out in the bay together. Neither spoke as Angus maneuvered the boat slowly out into open waters. Eleanor sat quietly and looked out over the glistening waters of Waterton Bay. Even though the sun was bright, the air on the bay was cool. Gulls cried, but most of the sounds were drowned out by the boat's motor as they made their way across the bay to the spit. There were several boats afloat on the mirror surface. Serious fishermen would have been at it for hours. Angus guided the boat to a protected cove, anchored and turned the off the engine.

"What a beautiful day!" Eleanor exclaimed.

"Near perfect," Angus replied. Somehow, they lacked their usual easy banter and conversation seemed forced and wrong.

"What do you think of the boat? Will you take it?" Eleanor asked.

"Of course, that was never in question. I love this boat." Angus' admission surprised Eleanor.

"So why the test drive?" she persisted.

"Seriously? I needed to get you somewhere alone to talk about us. I thought it would be romantic. I just didn't factor in the part about Walter being here too," Angus lamented. "First I hear that pesky parrot tell you he loves you in Walter's voice, and being on his boat isn't exactly neutral territory."

"So, what is it you want, Angus? Just tell me," Eleanor urged.

"I want you, Eleanor. I want you in my life. I want to look after you, protect you, and eat your cooking," he smiled as he admitted his hunger.

Eleanor smiled too. "I like it."

"You do?" Angus didn't think it would be this easy.

"Isn't that what we already have?" Eleanor asked.

"No, I want more. I want to see you every day and every night. I'm tired of being alone and I know you are lonely too." Angus looked deeply into her eyes. "I want to marry you."

"Angus, I'm a married woman. I still love Walter."

"But he can't be there for you anymore."

"Are you suggesting I divorce him?" Eleanor was shocked.

"I love you, Ellie. Walter doesn't know you," Angus argued.

"How do you know that?" Eleanor snapped.

"I've been to Rosewood Manor. I've visited Walter and I know about Alice. It must be awful for you, but you don't have to endure it," Angus said.

"Is this pity I hear?" Eleanor's pride was bruised.

"No, Ellie, this is a man who loves a woman and doesn't want to see her suffer. I think we are better together than we are apart." Angus reached for her hand and held it.

"I'm very fond of you, Angus. I do enjoy your company and I love cooking for you, but I won't divorce Walter. I'm a 72-year-old woman who has spent almost two thirds of her life married. It isn't you I don't want to marry, I just don't want to be married. For the last three years I've been totally independent. No one tells me how to spend my money, when to go to bed, or makes me feel guilty if I eat ice cream for dinner. I don't tell anyone where I'm going or when I'll be home, and I like it." Eleanor looked into Angus' eyes and saw disappointment but not defeat.

"Okay, I understand that. I respect that. Can we still be friends? Will you still invite me to dinner?"

"Absolutely, I'd be heartbroken to have it any other way. Maybe you could come over every Wednesday for dinner," Eleanor offered, knowing she would need something to replace her Wednesday of woe. Now it could be Wednesday of woo. She smiled and saw the light of hope return to Angus' eyes. She wondered what he was hoping.

"Let's get out of this boat and walk the spit," he suggested. "We can take this picnic basket with us and find a place to enjoy the view." And so they did.

Eleanor sat in her house alone looking out at the ocean without seeing it. She was exhausted, more emotionally than physically. She absently stroked Feathers as she pondered her options. Never in a million years had she ever considered being in this position. She enjoyed Angus' company more than she cared to admit. They had enjoyed the day on the water and even after her refusal they had laughed together without any awkwardness, but she could not get past her devotion to Walter and the vision she had of them growing old together. Walter had grown old without her and left her in ways she could never have predicted. Angus was handsome, smart, funny, and he liked her cooking.

The whole thing was just messy, and Eleanor did not tolerate messes. If she divorced Walter and married Angus what would happen to her finances? The will Walter and she had carefully crafted to benefit their children and grandchildren would need to be changed. There would be decisions about where to live and all the things they had accumulated over a lifetime sorted and redistributed. Making room for Angus in her life even mentally was just too much work.

Eleanor believed she could have anything she wanted, but not everything. She loved her freedom and independence but yearned for the comfort of knowing someone was there for her if she needed to share an idea, or reach into a high cupboard, or help make a difficult decision. Choices needed to be made, but now all she wanted was to close her eyes and fall asleep to the rhythm of the waves.

When she woke, disoriented, she began her morning ritual, but could not remember the day. Was it Monday or Tuesday? It was still daylight, but the sun was setting, coloring the sky a vibrant crimson. It was still Monday. She stretched and went to the kitchen in search of food. There was no one here to tell her what to eat or judge her for her choices. She opted for the banana split ice cream and smiled at her bad behavior.

Tuesday, June 20, there was nothing. Eleanor could think of nothing she had to do, nothing she had planned. It was a day full of possibilities. Of course, Walter wasn't here. Angus loved her.

She stretched, sat up and looked out the window. There was fog and a quiet grayness that mirrored her mood and made her wonder if a day full of possibilities was an adequate description for this day. She would choose to make it one.

Eleanor took her freshly brewed cup of coffee into the office and lit the gas fireplace. She looked around the room. It had been several days since she had been in it. A thin coating of dust covered her desk. Nora would come tomorrow. Her eye fell on the box shoved to the side, the box from Frieda. Why had she left it so long, unopened, as if it were unwanted? She felt a little guilt as she carefully pried the tape off and lifted the flaps out of the way. A beautiful lightweight lounging robe lay folded neatly on top. Eleanor shook it and held the soft, rich velvet burnout material up to her body. A faint lavender scent wafted from it as Eleanor put it on over her nightgown. Perfect, she would declare this a pajama day and refuse to get dressed. Just then the doorbell rang and Eleanor left the box to see who would visit this early.

No one was at the door, but Feathers guiltily flew to her shoulder whistling a show tune. Forgetting about the box for now, Eleanor returned to the kitchen and made herself a large omelet to make up for her poor choice of dinner from last night. She read the paper, completed the crossword puzzle and the Sudoku while she ate.

"Well, Feathers, it's been a long time since I've felt bored, but I think I'm bored right now. What are you doing today?" she asked.

Feathers refused to answer but flew to his perch by the wall of windows and looked out over the ocean that was slowing emerging from the lifting fog.

"I should go for a walk," she spoke to herself. "That always makes me feel better, but I've declared this a pajama day and I don't feel like getting dressed." Eleanor stroked the velvety robe. "Boredom sparks creativity. I shall allow myself to be superlatively bored and create something fantastic." She cleared her breakfast dishes, poured herself another cup of coffee and returned to her office. Here she pushed Frieda's box once more to the side and picked up her pen.

The Seedling

The sunlight filters through,

A drop of rain or two

Escapes

Into my prison.

Yet I remain the same

Although my friends have miraculously grown feet

And strayed away.

I look for blight and find nothing.

Look for mold and rot but find none.

Waiting for that upward surge

To thrust me into blue space

To feel the wind, the rain and sun upon my face.

Eleanor was ready to get dressed. She needed to feel the wind and sun upon her face.

The fog had evaporated revealing a dazzling day. As Eleanor walked down the hill past Bootsy's house, she once again noticed the vacant feel of the place. There is nothing sadder than an empty house, she thought. The dark windows seemed to watch her woefully as she left the road to check the hidey-hole. She was not surprised to find nothing there, and she hurried on eager to escape the mournful eyes that continued to haunt her. What would Jean Scattergoods think of her abandoned beach home with the "for sale" sign out front telling the world that it was no longer wanted? Just like all the treasures collected over a lifetime, so easily discarded as junk and dropped off at the nearest thrift shop. No one seemed to want the stuff connected to someone else's memories. She couldn't really blame them. She thought of Frieda's box and how even now it sat neglected in her office, and how indifferent she was to its contents. It's just stuff, she thought. It's not Frieda and she continued on her way to the beach forgiving herself for her disinterest.

Farther on and almost to the bottom of the hill, she met Nancy driving home.

"Hi neighbor," Nancy called out, stopping in the middle of the road and blocking it entirely.

"Hello, what's new?" Eleanor responded.

"Just went to the grocery store. Dennis wants to start up the barbecue and cook up a flank steak. Would you like to join us for dinner?" Nancy offered.

"That sounds delightful. What can I bring?" Eleanor loved Dennis's flank steak. He had mastered it to perfection.

"I think I have everything. Just bring yourself." Nancy responded.

"I have a very good cabernet that would complement that steak." Eleanor knew Nancy enjoyed her wine.

"Perfect, come over about six. I'll see you then." Nancy glanced in her rearview mirror and noticing a car behind her, drove off with a wave of her hand.

Eleanor's mind continued to wander as she strode down the trail that led to the shore. Several thoughts made their way into her brain like rain through a leaky roof. She didn't know where they came from or why. As she walked along, the sand moved under her shoes, the waves rushed closer, and gulls cried over the salty breeze that blew into her face, but she was so deeply into her thoughts that none of it registered. She thought about Walter and Alice and imagined a sick scenario where she confronted them and got into a hair-pulling cat fight that left Alice bald. Then she fancied herself with Angus in a most inappropriate and lusty activity where she conjured up visions of his naked body. It did not shame her to have such notions. Eleanor had enjoyed an active sex life with Walter and missed the intimacy they once shared. It was normal and human even for someone as old as she was to enjoy the touch of another. She remembered her final visit with Frieda and how the old woman expressed pleasure in the hugs they gave one another. Everyone needed to be touched.

Her mind turned to the evening's dinner plans and what she would wear, then continued to her dinner with Angus on the Wednesday of woo. What would she make? Her mind flipped through an entire cookbook, selecting and discarding possible recipes for wooing him, surprising herself with the pleasure it gave her.

From out of nowhere came the idea of poison and the Maude Squad. It seemed ages since she had given the murders any thought at all. She began a list of the known dead: Henry Ott, Gertie Frank, Lidia Garfield, Howard Welk, Edith Allen, Edward Eberlee, Frieda VanHorn, Jackie Ann Heart, Claire Dobbs, and Adele Grimes. Were there others? Jean Scattergoods wasn't murdered, but she had asked to be and there was the unknown woman in Silverton. Most were over eighty, but not all of them. This was a real thing. There were those ads in the newspaper. Eleanor wasn't sure how she felt about it. Were these all people who wanted to die? If so, who was she to tell them they had to keep living even though it might mean a painful existence. She didn't have any answers. Eleanor questioned her silence. Knowing what she knew, was she abetting murder or mercy?

Eleanor looked out at the vastness of the ocean and realized she had walked farther than she normally did. Time had flown and the tide was coming in. She would have to hurry back if she didn't want to get trapped by high water. She hustled as fast as her old legs would go.

At dinner that evening Eleanor learned that two more old people had died—natural causes. No one questioned it.

The telephone woke Eleanor the next day. "Ellie, this is Angus. Are we still on for tonight?" He must be an early riser thought Eleanor as she rubbed the sleep from her eyes.

"Good morning, Angus," she said softly, hoping not to croak in her morning voice. "Of course, I'm looking forward to it."

"Great! Shall I bring red or white?" he asked.

"White," she said. She did not want to reveal her menu but wasn't averse to a clue.

"Hmmmm, okay then, see you at six," Angus said, and he hung up.

Wednesday, June 21, day of woo, Walter would never know, Angus was coming for dinner, there was shopping to do, Nora would come to clean, Eleanor got up quickly and hurried through her morning rituals. She did not want to be caught in her nightgown by Nora. Neither did she want to be in the house while Nora cleaned, so she planned to drive into town, shop for tonight's dinner, and run some errands.

Feathers gleefully announced the arrival of Nora with silly parrot fanfare, "Da da da daaaaa!"

"Good morning, Mrs. Penrose," Nora said, smiling as she carried in her tub of cleaning supplies. "Are there any particular things you want done today?"

"Good morning, Nora. Just do the regular things today. If you have time maybe you could clean the windows on the west side of the house." They were always covered with a salty film from the ocean's mist.

"Yes, Mrs. Penrose." Nora began her work in the kitchen while Eleanor finished her grocery list.

"Did you hear about Mrs. Potts?" Nora asked.

"Yes, but I didn't know her. Did you?" Eleanor didn't like to gossip but was curious to know more about anyone dying recently.

"Yes, I cleaned for her," Nora said. "I was the one who found her dead in her bed when I went into her house on Monday morning. It was quite a shock. I knew she had recently been diagnosed with cancer and that she refused treatment, but I didn't think it would kill her so quickly." It was clear to Eleanor that Nora needed to talk about her experience.

"I'm so sorry," Eleanor sympathized. "Was she very ill?"

"No, that was the strange part. You wouldn't have even known she had anything wrong. The week before, she had a big party with her family and closest friends. It was like a wake only she was still alive to enjoy it. I helped clean up after. She seemed in great spirits. It's just so hard to imagine that she's gone." Nora continued. "If I had to die, that's the way I would want it: a big party and then a quick end."

"How interesting, Nora. Was Mrs. Potts very old?" Eleanor questioned.

"I'm not sure. She might have been seventy or eighty. She seemed ageless. I just loved her—always so full of life and fun." Nora sighed and began to scour the sink in earnest.

Eleanor finished her list and left for the fish market.

As she drove into town she pondered her own death and wondered what Nora would say about her if she found her dead in bed. She made a mental note to have more fun. Then she realized that Nora had no idea who she really was at all. Once a week, she came, cleaned, and left, hardly ever having a conversation. Eleanor was usually visiting Walter, or like today, on a mission to get out of her way. Eleanor didn't know Nora either, only that she was efficient, a hard worker, and trustworthy. Somehow that left her feeling sad. She determined to include Nora in her life. Next week Eleanor would stay home and make an effort to know more about her.

The farther she got from Sand Beach the clearer the sky became. A bank of fog seemed to hover over the little village but two miles away the sun was shining. Eleanor didn't care, but she knew that was the reason most of her friends chose to live inland. It seemed a small price to pay for the magnificent views she enjoyed. Of course, some days she could hardly see the ocean because of the fog, but she could hear its constant and reassuring rhythm.

She finished her errands quickly and decided to drop in on Dede to see if she wanted to go for lunch.

Dede's car was parked in her driveway, so there was a chance she might be free from her mayoral duties.

As she waited for Dede to answer the door, Dede's dog, Doogie, barked viciously thinking perhaps she was the mailman, but when Dede opened the door he sniffed at her feet and quickly lost interest in her.

"Sorry to stop by unannounced," Eleanor apologized, "but I thought you might like to grab a bite to eat."

"I'd love that," Dede said, truly pleased. "Come in. Let me get my purse and we can go. I'm starved, and Mark has gone to work on one of his projects, so this is perfect."

As Eleanor waited for Dede to fetch her things, she noticed a book on the kitchen table. "Are you reading this?" she asked, holding up the book titled *The Leftovers*. "Is it a cookbook?"

Dede laughed, "No, it's about the coming end of days. You know the Rapture: the time when all the good people are taken up and the rest are left behind."

"Oh, does it say when it's happening? Do I have time to repent?" Eleanor asked.

"The latest prediction is this Saturday, so probably not enough time, but take the book." Dede laughed but Eleanor wasn't sure she thought it was funny.

After lunch Eleanor dropped Dede off at her house and hurried home to begin her dinner preparations.

Nora was gone and the house was immaculate. Eleanor knew she would not have time to cook if she had to clean too. There would be no energy left either. Thank goodness for Nora.

As she worked in her neat and tidy kitchen Eleanor hummed a little song and baked a beautiful lemon meringue pie. Even she was impressed by the volume and texture of the meringue piled high on the lemon curd and delicate crust. She prepared the tomato vinaigrette, put the potatoes in the oven to roast, then washed and trimmed the collard greens. She would leave the halibut for last. She knew Angus would bring white wine, so she rewarded herself with a glass of red and went to relax in the living room. Feathers joined her there for a serious conversation about proper guest etiquette.

It took only a few minutes to set the table. Eleanor stepped away and admired her work. An artist does everything artfully, she thought to herself and then went to look at herself in the mirror. She studied the reflection as if she were Angus seeing her. Her graying hair was neatly coifed, blue eyes clear and bright, but lips needed just a touch of color. There was no denying the fact that she was old. There were crow's feet at the corners of those eyes and creases around her mouth. No scars or ugly warts with hairs growing out of them but there was a white whisker on her chin which she immediately plucked. Nothing more to do here she thought, and it was just as well because Angus was at the door.

"Good evening," Angus said, offering up the bottle of pinot gris along with a lovely bouquet of red roses.

"How lovely." Eleanor was suddenly reminded of the meaning of red roses and blushed. "Help yourself to a drink, Angus, while I put these in water." She quickly walked away and hoped he did not notice her obvious discomfort. White for purity, yellow for friendship, and red for passion, she thought. Walter always gave her pink roses.

By the time Eleanor returned with the roses in a vase, Angus had poured himself some Crown Royal, opened the bottle of wine and had poured a glass for Eleanor. He was peering in the oven at the roasting potatoes, making himself right a home.

"Smells good," he smiled revealing his charming dimples.

Something had changed, or so it seemed to Eleanor, but she wasn't sure if it was Angus or her.

"Sit down and relax," she said, "I just need to put the fish on the grill and put the greens on. It won't take long. Feathers will keep you company."

"I'd rather stay here and help you, if you don't mind." Angus stood very close behind her as she worked at the stovetop.

"I don't mind, as long as you're not trying to steal my recipe for grilled halibut with tomato vinaigrette," she teased and immediately felt the mood lighten.

"Why would I need it when I have you to make it for me?" Angus leaned in a planted a kiss on the back of her neck.

Something had definitely changed.

Thursday, June 22, and Eleanor woke with the realization that it was now officially summer. She could not recall one dream, but remembered the delightful evening spent with Angus. They ate the most delicious meal, drank the sweetest wine, shared stories, and laughed late into the night. They even danced to some oldies. It was fun. She could still have fun. Today she would work in her office, maybe catch up on some reading, and definitely take a long walk. She stretched and looked out the window to see that the fog had lifted and the sun shone brightly. Seeing the time, Eleanor was surprised at the lateness of the hour. She rolled out of bed and humming one of the oldies, she started her day.

Eleanor walked quickly down the hill to the beach. She passed Bootsy's empty house and only briefly noted the new "sale pending" sign attached to the "for sale" sign. She would quiz Nancy about it later. Her plan was to walk the beach and stop at Roseanna's for breakfast on the way back.

As she progressed at a brisk pace along the shoreline, her thoughts returned to the previous evening and she began to relive the entire event; the words, the feelings, the food, the music. It all seemed so magical. She never thought she would feel this way at her age. As her mind worked so did her feet, and before long she was back in the village with a full heart and an empty belly.

Roseanna's was dim after the bright sunlight outside the quaint café, but Eleanor recognized the four elderly women sitting at the table in the darkest corner. They called themselves the Do Nothings and as far as she knew that described them to a T. They must have been at least eighty and met weekly at Roseanna's to drink coffee, gossip, and do nothing. Eleanor stopped at their table to greet them on her way to a table by the window.

"Hello, Eleanor," Mattie May chirped as she approached.

Eleanor could not help but see the title of the book that lay on the table, *Book of Poisons*.

"Good morning, ladies. Or is it afternoon already?" She had no idea what time it was.

"Oh, plenty of daylight left on the longest day of the year," added Mavis Bench who discretely covered the book with a copy of the *Fish Wrapper* opened to the obituaries.

"What are you four up to these days?" Eleanor quizzed.

"Oh, you know us. We do nothing," Sybil Wendt quipped and suddenly all four began to laugh.

"Well, don't let me interrupt," Eleanor teased in return yet lingered to ask, "Do you know anything about Jean Scattergoods' house being sold?"

"Has it sold?" Eva Long seemed shocked. "That didn't take long, but property here is quick to sell. Who wouldn't want to live here and see this view every day?"

The other ladies simply smiled and nodded. Eleanor wondered if they also might be the Know Nothings as well.

"Enjoy your day," she added as she walked to the table and sat looking out at the absolutely stunning view.

As she ate her late breakfast of scrambled eggs and bacon, she once again recalled the previous night. The laughter from the Do Nothings brought her back to the present and she slyly peeked to see them pouring over the book that was now opened on the table.

Maybe they belonged to a book club, or perhaps one of them was writing a novel. Who knew? She was glad they seemed to find some joy in their old age. She realized they really weren't much older than she was and here she sat judging them as old busybodies doing nothing because they couldn't answer her need for gossip. She had passed them many times on the sidewalks of the village or in shops and didn't give them a second thought. They were just as invisible as the old people who were dying, and she was just as guilty as anyone who discounted them because they were old.

Later that day Eleanor returned to the box that Frieda had left to her. There was more in it than the velvet robe. Carefully wrapped in newspaper were two beautiful pieces of Frieda's delft collection: one ceramic plate with a bird and a blue delft ginger jar with a finial top. Eleanor had no idea of their monetary value. She only knew they were priceless because they had once belonged to her good friend who told her how she and her mother went on a shopping spree in Amsterdam when they were freed from the concentration camp. A little tear escaped Eleanor's eye as she put the pieces on a shelf and returned to explore what other treasures might be in the box. There she found three books: *How We Die: Reflections on Life's Final Chapter* by Sherwin B. Nuland, *Who Dies: An Investigation of Conscious Living and Conscious Dying* by Stephen Levine, Ondrea Levine, and *And Now and Here: Beyond the Duality of Life and Death* by Osho.

These she also put on the shelf with her other books, knowing she would return to them later when she was ready. Maybe Josephine would like to borrow them since they seemed to be in her area of interest.

Finally, in the bottom of the box in a leather-bound folder, Eleanor found what appeared to be the unfinished book Frieda had begun to write about her life. It was just all too much for Eleanor to take in on this beautiful summer day when she felt the blossoming of a new love. She quickly stored the folder in a desk drawer and took the box to the garage. These things would have to wait for a different kind of day.

Friday, June 23, coffee day, midsummer's day, Eleanor was totally looking forward to coffee with her friends. She almost jumped out of bed, made coffee, and finished the crossword puzzle, Sudoku, and the jumble in record time. Her mind was clear and she felt maybe 50 instead of 72. On the drive into town she wondered what her friends would say when she told them about Angus's proposal. She wondered if they would judge her. She wondered if she should even tell them.

Pearl and Cleo were already inside the Boat House sipping their coffee when she arrived. They were comparing scars from their skin cancer surgeries.

"I can't even see anything," Eleanor reassured them as she peered carefully at Pearl's cheek and Cleo's nose.

Josephine came in and sat in her regular spot.

"Dede isn't coming," Pearl informed them, "she has a meeting this morning."

"I saw her Wednesday. We had lunch. Did you know there is supposed to be a Rapture tomorrow?" Eleanor said. "Do you think Dede believes in that stuff? I saw a book she had about it on her kitchen table. She let me borrow it." She pulled it out of her bag. "It says in here that there are signs that indicate the end is near: war, dissension, earthquakes, famine, etc. At the Rapture Jesus will come like a thief and only believers will see him."

"So, the Rapture is happening tomorrow you say?" Cleo leafed thoughtfully through the book.

Pearl and Eleanor exchanged glances while Josephine poured Swiss Miss into her coffee cup and waited patiently for the waitress to return with coffee.

"I have an idea!" Cleo exclaimed. "We'll go to Dede's house tomorrow and leave our clothes on her porch and ring her doorbell. When she comes to the door, she'll see our clothes and know we have been taken in the Rapture and she has been left behind. It will be a hoot!"

They all laughed at the thought of the most religious of them being left behind in the Rapture while the pagans were lifted up. Then they seriously considered the plan and the details necessary to put the plan into action. It *would* be a hoot.

"That's not the only book I noticed this week." Eleanor shared seeing the Do Nothings at Roseanna's, and the books about dying in Frieda's box.

"Maybe the universe is trying to tell you something. There seems to be a theme here," Josephine commented. "Let's see, the Rapture, poisons, dying: is there something you aren't telling us?"

"Well, yes, but it has nothing to do with dying really, maybe rapture, but not dying, definitely not dying." Eleanor was babbling.

"What then?" Pearl asked, and Cleo and Josephine leaned in to hear what seemed to be something important.

"Angus has proposed marriage." Eleanor watched her friends carefully as they all leaned back and their jaws dropped. She waited to hear what they would say.

"You're already married. Won't that be bigamy?" asked Cleo.

"Will you divorce Walter?" asked Pearl.

"I had an Aunt Catherine who had dementia. Her husband divorced her for financial reasons but visited her at the home every day. When she died, he killed himself. It was just so romantic," Cleo related.

"What did you tell him?" asked Josephine.

"I'm married and will never divorce Walter, so I guess I said no," Eleanor said slowly. "I did say that I still wanted to be friends."

"Oooh, that line always kills a friendship. What did Angus say?" pried Cleo.

"Angus McBride, even at his age is still a hunk. It must have been hard to cut him loose," bemoaned Pearl.

"And . . .?" prompted Josephine.

"We think we can make it work. He still wants to be friends. He still wants to come for dinner every Wednesday night. We had the best time ever last Wednesday, so I think we can still be friends and not be married." Eleanor heard the words as she spoke them and wondered if it really could work.

"Do you mean friends with benefits?" Pearl had gone where the others dared not go.

"If cooking for him is a benefit, yes, and if helping me with some household chores is a benefit, yes." Eleanor would go no further. Even friends had their limits. She would not tell them about the kisses, the snuggling, or the dancing.

"I think that's great!" Josephine remarked.

"Well, what's really changed?" asked Cleo. "Wasn't he already trading chores for a home-cooked meal?"

"Everything has changed," Eleanor almost whispered the words, "everything."

"You love him, and he loves you and now you both know it," Josephine said. "That is what's changed. I can see it in your face. He's someone you can count on. It's what you lost when Walter went ill. I'm happy for you Eleanor."

"Of course, we are all happy if you're happy, Eleanor," Cleo chimed in.

"Just don't be surprised if you become fodder for the gossip mill," warned Pearl. "The Do Nothings have eyes everywhere and do a lot more than you think."

Eleanor grimaced and then revealed her own prejudices about old people.

"I guess I don't think of myself as that old," she admitted, "but I'm guilty of practicing the very things I call ageism when I see others doing it. I guess that makes me a hypocrite."

"Well, you are a nice hypocrite," comforted Cleo.

"It's like Maya Angelou said, 'We do better, when we know better.' Maybe Oprah said that. I'm not sure, but when you know old people, you like them. We're old and you like us. You have lots of old friends," Pearl rambled.

"Yes, maybe you just ignore the ones you don't know. Maybe you ignore all people you don't know and it has nothing to do with age at all. You are just a snob, Eleanor. And now that you know that, you can do better," Cleo teased.

They all laughed, and Eleanor was happy.

Eleanor woke on Saturday, June 24, with the ringing of the telephone.

"Good morning, Ellie." It was Angus. True to his word he was doing his best to be the first thing she thought of each morning and the last thing she thought of each night. "Did I wake you?" he asked.

"Yes, but it was time for me to get up," Eleanor admitted.

"I'd like to drive you to Rosewood Manor on Sunday. It's been a few weeks since I've visited Walter and I just thought it would be nice to go together. What do you think?" Angus always cut to the chase.

"Hmm, let me think about it." Eleanor wasn't fully awake and couldn't foresee any problems with Walter's good friend visiting him along with his wife. "Yes, I'd like that. I think that would be great."

"Okay then, I'll pick you up at 9:00 on Sunday." Angus hung up.

Eleanor lay back on her pillows and began her mental list, Saturday, June 24, thoughts of Angus and Walter together at Rosewood Manor distracted her. She imagined Walter seeing them together holding hands as they entered Walter's wing. Walter approached and punched Angus in the face. Then the slutty barroom skank that was Alice rushed to help Angus. The next scene was Alice laying a sloppy lip lock on Angus. Eleanor shook her head. "Where do these ideas come from?" she muttered to herself. "Maybe I've been watching too many Hallmark movies." Now she was answering her own silly questions. Back to her plans for Saturday, June 24.

She was supposed to meet the coffee group ladies to play a prank on Dede! She had almost forgotten the whole thing. Eleanor looked at the clock and leaped out of bed. Sometimes a ridiculous plan was needed to get the day started.

The ladies parked around the corner from Dede's house. They got out of their cars.

"What are we doing?" asked Pearl.

"We need to sneak onto Dede's porch and leave our clothes there. Did you bring your clothes, Pearl?" Cleo seemed to be in charge.

"Yes," Pearl whispered as if Dede might be near.

The ladies moved stealthily around the corner and approached Dede's house.

"Her car is in the driveway," whispered Josephine, "so she must be home."

They crouched under the windows and quietly took the steps leading to her front door.

"I hope Doogie doesn't give us away," fretted Eleanor as she spread her clothes on the porch.

"Make it look like you just evaporated and the only thing left is your clothes," ordered Cleo.

"Let's leave our purses here too," suggested Pearl. "She will definitely recognize them and know it is us."

Eleanor thought leaving the borrowed book about the Rapture on the porch was an excellent touch.

They finished their work and slinked off to hide in the bushes under the window where they could watch unseen.

"Someone needs to ring the bell," Josephine reminded them.

Cleo rushed up the steps, rang the bell, and almost tripped on the bottom step as she breathlessly returned nearly falling into the shrubbery.

Inside Doogie barked a warning and Mark appeared in the window looking down on their hiding place with puzzled amusement.

"Caught!" cried Pearl.

They met Mark on the porch just as he opened the door and observed their handiwork. A wide smile spread over his face as understanding dawned.

"Dede is over at the church planning for tomorrow's mass," he offered, "I'll go bring her back. You can hide inside." And with that he was out the door to walk the two blocks to Saint John's Catholic Church.

All four friends scurried inside and rushed to find the best hiding spot: one where they could witness her reaction.

As Eleanor waited, heart pounding, she could see Mark and Dede ambling toward the house. It was a picture so sweet it made tears well up in her eyes. They chatted as they walked, gray heads together, and the looks they gave each other testified to their mutual trust and respect. She didn't know what he told her to get her to come with him. It could have been anything, even the truth. Whatever it was, Dede believed it.

It didn't take long for Dede's surprised response to reach them. She bent over with laughter and slapped her knee, then wiped the tears of hilarity from her eyes.

"I don't believe it!" she cried, "You guys are the best!"

She hugged them all and invited them in for pie. Of course, no one refused, because to eat one of Dede's pies was to experience true rapture.

Later, Eleanor stopped by the local pharmacy to pick up a prescription. Mattie May was in line ahead of her. Eleanor overheard the conversation between the pharmacist and Mattie unintentionally because it was so loud. Mattie must be hard of hearing, thought Eleanor.

The pharmacist spoke slowly and clearly. "I see Dr. Shaw has increased the dosage of your prescription, so discontinue it if you become dizzy or confused."

"I know all that!" Mattie May snapped angrily. "I'm old but I'm not an idiot, you know." She snatched up the small bag and left in a huff.

Eleanor stepped up to the counter with raised brows.

The pharmacist merely shook her head and apologized, "Sorry you had to overhear that. Sometimes it's difficult to talk to people who already know everything. Doctors and pharmacists are the worst."

"I didn't realize Mattie was a health professional," Eleanor said.

"Oh yes, years ago, but she was a very good pharmacist. Still mentally quick and up on the latest medications too. I'm sure she reads the medical journals. Let me get your prescription," she said, and she was off.

Eleanor pondered her own biases about older people, including Mattie May. She had never given any thought to any of the women in the Do Nothing club. She never wondered how they spent their time or what they once achieved in their professions, or if they had professions. She just assumed they did nothing and knew nothing. She was an ageist, and she didn't want to be. She certainly didn't want others to think of her in that way when she was old. Was she old? Probably many people considered her old, invisible, and useless. Eleanor determined to learn more about the older citizens that lived in her neighborhood.

When she returned home, she Googled Mavis Bench but only learned about various storage benches. Then she tried Mattie May but only found the lyrics to a song by Rod Stewart. Sybil Wendt turned out to be an 85-year-old doctor from California who retired to Sand Beach, Oregon 10 years ago. Eva Long was a retired nurse who specialized in geriatrics. How strange was it that at least three of the four Do Nothings had worked in the medical field? Maybe it wasn't that odd. All of her friends in her coffee group were connected in some way to education. It's true, thought Eleanor, that birds of a feather flock together. That made Eleanor think of Feathers who she hadn't noticed for some time. She found him on his perch by the windows facing the ocean, gazing sadly at the free-flying gulls outside. Gently stroking his gray feathers, she spoke to him in a soothing voice.

"I'm sorry I'm not Walter," she apologized. "I know how much he loved you. You must miss him very much. I have lots of friends, but you had only Walter and now mostly me. I'm not much of a replacement, am I? You must be so lonely and so sad." Feathers made a noise that sounded like a sigh.

Eleanor had never given much thought to Feathers' emotional health. She wondered if he was depressed and decided that she would take him to visit Walter tomorrow. She only hoped there would not be trouble if Angus went too.

Sunday, June 25, broke clear and sunny. Eleanor cleared her mind of sleep and reminded herself that today Angus was driving her to Rosewood Manor to visit Walter. She would insist on taking

Feathers. Maybe Feathers needed Walter more than Walter needed him. Eleanor was certain she did not need either of them.

Angus appeared at her door at exactly 9:00. He greeted her with a polite peck on the cheek and did not bat an eye when she brought the caged parrot to the door, but simply took possession of it and loaded it in the backseat of his pickup truck. Maybe he thought it was the usual routine to bring the pet that Walter loved so much. Eleanor only brought Feathers on occasion, but he didn't know that.

As they drove the many miles to Rosewood Manor, Eleanor and Angus chatted easily about their activities of the past week. Every now and then Eleanor caught herself studying his handsome profile as he expertly maneuvered their way through the twists and turns of the highway as it wound through the forest. He laughed when she shared the adventure of the Rapture, and she reacted with disbelief at his outlandish fish tales.

"What do you know about the Do Nothing club?" Eleanor suddenly asked.

"As far as I know they do nothing," he joked.

"Yes, but who are they? I mean what did they do before they did nothing?" she persisted.

"Why? Are you planning to join?"

"No, I'm just curious," she said, admitting her fear of becoming an old ageist.

This made Angus chuckle, "I'm trying to remember who is in that group. I don't believe any of them are felons. Mattie May was a pharmacist for a long time before she retired. She's a strong-willed woman, if I remember right. As a matter of fact, I think there are four opinionated women in that group who all had successful careers. One of them was a research scientist at OSHU before retiring here. I can't recall her name."

"Was that Mavis Bench?" asked Eleanor.

"Yes, I'm sure of it. I think she received an award of some kind for her Alzheimer's research," he added. "I remember reading about her in the *Fish Wrapper* years ago, probably when she first moved here."

"Interesting women," mused Eleanor. "Do you think I would like them? I'd like to expand my network of friends."

"Hard to say," Angus said, undecided. "They seem to be a very tight group. You might do better to make some younger friends, you being an ageist and all."

Eleanor smiled and turned up the radio. This conversation was over.

When they arrived at Rosewood Manor, Eleanor couldn't help noticing how easy everything was for Angus. He moved like a well-oiled machine as he retrieved the caged Feathers and entered through the tall oak doors. He greeted all the aides as if he were a regular visitor, signed the log, and punched the proper code that allowed them access to the memory care unit, all the while holding doors and guiding Eleanor as if she were a first-time guest. She sort of liked and hated it at the same time.

When they reached the common area, Angus put the cage down and uncovered one grumpy gray parrot. Seeing Angus, Feathers at once went into his angry rant, "Intruder, intruder, Ellie, get your gun!"

Residents slowly found their way over to the table to point at and chatter to Feathers. They absolutely loved him. On his previous visits, Eleanor had only taken Feathers to Walter's private room. This was new and unexpectedly rewarding. She saw Walter approach with Alice shuffling behind holding on to his belt. When he saw Feathers, a wide smile lit his face. He made his way to the table and opened the door to the cage. Feathers recognized his friend at once, climbed onto his hand, walked up his arm, and gave him a sweet bird kiss.

Eleanor was surprised to hear her own voice coming from Feathers' mouth, "I love you, Walter."

The residents laughed and some of them clapped as Feathers did a host of tricks and offered odd bits of bird wisdom. It was obviously the highlight of their day. Many of the aides enjoyed the show too as they pushed those in wheelchairs closer so they could see. But the best part was watching Walter. The smile never left his face. He had eyes only for Feathers and it seemed as if the old Walter had reappeared as he reenacted the many silly tricks he had taught his pet. No one was prepared for the performance that followed as Walter moved to the piano with Feathers on his shoulder.

Walter began to play as he always had, and Feathers began to sing.

Walter chose one of his favorites from the Temptations, *My Girl*, and every time he sang the words, Feathers would repeat, "My girl, my girl."

Eleanor realized tears were streaming down her smiling face and she didn't even bother to wipe them away, until Angus offered his handkerchief. His large warm hand found hers and wrapped around it offering a comfort she didn't know she needed.

Suddenly Feathers was in the air flapping his wings high overhead. He swooped down and up again enjoying the little bit of freedom the high ceilings and long hallways provided. After a time, he returned to Walter's shoulder and nuzzled his ear.

The show was over, and the residents were guided to the eating area for lunch. Feathers came too. As they moved to their table, Eleanor spotted Bootsy and waved her over to sit at their table. And that is how Eleanor sat next to Walter and Angus and looked across the table to see the barroom skank that was Alice who sat next to Bootsy. They chatted amiably as they ate their meatballs and mashed potatoes covered in gravy. Walter fed his carrots to

Feathers and no one seemed to care. They were stars and could do no wrong.

After lunch, Angus challenged Bootsy and Alice to a game of Go Fish and they left Eleanor and Walter to share a walk outside in the atrium. Feathers perched near the window and eyed them suspiciously.

"I'm glad I bought Feathers today." Eleanor began. "He has missed you I'm afraid."

Walter gazed off in the distance and did not reply.

"Do you remember Angus?" she continued to chat as she always did. "He drove me here today. Remember how you used to go fishing with him?"

Walter wrinkled his brow as if trying to remember. "I can't take care of myself any more. I have to stay here now."

It was the longest statement he had made since she could remember. She wondered if it meant that he was getting better, but she knew that wasn't true. He was having a good day. That was all.

She touched his hand and caressed his cheek. "I love you, Walter," she whispered.

"Ellie doesn't live here. She does her own thing and I do mine," he explained. Then his eyes went blank and there was only silence. He didn't know her.

Eleanor could have been sad. She could have gone into the restroom and cried, but for some reason, she felt strong. She could handle this. She walked Walter back to his room where he lay down on his single bed and fell asleep to her soft voice as she told him about the Do Nothing club, the Rapture, and how she thought she was in love with Angus. When he began to snore, she covered him with his favorite afghan and quietly left.

"I've won every game," bragged Bootsy as soon as Eleanor returned.

Angus merely hung his head in defeat.

"Congratulations! Do you want to go for ice cream to celebrate your victory?" Eleanor suggested. "Maybe if you don't gloat too much, Angus will give you a ride home."

The thought of ice cream brightened Angus's face. "Great idea!" he exclaimed as he rose to go.

"I'm not sure I can stop gloating," Bootsy said, winking at Eleanor, "But I'll try." She seemed to be taken with Angus, who had gone in search of Feathers.

The resident manager approached Eleanor. "Mrs. Penrose, I'm glad I caught you before you left. Watching the parrot today and the way the residents reacted to it, I just wondered if you might be willing to leave it here for a bit."

Eleanor's surprise showed clearly on her face. She had seen their reaction too but hadn't prepared herself for this. She hadn't prepared herself for losing Feathers too.

"We could keep him until you come for your next visit and see how it works, a sort of trial." She continued. "I think it does Walter a world of good. He hasn't been this animated in a long time."

Eleanor could not argue that point. "I didn't bring any extra food for him."

"I'll take care of everything," she reassured. "If it doesn't work out, I'll let you know, but pets make people happy and these people need all the happiness we can give them."

Before they left Feathers at Rosewood Manor, Eleanor wrote three pages of directions for the care and feeding of the pet she thought she didn't love.

Monday morning, Eleanor woke early. A coastal drizzle had moved in overnight, leaving the world around her dark and gray. She lay in her cozy bed thinking: Monday, June 26, Walter wasn't here, Feathers wasn't here, a deep empty feeling came over her. She heard her heart beating in her ears and anxiety settled on her chest like a heavy stone. Eleanor was alone. She knew she had to get out of bed and move.

The house felt empty because it was empty. As Eleanor walked by the table where Feathers' cage usually sat, she once more felt a pang of great loss. Who knew? She hadn't admitted to herself how much she depended on that silly bird for company.

As she sat down with her coffee and crossword puzzle, she began to feel better. A routine was important. Exercise was important. Sleep and a good diet were important. Friends were important. Eleanor's recipe for good mental health was interrupted by the telephone.

"Good morning, Ellie." Angus sounded unusually chipper.

"Is it?" she questioned.

"What's wrong? You don't sound like yourself." He was quick to pick up on her tone.

"Just missing that silly bird," she confessed.

"Oh, I don't suppose the weather is helping either. It's quite a change from yesterday," he noted.

"Yes, I'm wondering if this drizzle will stop so I can get my walk in this morning," Eleanor remarked.

"You might think about joining the YMCA. I've already had my workout this morning and the rain didn't bother me one bit," Angus bragged.

"Hmmmm, you know I like to be outside when I exercise. I think I'm not too fragile to get a little wet." Walter had always told her she wasn't sweet enough to melt but she kept that thought to herself.

"The reason I called was to tell you that I can't make it to dinner Wednesday. I'll be out of town for a few days, taking care of some business in California," he said. He didn't sound regretful.

"Oh, that's too bad, I was looking forward to it," she admitted.

"Well, next week then. Bye." And he hung up.

Eleanor glared at the phone. She really was in a funk now and needed to do something to change her mood. It was much too early for wine, she thought, and the drizzle outside did not look appealing. The Do Nothings came to mind and she decided to act on her desire to expand her circle of friends. She would host a tea party! Eleanor immediately scurried into her office in search of invitations. Within 30 minutes she had found all of their addresses and filled out the invitations for an afternoon tea party to be held on Wednesday afternoon. She dressed in her most water-resistant outerwear and ventured out in the drizzle for a wet walk to the post office.

As she walked she made a mental list of things she would need at the grocery store to put together an impressive tea for her new friends. Should she bake or just pick up some savory scones from the bakery? She wondered if any of them had dietary restrictions. Many older people suffered from diabetes or were lactose intolerant. What if they were on a gluten-free diet? She finally decided she would provide something to cover all possibilities. A trip to The Sweet Life Bakery was in order since Nora would be cleaning that day and Eleanor didn't want to be in the kitchen baking. She remembered her commitment to befriend Nora as well. There was a great deal to do. Who needed Angus anyway?

As luck would have it Eleanor spotted Eva Long inside the post office.

"Eva, how fortunate to catch you here!" she spoke with genuine delight.

Eva turned slowly, and a beautiful smile lit her face. Eleanor could only imagine the impact that smile had on her patients when she was a nurse.

"I have an invitation here for you," Eleanor offered the envelope and as Eva reached out for it, she noticed the tremor in her liver-spotted hand.

"Thank you, Dear." Eva opened the invitation on the spot. "How lovely, I'd be delighted to come."

"I'm also inviting the other members of the Do Nothings. Do you know if they have any dietary restrictions?" Eleanor questioned.

"How thoughtful you are to ask! So many people these days don't bother. We all have our issues but each of us knows what we can and cannot tolerate. Don't give it another thought. If you serve something we shouldn't eat, we just won't eat it. After all it is only tea and none of us is starving." Eva's remarks didn't help Eleanor in the least. "The others are still over at Roseanna's finishing up their coffee. You might catch them before they leave if you hurry."

Eleanor glanced toward Rosanna's and decided it might be wise to do as Eva suggested. This way she could get the facts from each of them including whether they intended to accept her invitation or not.

She thanked Eva and waved goodbye.

As she entered Roseanna's, she spotted them right away. They were seated at the same table as the last time she had seen them. The same book was on the table. Maybe it belonged to Rosanna's.

"Good morning ladies," Eleanor greeted them with her friendliest smile. "Sorry to interrupt but I wanted to invite you to a tea party. I met Eva at the post office and she told me you were here."

Eleanor passed out the invitations and the ladies eagerly opened them and expressed their delight and intentions to attend.

"I'll be off for my walk then. See you Wednesday afternoon."
Eleanor slipped back outside into the drizzle. She was delighted at
their apparent enthusiasm and once again began planning her menu
heedless of how wet she was becoming.

When she returned to her house, she was once again surprised
by the emptiness she felt now that Feathers was no longer here.
There was no silly bird to flutter onto her shoulder in greeting, no
one to say "I love you, Ellie," in Walter's voice. Yes, and no cage to
clean or anyone to interrupt her work with bird-brained criticism.
Maybe she could get used to it. Eleanor spent the rest of the day
doing chores around the house and even squeezed in a nap.

Tuesday, June 27, Eleanor woke early enough to watch a pink glow
infuse the sky. It's a clear day, callooh callay. Today she would finish
her list and make a trip into town. She got up with purpose and
hummed a little song as she put on coffee and picked up the daily
paper. Sunshine did make a difference in one's mood she thought,
and she totally understood the need for the snowbirds she knew
who traveled south in the search for year-round sunlight. She
had never thought before that she needed such a thing. Now she
wondered.

Eleanor decided to break with routine and take a different route
for her daily walk. Instead of down the hill to the beach, she went
east along a wooded path. As she hiked along she had to jump over
several puddles and detoured along the way to avoid the marshy
ground. Just as she was determined to turn around she noticed
the trail had led her to the house that had been Henry Ott's. She
approached from the back and saw a pickup truck parked in front

of the garage. A man loading a wooden box into the back seemed startled to see her.

"I didn't mean to scare you," she apologized.

"Lost in my own thoughts, I guess," he confessed. "I'm just clearing out some of my father's junk."

"Oh, you must be Henry's son, Norman."

"Yes, did you know my father?" Norman asked.

"Not well, I saw him every now and then, but he pretty much stayed to himself. He was a quiet man," Eleanor remarked.

"I'm throwing out my grandfather's old trunk. I don't know why my dad kept it. It's rotten and falling apart." He seemed to think he needed to justify his actions, but even as he spoke the words that detached him from the object, a single tear rolled down one cheek.

"You know the trunk is not your grandfather. It's just stuff. There's no need holding on to it. Just keep the memories," Eleanor offered wisely.

"Right," he said, after dashing the tear away. "Unfortunately, there's a great deal of stuff here that isn't attached to any memories for me. It's hard to understand why dad kept so much of it. I can't see why anyone would want it."

Eleanor understood. "It has to do with his memories. People put it off and then they're too old to do the big clean up."

"We tried hiring a housekeeper for him, but there was too much clutter," he admitted. "It would be nearly impossible to clean around all his treasures."

"One man's junk is another man's treasure," quoted Eleanor. "Just be careful not to toss anything that might have value."

"That's what's taking me so long. Sorting through everything is time consuming," he lamented.

"I can see you have a lot to do, so I'll leave you to it." He seemed like such a sweet man. She wondered why anyone would suspect him of murder.

Eleanor took the road in front of Henry's house back home. It was much drier, and she suddenly had the desire to throw out some of her stuff.

After filling two large bags with books and old clothes, Eleanor sat at her desk and picked up her pen.

Where to go? Where to go?
The path lies under water.
The ground, rain soaked,
Begins to suck feet under.
Puddles much too wide to leap,
Too deep to plunder.
Wanderer returns, feet dry
Not to wander, but to wonder.

With nothing more to do, Eleanor gathered her shopping bags and headed to town to complete her errands.

Entering The Sweet Life bakery, Eleanor saw Cleo drooling over the pastries behind the glass cabinet.

"Starting a new diet?" she whispered in Cleo's ear and watched her friend jump.

"Eleanor, you almost gave me a heart attack!" Cleo exclaimed.

"Sorry, are you buying anything here or just window shopping?" she asked.

"I've got a craving," Cleo admitted.

"Why don't you help me pick out a few things for my tea party tomorrow? I've invited the Do Nothings over and I'm sure they must have some restrictions. I was thinking about some of those blueberry scones."

"I think you should definitely get that lemon pudding cake," suggested Cleo. "It's covered with lemon curd. Those raspberry tarts look delicious and you definitely need something with chocolate."

"Looks good," Eleanor agreed. "Those ladies will never eat all this, I think you should come over and help me with the preparations and stay for clean up."

"Perfect, I'll be there at 3:00." And Cleo was out the door without buying a thing.

Eleanor did not regret her last-minute invitation. She knew Cleo was an excellent judge of character and would tell her exactly what she thought of the Do Nothings.

Wednesday, June 28, Eleanor woke and made a mental list of what she knew: Nora was coming to clean, Walter was at Rosewood Manor but today was not the Wednesday of woe, Angus loved her but was not coming for dinner, so it wasn't a day of woo, the Do Nothings were coming for tea, Cleo was coming to help, Feathers wasn't here. She didn't really have much to do—set the table for the tea party and stay out of Nora's way. That would be a problem. She had determined to befriend Nora, but if she followed her around the house, Nora wouldn't be able to get her work done. Nora was younger than most of Eleanor's friends, but it was important to make new friends because no one lives forever. With that dark depressing thought, Eleanor crawled out of bed to start her day.

When the doorbell rang, there was no Feathers to chide for imitating the ring. Eleanor knew Nora had arrived.

"Good morning, Mrs. Penrose," she politely addressed Eleanor, "Are there any special instructions for today?"

"Just do the normal cleaning, Nora. I'll be out for a walk now, but I'll be back before you leave." Eleanor said as she left for her morning exercise. She would give Nora time to get her work done before she started the friendship process.

Eleanor started down the hill for her beach walk. As she passed Bootsy's old house, she noticed the "For Sale" sign now had a SOLD banner across it. I wonder who it will be. Maybe someone's second home, and they will only be here on weekends. Maybe it will be a family with children. She missed children. She wondered if Nancy knew. Eleanor veered off the road to the hidey-hole and retrieved a note hidden inside. Had Bootsy been here?

She unfolded the neatly folded note and read the forceful dark lettering:

*The fountains mingle with the river*
*And the rivers with the ocean,*
*The winds of heaven mix forever*
*With a sweet emotion;*
*Nothing in the world is single;*
*All things by a law divine*
*In one spirit meet and mingle.*
*Why not I with thine?*

*See the mountains kiss high heaven*
*And the waves clasp one another;*
*No sister-flower would be forgiven*
*If it disdained its brother;*
*And the sunlight clasps the earth*
*And the moonbeams kiss the sea;*
*What is all this sweet work worth*
*If thou kiss not me?*

There was no signature. It was definitely not from Bootsy. The handwriting was too mature, and masculine. Eleanor hesitated to take it. Maybe it wasn't meant for her. Could someone else know about the hidey-hole? She stuffed the note back in the hole and walked slowly away looking around as if she might see whoever placed it there watching her. It puzzled and made her uneasy. She picked up the pace. By the time she reached the beach, she remembered why the words were familiar. They were from *Love's Philosophy* by Percy Bysshe Shelley. Maybe the new owners were lovers and had bought the house for their trysts. Eleanor would have to let the hidey-hole go. It wasn't hers any more.

By 3:00, Nora had finished with the housecleaning and hurried off to her next client. Eleanor had spent most of that time hiding in her office pouring over various love poems and chatting on the telephone with her sister in California. She had learned that it is not easy to make friends when someone is working for you, her sister talked too much, and love is elusive when you are fickle.

True to her word, Cleo arrived to help Eleanor set up for the tea with a lovely bouquet of pink and yellow roses she had cut from her garden. Together they created a table that would rival the Queen's own. It was dressed in Eleanor's finest cream-colored linen cloth sprinkled with small pink flowers. Each place was set with fine pink china tea cups, silver, and cream napkins. The artist in them both caused them to gaze in a satisfactory manner long after they were finished. The doorbell broke the trance. The Do Nothings were early.

Mattie May, who liked being in control, had driven them all up the hill in her vintage Lincoln Town car.

"Please come in." Eleanor welcomed them with a warm smile. "This is my friend, Cleo."

"So happy to meet you," Cleo smiled as she was introduced to each of them in turn.

Eleanor collected their sweaters and purses while they milled around her rooms checking things out.

"What a lovely home you have, Eleanor," Mavis remarked all the while nodding her gray head on her thin little neck in approval.

"As well as a magnificent view," added Sybil who was immediately drawn to the large windows.

"I've always admired this house. How lovely to find it is just as beautiful inside as out." As Eva smiled her entire head shook as though to negate her positive remarks.

Mattie had already seated herself at the table. She obviously had no interest in home décor.

"Please sit down and make yourselves comfortable. I'll be just a minute while I get the tea," Eleanor said as she went to the kitchen.

She returned with two pots: one in a yellow floral tea cozy and the other in pink. "I've made a pot of herbal for those of you who prefer decaf," she informed them.

"I'll drink what you're having," said Mattie as she waited for Eleanor to fill her own cup first.

Eleanor quickly filled her cup from the yellow pot and then also filled Mattie's.

"I simply can't drink caffeine this late in the day," confessed Cleo as she picked up the pink pot and filled her cup.

Everyone suddenly sighed for no apparent reason, each of them filling their cups, straining their tea leaves, and politely sipping their brews. Cleo caught Eleanor's eye and her brows shot up and down in puzzlement.

Mattie filled her plate with scones, tarts, and cakes while the others politely nibbled on a few cookies.

As they ate they made polite conversation until Mattie began to ask about Walter.

"How is Walter anyway?" she quizzed. "We never hear about him. Did he die?"

"He's at Rosewood Manor, dementia I'm afraid." Eleanor knew you couldn't make friends without giving up something about yourself. She was no longer ashamed of his ailment and they need never know about Alice.

"That is a lovely place, if you have to be someplace." Eva spoke from experience. "I worked as a geriatric nurse for years and loved those old people. I can't believe I'm one of them now."

"None of us have men anymore," Sybil offered. "It's a blessing and a curse, I say. There is the freedom of it all and then the horrible loneliness as you must know. It is a mixed bag."

Eleanor didn't want the conversation to go there but had no power to stop it.

"I remember when I had my practice and a marriage," Sybil continued, "I had a very difficult surgery to perform. The patient had been in a car accident, there was blood everywhere, compound fractures of both legs and internal bleeding. It was hours before I could finish, and I was totally exhausted, but when I got home, my husband demanded dinner. Men, they are just so spoiled and selfish."

Eleanor could see Cleo turning green at the mention of blood. She alone knew how squeamish Cleo was.

"Do you like the chocolate-covered macaroons?" she asked in an attempt to steer the talk back to food.

"Never touch chocolate," stated Mattie. "It gives me an upset stomach like you would not believe. It starts with a rumbling and then it's 'Thar she blows'. It must be allergies. By the way, look at this rash, Sybil, it came on this morning and is horribly annoying."

Here, Mattie pulled up her top while Sybil inspected the rash around her middle and declared it a reaction to her laundry detergent. No one seemed phased by any of it and the conversation continued in that vein until each had shared at least two medical procedures and three scars, some of which belonged to people not at the table. Cleo excused herself and was in the restroom for at least 15 minutes.

"Are you alright, dear?" questioned Eva when Cleo returned. "You look a little green around the gills."

"I'm fine," she lied, "probably those macaroons."

"You really should keep a food journal," began Mavis, "if you write down everything you eat, you can track your episodes of diarrhea. Of course, you will need to eliminate everything from your diet at the beginning and then add one thing to it at a time. It really is the best way to discover sensitivity to any allergen. I'm sure I have such a journal at home. I could drop it off at Eleanor's later and she could get it to you or . . . do you live with her dear?"

"No, and no. Really I'm fine. You don't need to . . ." But Cleo didn't finish before Mattie began again.

"It could be an interaction with the drugs you are taking. One must be very careful of interactions of any kind. There are so many prescriptions these days. It is very difficult to keep track of how they combine with each other and the foods you eat. Are you on any medications, Cleo? You know that reminds me. I read an article about this very topic the other day and how nursing homes often overprescribe to their patients in an effort to keep them sedated. It really is alarming, Eleanor. Please make a point of checking Walter's dosages at Rosewood Manor. I've actually heard of cases where there was no dementia at all, just too many drugs interfering with the body's natural functions."

"Yes, there was an investigation," Mavis picked up the thread, "that revealed the use of Nuedexta, which is a drug used in treating those with pseudobulbar affect, you know where they cry or laugh uncontrollably, on patients with dementia or Alzheimer's disease. Totally inappropriate! Most patients of dementia don't exhibit those symptoms at all. I believe they may have been pushing this drug on the most vulnerable patients just to make money. Do you know if Walter is unruly, Eleanor? Do you know what medications he is taking? Do you visit regularly?"

"No, Walter is not unruly," Eleanor began but could not finish before Eva spoke with her vibrating head.

"I'd be happy to go to Rosewood Manor with you, Eleanor, and help you sort out this mess. It would be no trouble at all. Mattie could come too and look over his prescriptions, just to make sure. It must be so overwhelming for you. Do you still visit every Wednesday?"

"Today is Wednesday, Eva," Mavis reminded her.

"No worries, really, you ladies are so very kind, but I have my finger on the pulse of all things Walter." Eleanor finally was able to speak. She could only imagine visiting Rosewood Manor with four old women tottering behind her. "Would you ladies like to go out on the deck for some fresh air?"

"Oh no, thank you so much for the lovely tea, Eleanor, but shouldn't we be on our way?" Eva looked at Mattie and the others and they began to rise. Sybil helped the somewhat shaky Eva to her feet.

"It really was refreshing to meet some younger people," admitted Mavis. "It's so hard to make new friends when you are over eighty."

"Yes, it was nice to meet you both, maybe you'd like to have coffee with us sometime at Roseanna's," offered Sybil.

"Of course," answered Eleanor. "Thank you for coming."

"Bye now," Mattie spoke as she exited.

As soon as Eleanor closed the door and the Do Nothings had driven away, she looked at Cleo and they both began to laugh and laugh. Cleo pretended to swoon on the sofa. "I think we have pseudobulbar affect. Why else would we be laughing uncontrollably when everything is so sad? And that is why old people have few friends," giggled Cleo as she pulled herself up to a sitting position.

"Why is that, Cleo?" Eleanor asked. "I can't believe you are being so mean."

"They are B-O-R-I-N-G." Cleo spelled it out.

"They would most likely think we were boring too if they came to our coffee meeting and listened to us talk." Eleanor argued.

"Let's make sure that never happens." Cleo made Eleanor pinkie swear and then the laughing began again.

"At least they have each other," Eleanor mused.

"Do you have any wine?" asked Cleo.

Thursday, June 29, and as Eleanor lay in bed an emptiness filled her like gray fog sifting into every corner of her being. She could hear her heart beating over the waves that broke on the shore below, yet it was the total silence in her house that brought on the anxiety she was feeling. She hadn't slept well. Her thoughts kept returning to the Do Nothing tea party and the loneliness of the older women. At least they had each other, but what if they started to die as she knew they would. What if her coffee friends began to die? Walter was already lost to her and the memories he held were no longer available. Who would remember her as a young girl? Anyone who met her now would only know the old Eleanor, with graying hair and crepe skin, and wild whiskers shooting from her chin. Her children and grandchildren had busy lives of their own with so much to plan for and anticipate. Most of her anticipated joys had passed. What was she planning? She definitely was not looking forward to visiting Walter. Coffee was always a treat. She absolutely loved her friends. Maybe it was time for a girls' trip or at least dinner and a movie. She would suggest it tomorrow when they met at the Boat House.

Slowly she forced herself up and out of bed. There was no Feathers to care for or make her laugh. Maybe a brisk walk would perk her up.

Eleanor had to walk fast just to keep warm. The fog had brought a chill to the air and a wind began to blow as she neared the bottom of the hill. She remembered a phrase she had heard somewhere about there being no such thing as inclement weather, only inadequate clothing, and decided she had not dressed appropriately. She continued a short distance along the shore but cut her walk short and returned home.

After a hot shower, Eleanor decided music might lift her mood. She put on an old Van Morrison album, poured herself a cup of coffee and sat with the crossword puzzle. Her mind wandered away from the puzzle as she sang along with *Brown Eyed Girl*. But Eleanor's mind snagged on the words "transistor radio" as her thoughts went back to an earlier time—a time when she owned a transistor radio with a single earbud that she plugged in to listen to her music.

Her friends would remember transistor radios, but what if they were gone and there was no one to remember with her; her youth some forgotten era dismissed by the young and knew that she had no control over at all. Worse, what if she could no longer recall what a transistor radio was! What if she were all alone and there was no one to visit her. What if she lived the life of a shut-in like some of the old people she knew. If she became as boring and dry as the Do Nothings, no one would want to visit her, and she would be all alone. The grayness of the day pressed down on her until the closeness of the sky made it impossible for her to breathe. This thinking was intolerable. Eleanor got up, put on her coat, grabbed her purse, and drove to town to do some shopping.

You can control your thoughts, she told herself as she drove. There is no reason to let these ideas take you to a dark and lonely place. You can choose to think about other things. Think about Angus and what you will make for dinner next week. Just breathe in and out.

Eleanor parked on the street outside The Boutique, one of only three dress shops in town. It didn't take her long to search the racks, find a new sweater and pair of pants, and return to her car. She wasn't in the mood for chitchat. Just as she got back into her car she saw Angus entering a restaurant down the block, but it wasn't his handsome face that make her heart skip a beat. It was the attractive woman on his arm. Eleanor was positive he had not seen her, but she was heartbroken that she had seen him.

As she drove home she puzzled over what it could mean. Who was this other woman so comfortable with him that she would hold his arm like that? Eleanor was sure she had never seen her before. Was Angus a cad? Was he simply toying with her? She couldn't believe how crushed she felt, betrayed even. She knew many women admired him, but she had never known him to flirt or carry on with anyone other than his wife, and then with Eleanor, of course. Perhaps she didn't really know Angus. Heck, she didn't seem to know herself! The strength of her emotions surprised and embarrassed her. Good grief, you would think she was a love-sick girl of 15 instead of a mature woman of seventy-two. Could this day get any worse?

Eleanor poured herself a stiff drink when she got home. She drank it down and poured another. Then she put on her pajamas and turned on the movie channel. When the telephone rang later that evening, she let it ring.

Friday loomed foggy too. It was June 30, for heaven's sake, thought Eleanor, when would summer arrive? She knew the locals said summer weather only came after the Fourth of July, but Eleanor was desperate for some light. There was her coffee group. Hopefully they would shed some light on her darkness.

As she drove to the Boat House, she relived her betrayal and humiliation at the hands of Angus McBride and could only be thankful that no one else had witnessed it. Was this Walter and Alice all over again? Was there something wrong with her? Maybe her refusal to marry Angus had pushed him into the arms of another woman. How trite and ridiculous can one woman be, wondered Eleanor.

Oddly enough, everyone was already at the Boat House when Eleanor arrived. They were drinking coffee and talking animatedly.

"What's new?" Eleanor asked hoping they were not talking about her. Could Angus's new romance be grist for the rumor mill already?

"Well, Eva Long has died!" Dede related.

"That means there is an opening in the Do Nothings," teased Cleo.

"What happened?" asked Eleanor, who was honestly shocked. She remembered the kind smile and the palsied hands.

"Evidently she has suffered from some neurological disorder for quite some time. Mavis Bench found her dead in her favorite chair yesterday afternoon. I guess she didn't show up for their lunch date," Dede filled them in on the details she knew.

"No trace of poison?" probed Josephine.

"Too soon to tell, but maybe Angus will know. You'll have to interrogate him, Eleanor." Dede prompted.

Eleanor shook her head, "I haven't seen him lately. He's been out of town."

"I just saw him yesterday," Dede said, full of information. "He was with his sister, Fiona. She's visiting here from California. I'm surprised he didn't tell you about her."

"Me too," Eleanor said, needing a minute to wrap her mind around these new facts. "I didn't even know he had a sister, but he probably doesn't know I have a sister either."

"Maybe he's planning to surprise you," offered Pearl.

"I wonder if she's moving in with him?" wondered Cleo.

"I believe she has some health issues, so maybe she's moving into assisted living or something. He didn't really say, and I didn't want to pry. She didn't seem that old, but I gathered she is his older and only sibling." Dede always knew the important facts and Eleanor really wanted to hug her right then, but she remained quiet.

"Not to change the subject, but getting back to the issue of poison, I noticed something strange at the tea party the other day. Eleanor, do you remember how they didn't drink their tea until we drank it? Maybe they thought we were trying to poison them," Cleo mused.

"I do remember thinking that was odd. Why would they think we would poison them, unless they know about the Maude Squad and suspect us? Wouldn't that be terrible if they did? Now Eva is dead, and they probably think we killed her!" Eleanor was floored by the thought.

"Maybe they are the Maude Squad and think we want to get them for killing those old people," suggested Pearl.

"They have to know the relationship between Eleanor and Angus. Surely if that was the case, they would think Eleanor would just report them to the police," reasoned Dede. "They wouldn't assume that everyone is a killer just because they are."

"What makes sense though is that the Do Nothings are the Maude Squad. We may have been looking at this from the wrong angle. They are all over eighty, but their victims were not." Eleanor

182

was thinking out loud. "I saw them with a book about poisons at Roseanna's two separate times. Just think about their collective knowledge: pharmacist, research scientist, geriatric nurse, and doctor. Who better to know how to kill and make it look natural?"

"Do you think they killed Eva Long?" questioned Josephine.

"Should we ask them?" Cleo inquired with a giggle.

Pearl shivered. "This whole thing is giving me the creeps. Do you think they are dangerous?"

"If they murder people, they are definitely dangerous," Josephine said, tossing in her two cents. "But are they really committing murder or just giving people the means to take their own lives?"

"The cocktail of death," exclaimed Cleo. "They must know the ingredients and it has to include pentobarbital. There may even be other drugs involved."

"They might have an entire pharmacy of poisons," ventured Pearl.

"Some of them could be derived from plants that a research scientist would know about," Dede surmised.

"What if they used a variety of poisons? That would make it even less likely that anyone would suspect a single murderer," Josephine added.

It was suddenly very quiet. They looked around the restaurant and wondered if anyone had overheard their conversation.

"I wonder if we asked them for it, if they would give us the recipe for the cocktail of death," Cleo whispered. "We might need it someday, and they aren't going to be around forever."

Eleanor returned home to find her house just as empty as when she had left it. No sooner had she closed the door behind her than the telephone began to ring.

"Hello," she answered.

"Oh, thank goodness, you're alive!" It was Nancy Wilson. "Angus has been calling all morning and asked me to check on you since you don't seem to be answering your phone. Please call him and put him out of his misery."

Eleanor smiled, "Sorry, Nancy, I wasn't feeling well last night and didn't answer the phone, but I'm fine. Thank you for caring."

"I wasn't the one who was worried," Nancy explained. "He must have called a dozen times this morning. I convinced him not to drive out here, told him you were a big girl."

"I'll call him right away," Eleanor reassured her.

"Maybe he should have your cell number. Are you two an item now?" she pried.

"Thanks again, Nancy. Maybe we should have lunch next week. I'll call you." Eleanor hung up and dialed Angus's number. He was turning out to be worse than her mother, but for some reason it made her happy.

The doorbell rang promptly at six, because Angus was the kind of man who didn't make a lady wait.

"Hi, are you ready? I left Fiona in the car." Angus was sporting a sports jacket and blue jeans. Eleanor thought he had never looked more handsome.

"Yes, I just need to grab a sweater." Eleanor wore the new outfit she bought while in deep despair. "Are we going to the Galley?" she asked.

"No, that's our place," Angus said as he draped the sweater over her shoulders.

"Our place, I didn't know we had a place." Eleanor hurried out the door. "Do we have a song too?"

"Sure, *Dream Lover.*" He smiled a wicked smile as he put her in the car and closed the door on her blushing face.

After dinner, Angus took Fiona home and then drove out to Eleanor's house for a nightcap and debriefing.

"So, what do you think of my big sister?" Angus asked as he sipped his Crown Royal.

"I think she is stunning. No one would ever think she is in her eighties, for heaven's sake!" Eleanor exclaimed.

"It's all fake," Angus revealed, "but don't tell her I said so. She and Margo bought in to the Los Angeles lifestyle years ago. It takes a great deal of energy and money to maintain that kind of façade. I think she may be tired of it. Coming here will give her a different perspective on how real people age."

"Are you talking about me?" Eleanor didn't know if she was offended or not.

"Ellie, you are as real as that horse in *The Velveteen Rabbit* and just as beautiful inside as out." Angus added a whiskey flavored kiss just to punctuate his comments.

It touched Eleanor to know that Angus was familiar with a classic children's tale. "What do you know about the Skin Horse?"

"I know he was real, and his hair was rubbed off by love. You can bet Fiona wouldn't allow that to happen," Angus speculated. "Neither she nor Margo would let something like love ruin their idea of an ideal body."

"Fiona has no children?"

"No children, no grandchildren, no one but me, and you may notice I have all my hair. Now I guess she's lonely." Angus sighed.

"Well, I like her," Eleanor declared. "She's funny and smart and tells a good story. If she stays, maybe she could write her memoirs. The things she shared at dinner were amusing and very illuminating."

"Who would read them? There aren't any interested parties." Angus seemed stuck on the fact that he was the last of his line. Eleanor began to get a hint of his baggage. She didn't know the Angus who had a sister depending on him.

"I'd read them. People like to read about the lives of others, even if they aren't related to them. That's how we learn. Sometimes it keeps us from making the same mistakes they made or inspires us to do more than we think we can." Eleanor rubbed Angus's back. He turned and took her gently in his arms.

"I love you, Eleanor Penrose," he whispered in her ear.

"That's good, Angus, just don't rub off all of my fur."

Eleanor could not sleep. She had completed her nightly routine, but for some reason she was itchy all over. After several minutes of tossing and turning, she got up and went to the kitchen for a fresh glass of water. Maybe what she needed was a good moisturizer. Just as she headed to the bathroom, she saw headlights slowly approach. It was very late. Who would be driving up her road at this time of night? She watched as the car stopped and the lights went off. Eleanor felt a tingle of fear. She knew that big car with the slanted headlights. It was Mattie May's Lincoln Town car. She waited and then went boldly to the front door and turned on her porch light. The car slowly rolled down the road. What was that? What was Mattie May doing? Eleanor had an uneasy prickly feeling and moisturizer didn't help.

Daylight finally came just as Eleanor fell into a deep sleep. Most of the night she dreamed of a faceless someone chasing her in a dark Lincoln Town car as she ran through a swamp. The driver was able to skim over the dark ominous water with no trouble while Eleanor stumbled and fell repeatedly. Angus appeared in the dream, but he was too busy pushing Fiona in her wheelchair to notice her distress. As Eleanor ran through the fog from the encroaching car, she saw Angus in a clearing all alone in the dark. He was crying. Her dreams made no sense and she woke exhausted and headachy. It was Saturday. Thirty days has September, April, June, and November. Today was the first of July, she would visit Walter and Feathers tomorrow, but what was she doing today? Her mind was blank. She stretched, rolled over and remembered the Lincoln Town car and the late-night visit. She was certain it was Mattie May but couldn't think of any reason for such a visit. There was nothing that the ladies left behind the day of the tea party. Surely Mattie and the other Do Nothings were deeply mourning the loss of their friend, Eva. Maybe Mattie couldn't sleep either and was just taking a drive.

Eleanor got up. She would walk down to the village. Maybe she would see Mattie, Mavis, or Sybil down at Roseanna's. Before she left her house, she called Cleo and asked her to invite the rest of the coffee group to come for lunch. They needed to get to the bottom of this.

There was no sign of the Do Nothings in the village. If Mattie was up until the wee hours, perhaps she was still in bed this morning. Eleanor ducked into the store to buy some cold cuts and cookies for lunch.

On the way home, she stopped again at the hidey-hole. The poem was still where she left it. She looked around suspiciously wondering if someone was watching her. Everyone who lived on the hills of Sand Beach owned a telescope. Anyone could watch her as she came and went on her daily walks. Many of her neighbors knew her routine. Suddenly her friendly little village seemed dark and sinister. Maybe Mattie May had watched her leave her house. Maybe she was there now searching for something Eleanor didn't know she had that might incriminate her. Eleanor's mind raced. Her friends would come over. They would eat lunch, lay out the facts they knew, and settle this one way or another.

As she put away her groceries, Eleanor heard the telephone ringing.

"Hello," Eleanor answered.

"Mrs. Penrose, this is Nurse O'Hara from Rosewood Manor. Don't be alarmed. Walter is well, but we have had an outbreak of norovirus and won't be admitting visitors until we have it under control. I hope this doesn't disrupt your plans for the weekend. We will let you know when the lockdown is over."

"Thank you very much for the call." Eleanor bit her lip. This had happened before during flu season, so it wasn't unusual. It just meant she had a free Sunday. She felt a mixture of elation and guilt. Maybe she was finally ready to let Walter go. She didn't want to think about him now. She had bigger fish to fry.

After preparing a tray of meats and cheeses, lettuce, tomatoes, and pickles, Eleanor covered everything and put it in the refrigerator along with a bottle of chardonnay. She set the table in the dining area and cleared the nearest wall to create room for all the information they knew. She set up her whiteboard on an easel and gathered pens, yarn, Post-It notes, and various other items that might be helpful. Then she sat down at her computer and began to surf the web for helpful images. The first picture she printed was the image of a 1960 vintage Lincoln Town car while it was still vividly etched in her mind. She was able to find pictures of all the Do Nothings from the local Sand Beach newsletter and several obituaries that were printed in the *Fish Wrapper*. Using Tacky-Tack she put up a huge sheet of butcher paper and posted the names of the many victims in one column and suspects in another. She printed a map of the county and was just about to pinpoint the location of the murders when the doorbell rang.

Cleo had successfully contacted the entire coffee group and convinced them of the importance of this lunch meeting. Somehow their friend, Eleanor, was in trouble and they needed to help.

"Oh, I'm so glad you could all come," Eleanor sighed. Suddenly she didn't feel like she was in this alone.

"Cleo told us it was an emergency," Dede said as she set down her offering of blueberry pie.

"I wasn't doing anything interesting, and Cary went to the casino with Richard so I'm happy to be here," Pearl said.

"Well, I'm genuinely intrigued," Josephine said. "I love a good mystery. Are there new developments?"

"Let's plate up some lunch and I'll tell you what I know." Eleanor led them into the kitchen where Cleo was already opening the chardonnay.

As they sat around the table, they couldn't help but notice the information Eleanor had on display.

"What's happened to set this in motion?" Josephine wanted to know.

"Late last night, a black Lincoln Town car stopped outside and turned its lights off. When I lit the porch light, it drove off. Frankly, it gave me the creeps and set me to wondering if maybe we know more than we think we do. I thought if we got together and put down everything we know for sure, we might come up with some connections or new facts. Perhaps we will recall things we've forgotten," Eleanor explained.

Each of the ladies nodded in agreement that this was indeed a good idea, maybe a great idea.

"Before this, I must admit, I thought we were just being silly," Pearl confessed, "but I see now how serious this is and how frightened you must be, Eleanor."

"I know that car, Eleanor, and so do you!" Dede was hooked. "You know Mattie May drives that car all over the county."

"I remember seeing a car like that behind us when we went to the Silverton address. Do you think Mattie May could have been there?" Cleo wanted to know.

"Maybe, and maybe not, there are probably lots of old cars like that." Pearl couldn't tell one car from another.

"There are most likely a number of reasons why Mattie May would be driving by your house, Eleanor." Josephine offered.

"Like what?" asked Cleo.

"Maybe she couldn't sleep and just happened to drive up here. People often have difficulty sleeping after suffering a loss," Josephine explained.

"Or a guilty conscious," added Dede.

"So why stop and turn her lights off?" Cleo persisted.

"Maybe she was with her boyfriend and they thought this was a good make-out spot," giggled Pearl. "Was she alone?"

"I couldn't see who was in the car," Eleanor said. "This is a good spot for looking out over the ocean. Maybe she was just trying to find some peace. Do you think I'm overreacting?"

"No," Josephine did not hesitate. "Your instincts are good, Eleanor. I'm sure Mattie May is involved in this some way. We just need to find the connection. Does anyone know anything more about Eva's death?"

"The police have given up searching for a serial killer," Dede informed them. "Instead of homicides, they have ruled all of the pentobarbital deaths accidental overdoses or suicides. They just couldn't find a link other than old age."

"So, the authorities no longer suspect murder, or just can't prove murder?" Josephine asked.

"I assume it isn't a priority and they're no longer testing for pentobarbital because of the cost and time involved," Dede remarked. "Old people are often sick, and they die. There is nothing suspicious about that."

"Is it a priority to us?" Eleanor wondered.

"Yes!" Cleo was clear. "We need to know if this is a case of murder or mercy. We definitely know some of these people on the victim list received help dying. We know there is a Maude Squad. We know they communicated through personal ads."

"What happens if we find out who is doing it?" Pearl asked. "Do we turn them in or give them an award for kindness?"

"I don't know for a fact, but I just know it is true that Mattie and the Do Nothings are up to their eyeballs in this," Eleanor said. "I want to find out for sure. If it is them, I suspect it is done as a kindness, but if it isn't them, there may be other sinister characters at work."

"I just want the recipe for dying in case I need it," repeated Cleo.

"Let's get to work," said Josephine. "We need to determine what the victims have in common."

"Does someone want to pinpoint the deaths on this map?" Eleanor asked.

"I'll look the Do Nothings up on the internet to see what I can find out about their histories," offered Dede.

"I'm just calling Mattie May to ask her to come over so we can grill her for information," Cleo quipped as she poured herself a glass of wine.

Several hours passed as the coffee group worked quietly at their laptops and computers. As they discovered each detail, they added it to the information board that hung on the wall.

"I'm tired. Let's break for pie and look at what we've learned," suggested Pearl. No one objected.

They moved into the kitchen where Eleanor served up the blueberry pie topped with vanilla bean ice cream. As they ate, Cleo leafed through the local telephone directory that she found in a drawer by the phone.

"Mattie would probably enjoy a piece of this pie," Cleo commented. "She wouldn't even have to know we were investigating her." Suddenly her eyebrows shot up. "Did you know Mattie's real name is Matilda? It says so right here in the phone book!"

"Yes, I found her on the web as Matilda May nee Matilda Bigs. There are even pictures of her from when she was young. It looks like our Do Nothing Girls knew each other in college, before they were married. At least there is a group here with all the same first names," reported Dede.

"What does the caption read?" asked Eleanor.

"Let me print these photos so we can enlarge them," Dede said.

"It seems as though these women all attended the same school and belonged to a science club," Dede continued as she attached the enlarged photos to the information board.

"I think I found a connection to Frieda too, but that picture is much later."

They all gathered to view the pictures. It was all so interesting to see these old women as young girls and imagine what their lives were like back then when they definitely planned to *Do Something*.

"That must be Eva. She had a beautiful smile then too," Eleanor commented. "And that is Sybil Wendt. She either never changed her name or went back to it after her divorce."

"I would never recognize Mavis from this picture," Dede said. "Look how studious she is with those big round glasses."

"This picture of Frieda is much later, after she was in nursing school. Mattie is the only Do Nothing pictured with her. I didn't know they knew each other. Frieda certainly never mentioned Mattie to me in all our conversations. You'd think they would have been friends," Eleanor said puzzled.

"The caption says this group was responsible for formulating a special numbing agent used in surgery," Dede said. "It seems as though Mattie and Frieda were chemical research scientists, but this is a Frieda Jansen, not VanHorn. Are they the same? The picture is from a medical journal."

"Maybe that's the connection Mattie has to you," suggested Josephine. "Didn't Frieda leave you a box of her things? Perhaps there is something in it that ties Frieda to Mattie and Mattie to the Maude Squad."

"That might explain Mattie's visit. She may be afraid you know too much or have something she wants," Pearl inferred.

"The other interesting bit is that Maude is a nickname for Matilda," offered Cleo as she stuffed the last of her pie in her mouth.

"Do you still have the box?" asked Dede. Suddenly everyone had a second wind.

"I'm sure I threw the box out, but there wasn't that much in it," Eleanor said as she led the others into her office. It didn't seem that long ago that she pulled the velvet robe from the box. On the bookshelf sat the three books Frieda had packed for her along with the two beautiful pieces of delft Eleanor had left for later to store away.

Josephine examined one of the books carefully while Cleo shook the others hoping something might fall out, but nothing did.

"These are all about death," noted Pearl. "Is that all that was in the box?"

"No," Eleanor said, remembering that she had placed Frieda's manuscript in its leather folder in the desk drawer. She opened the drawer and was relieved to find it there. "This is Frieda's memoirs. She lived a very interesting life. I only know a little of her story as she told me in bits and pieces. This is what she wrote. I don't know if she finished it."

"Boy, there are a lot of pages there," observed Cleo, who suddenly seemed eager to go home.

"All the answers may be in there or maybe not," added Pearl.

"May I borrow these books, Eleanor?" asked Josephine as she gathered the three books about death into her arms.

"Sure. You've spent all afternoon working on this and I know you need to get home to your families. Thank you for coming." Eleanor was just as eager to begin reading Frieda's manuscript as they were to leave.

"Will you be okay here, alone?" Dede asked worriedly. "If Mattie comes looking for the manuscript, it could be dangerous."

"I'm not afraid of Mattie May," Eleanor reassured her. "I'm sure I could take her if it comes to that."

"She might not play fair, Eleanor," cautioned Cleo. "Keep your doors locked." Then with hugs and goodbyes they were gone and Eleanor was alone.

Eleanor was exhausted. After the long afternoon of researching on top of a sleepless night she was delighted to crawl into her cozy bed and snuggle down into the comforter with Frieda's manuscript. Just as she started to read, the telephone rang.

"Hello, Angus," she answered on the second ring.

"Hey, Ellie, do you have caller ID now?" he asked.

"Who else calls me to say good-night?" she responded tenderly.

"So, is my plan working? Are you thinking about me? Am I in your dreams?"

"Absolutely." Eleanor did not tell him they were nightmares. She had thought about him in ways that had never occurred to her before, not as a strong, confident man but more as a sad, lonely little boy who just wanted to be a part of a family. "Rosewood Manor is on lockdown due to norovirus, so why don't you bring Fiona over for Sunday supper tomorrow?"

"Are you sure you want to cook for her? She doesn't eat anything—won't touch bread or meat. She's hard to please." Angus sounded sad.

"Don't worry. I'll grill some chicken and make a big salad. You can help me. If the weather is nice we can eat on the deck and drink beer. She can eat or not. I won't take it personally unless you don't eat." Eleanor's offer was heartfelt.

"I'd be a fool to pass up that proposal."

"Come over around three," she said sweetly.

"Yes, dear, good night, dear," he joked and hung up.

Eleanor was happy that she had made Angus happy. Maybe that was love, she thought as she drifted off to sleep with the first page of Frieda's story still in her hand.

How lovely to wake slowly from a deep and satisfying sleep! Eleanor wriggled her toes and flexed her ankles under the covers.

She remembered that this was Sunday, July 2, and she did not need to drive to visit Walter. She could lounge around in her pajamas, read the Sunday paper and just relax. There was Frieda's manuscript to read. Eleanor noticed it was still on the bed and only slightly crinkled. She quickly put the papers back in the folder and continued her plan for the day. She would take some chicken out of the freezer for grilling later. Her mind went to menu planning. It was the Fourth of July weekend and the sky was clear. Most likely there would be fireworks on the beach tonight. Things were looking up.

When Erin called later, she invited her and her family to come for dinner and stay the night. She imagined the family barbecues of the past taking place for Angus, but they had already made holiday plans and politely declined. It's what is expected as families grow up and move on to create their own traditions. At least she had called. Eleanor would not be sad. She was moving on too.

At 3:30, Eleanor began to fret. Angus was never late. It was a holiday weekend at the coast so maybe there was traffic or an accident, but just as she picked up the phone to call, the doorbell rang.

"Hello Beautiful, I brought a bottle of wine even though you said there would be beer, but I know you don't drink beer," Angus said babbling. It was so not like him. Whatever was wrong?

"I'm the reason we are late, Eleanor. Can you please forgive me before Angus gives himself a stroke? I've never met a man so anal in my life." Fiona entered behind Angus and leaned in with a hug for Eleanor.

"No big deal, although I was beginning to worry a bit, since Angus has never in all the time I've known him, been late for a meal." Eleanor succeeded in putting her guests at ease. Angus even smiled as he put his contribution in the kitchen.

Fiona wandered through the house commenting on Eleanor's good taste in all things décor.

"Who did the decorating for you?" she asked.

"I just filled the house with things I love, so I guess I'm the decorator. My husband, Walter, and I traveled quite a bit and brought a few items back with us." Eleanor explained.

"Well, you have done a marvelous job. I just love your view too."

"I had nothing to do with that," laughed Eleanor. "Would you like something to drink, Fiona? I'm having a gin and tonic. Do you want your usual, Angus?"

They found themselves on the deck with drinks in hand sharing stories of their youth when the black vintage Lincoln Town car slowly drove by. It was clearly Mattie May behind the wheel and by the look on her face, she was stunned to see Eleanor at home entertaining a former homicide detective. In her rush to drive away, she almost hit Angus's pickup truck.

"What was that?" Angus was riled. "It might be time for Mattie to give up her license."

"Don't let a silly old woman ruin your fun," chided Fiona, who obviously didn't know who she was talking about. Mattie was most likely the same age as Fiona. In the bright light of day, Eleanor could see age written on Fiona's face and she noticed her long, dark hair was made of extensions. Fiona was thin to the point of emaciation. From a distance or in a dim room she looked fine, even pretty, but no amount of nipping and tucking could make an old woman young.

Angus left to check his pickup for damages and Eleanor had a private moment with Fiona.

"What are these pretty pink flowers," Fiona asked as she fingered a blossom from the start that Frieda had given her.

"I don't know what they are called. A friend gave me a start and now I can't seem to kill them, Eleanor joked.

"You know Angus is quite taken with you, Eleanor. I hope you're not stringing him along. I understand you have one husband already." Fiona had pulled out her claws.

"It's complicated," she said. Eleanor had no intention of explaining herself to Fiona. "I'm very fond of Angus, so I'd never string him along. He knows I'm not looking for another husband."

"He's my baby brother. We are all we have of family and I can't live forever, although I'm planning to try. I know he doesn't approve of my ways, but I'm not going to change. I just don't want him hurt. He doesn't have any money, you know."

"No, I didn't know. Do you think he's after mine?" Eleanor countered.

Before Fiona could respond, they heard Angus.

"Better check that chicken, Ellie. It's starting to smell delicious." Angus refilled his drink and returned to the deck satisfied that there was no damage. He seemed oblivious to the fact that the two women had been talking about him, but that brief moment had changed Eleanor's perception of his older sister.

When the meal was served, Fiona simply moved it around on her plate with her fork and ate very little. She tried to be charming by telling amusing tales of their childhood, but they were the same stories she had told the night before. Eleanor wondered about her mental and physical health and worried that Angus might find himself saddled with a sister he could not care for.

It wasn't long before Fiona said she was tired and pleaded with Angus to take her home.

"Is Fiona ill, Angus?" Eleanor's concern was real.

"No, Ellie, she's not ill. Fiona's tired. I'll take her home and come back for pie and fireworks. You wait for me."

Eleanor tidied up and washed the dishes. She thought about Fiona and how lonely and afraid she must feel living by herself with no family near. It was easier for Eleanor to put herself in Fiona's place than it was to do the same for Angus, yet he too must feel lonely and maybe afraid with no family near. They both had friends. Sometimes friends were better than family. Eleanor comforted herself with that thought.

She wandered into her office where she had hastily hidden the coffee group's investigation data. There was no way she wanted Angus involved in it. If Mattie May was guilty of mercy, Angus would be obligated to turn her in for murder. She checked on Frieda's manuscript in the desk drawer and resisted the impulse to start on it again knowing Angus would be back soon. Hearing his pickup on the drive, she quickly closed the drawer and left the office to greet him.

"You were speeding," Eleanor accused him.

"Can you blame me? I need pie." Angus didn't seem upset by Fiona's departure but more like himself than before.

They took their plates out on the deck and watched the waves and crowds of people on the beach as they ate dessert. It was a pleasant day. A gentle breeze blew off the ocean and the sound of the surf mingled with the cries of seagulls and children laughing. Everyone below scurried to save their spot with their beach towels, picnic baskets, and sand buckets. It made Eleanor happy to watch.

"Thank goodness, we're not down there!" Angus remarked. "I haven't seen the beach crowded like this before. It's crazy. Just look at all the cars parked at the wayside."

"It's a holiday weekend and the weather is wonderful. The fog is not making an appearance and I daresay that breeze will die down as soon as the sun sets. It all adds up to a perfect evening for fireworks," Eleanor said, summing it up nicely.

"It's not even the Fourth of July yet. These tourists will be here until Tuesday when they'll all hurry home causing traffic jams and accidents. They are probably all overindulging right now," Angus speculated.

"But you, my friend, are up here above it all, just relaxing and able to enjoy the best of it without the hassle. Do you want another piece of pie?" Eleanor inquired as she rose from the table and began collecting their plates.

"Yes, I do, but I don't think I have any space for it," Angus lamented as he followed her to the kitchen. "I wish I saw the world as you do, Ellie, all bright and shiny with good people doing good deeds for other good people."

"Really?" Eleanor was surprised. "How do you see it then?"

"I know the dark places in men's hearts and where they go to commit evil. I've followed them there and it's never good." Angus had his gaze fixed out the window, but he was looking inward. "You are my light in the darkness, Ellie."

Eleanor had no answer for that other than to wrap her arms around him and squeeze his heavy heart and his pie too.

The summer sun created its own fireworks as it set over the Pacific with vibrant reds and oranges spreading out across the sky and spilling into the water. Angus and Eleanor snuggled together under a fleecy blanket and waited for the man-made fireworks to begin.

"Do you think Fiona is okay?" Eleanor asked, thinking how much she was enjoying the evening.

"She's fine. She lives in a little apartment in a big city and doesn't appreciate what we have here. Most likely she's sleeping."

"How long will she stay?" Eleanor pried.

"Not long. She can't survive in a rural environment. She was made for concrete and city lights." Angus did not judge.

"Do you think she is lonely?"

"No, there are more people like her than there are people like you, Ellie. She surrounds herself with her friends and they are devoted to her. She is really quite brilliant, and her friends aren't bad people, just different. I think she's happier there."

"What did Fiona do for a living?" Eleanor was curious about her.

"You won't believe it, but she was a research scientist for a big pharmaceutical company. I think she was always looking for a cure for aging. She never wanted to look old. I think she tries too hard, but that's my opinion." Angus didn't want to tell tales about Fiona.

Eleanor scolded herself for finding pleasure in knowing Fiona would not be staying in her world. She snuggled deeper into Angus's embrace. When the fireworks lit up the night time sky, there was no more talking.

Angus stayed well into the night. Eleanor thought she knew why he didn't want to go home; maybe it was the drive, or Fiona, or that second piece of pie, but Angus stayed for the light in the darkness.

Eleanor was tired on Monday morning. It wasn't her habit to stay up until the wee hours, so when the telephone rang at a respectable time, she was still asleep.

"Hello," she mumbled into her sheets.

"Eleanor? Are you still in bed?" Josephine seemed shocked.

"Late night . . ." was all Eleanor could get out before Josephine continued.

"Listen, I found something in one of Frieda's books and I'm coming over with it. Get up and put on the coffee." Josephine hung up.

Doesn't anyone say goodbye anymore? Eleanor rolled out of bed, shocked at the lateness of the hour and managed to ready herself for a visitor. By the time Josephine arrived, she was antsy with curiosity.

"I can't believe you found something in the books," Eleanor said, welcoming Josephine with a hug. "Didn't we shake the dickens out of them?"

"It's an envelope addressed to you, Eleanor, but just look how thin the paper is. It was wedged tightly in this book, *How We Die: Reflections on Life's Final Chapter.* She didn't want it falling out. I didn't open it, of course, but I really wanted to." Josephine paused for a breath as Eleanor fingered the onion paper.

Slowly, and with great care she opened the delicate envelope. There in Frieda's spidery old lady handwriting was the following:

*My Dearest friend Eleanor,*

*I write this letter to you before I die. There are a few things I need to say, first how much I have loved and valued our friendship, second to ask a great favor and, third to confess the sins of an old soul. I know your heart and am confident that you will not judge me harshly for my failings. You may, in your great kindness, even count them as blessings. Because I feel that we are similar in spirit, I trust you, and no one else with my life's secret. There are others who would use and abuse this knowledge, and many thought I had destroyed it. Perhaps that is what I should have done, but I will not take this to my grave.*

*Long ago, as you know, I suffered at the hands of the Japanese in their concentration camp during World War II. I witnessed many atrocities and swore to do whatever I could to stamp out pain and suffering wherever I found it. As fortune would have it, I was given a great gift. As I studied to be a nurse, I discovered I had a talent and love for chemistry. A few of my colleagues and I perfected a formula for a medicine that would alleviate pain and bring on a peaceful death. It leaves absolutely no trace of its use and looks as though the patient has died peacefully in sleep. Knowing how something like this could be misused, I have hidden the formula and never used it. Only I knew the entire recipe. My colleagues pressured me to sell it to a large pharmaceutical company, but my fear caused me to argue and finally break off contact with them. I know they have sought me out.*

*I am tired and in great pain now but lack the courage to end my life even as I feel death is near. Now for my final request:*

*I have not finished my memoirs. The pages I have completed are in the box I have left for you. Please edit them and put the final chapter in place. Within the pages of the manuscript you will find the formula for my death cocktail and in the box a small vial of the poison. Whatever you decide to do with it, will be what needs to be done with it. My trusted friend, I leave you with a heavy burden and for this I am sorry.*

> *Your friend,*
>
> *Frieda VanHorn aka Dr. Frieda Jansen*

Eleanor read it silently and looked up at Josephine when she finished.

"I'm sorry you rushed over here for no good reason. It's just a letter asking me to edit and finish her manuscript," Eleanor lied.

"You are a horrible liar, Eleanor Penrose! I watched your face as you read that letter and there was more to it than that." Josephine suddenly wished she was not always the most honorable person in the room. "I wish I had opened it and read it. This will kill me."

"Frieda has entrusted me with a secret I cannot share. Sorry, Josephine. Would you like that coffee now?" It was all Eleanor could offer.

"Is there pie?"

After Josephine left, Eleanor went immediately to her desk and opened the leather folder that contained Frieda's manuscript. There was more than 300 typewritten pages. Somewhere among them was a recipe for dying that was probably worth millions of dollars. Her sweet Frieda had hidden this secret for fear of what others would do with it, and denied thousands, including herself, relief from a painful existence. There was a fine line to explore here. What was the moral choice? Where was the vial of poison?

Eleanor reread Frieda's letter. She did not remember seeing a vial in the box. She checked the pieces of delft—nothing. She searched the pockets of the robe and still found nothing. The folder containing the manuscript had no room for a vial. Could it be hidden in one of the books that Josephine had? Eleanor had taken the box to the garage. Hopefully she hadn't put it in the trash or recycling.

Eleanor spied the box sitting in a corner on the floor beside the trash can. She carefully sifted through the wadded newspapers and on the side of the box discovered a small vial taped to the inside of the box. It certainly was not what she would have expected from Frieda. How easily this could have gone undiscovered and how dangerous to leave a vial of poison here. Maybe Frieda was losing her faculties at the end.

Eleanor carefully released the vial and held it in her fingers, eying the contents suspiciously. There was a clear harmless-looking liquid inside, a little thicker than water with maybe a hint of pink. Where would she keep it safely, and what would she do with it ultimately?

Eleanor returned to her office and placed the vial in a safe she had behind a picture that hung on the wall. She sat down at her desk and looked at the information board they had created.

What was Mattie Mays' interest in this formula? Maybe she suspected Frieda gave it to Eleanor. That might explain her visits. She might have been looking for an opportunity to snoop around for it. Mattie and the other Do Nothings might know of it and perhaps even helped create it. They could be the colleagues Frieda spoke of in her letter. Were they after the money it could earn them? Did they want recognition and fame, or were they only interested in helping relieve the suffering of others and themselves? It was difficult to know the answers to these questions and that made it difficult to know what to do.

Eleanor already suspected the Do Nothings of mercy killing, but what if their real motive was to find Frieda to get their hands on the formula? When she didn't cooperate, they killed her. She would just be one of many old people who died of natural causes and if there was suspicion to the contrary, just one of many poisoned by a serial killer passing through. How would Eleanor know? What could she do to find out? She certainly was not eating or drinking anything they offered. Eleanor laughed out loud when she remembered her tea party and how reluctant they were to drink anything she did not drink herself. They were afraid of her. They must think she knew more than she did. She would have to change that. She would have to know more than they did. Eleanor began to read Frieda's memoir.

After an hour of delving through Frieda's manuscript Eleanor needed a break. She had made progress but hadn't found the formula. She stood, stretched, and gazed at the picture of Frieda from the medical journal. Eleanor liked thinking of Frieda when she was young. She and Mattie stood next to another woman. All were young, vibrant, and beautiful, especially the tall dark-haired one next to Frieda. The photo was old and a little grainy, but Eleanor recognized her at once. She hadn't seen it before because she was focused on Frieda and Mattie, but it was clearly Fiona McBride.

Eleanor felt the room tilt and spin. Her center was coming apart. What could this mean? How could all these people be connected? Why would they all converge in a small town on the Oregon coast? Who were the good guys? How was Angus involved in all this? She could not wrap her head around it and she no longer knew who to trust because nothing made sense.

Eleanor searched for a common thread and knew it had to be Frieda and her formula. The Do Nothings had gone to school together. Frieda, Mattie, and Fiona were involved in chemical research together. They had created a numbing agent for surgeries, but had they also created the death formula together? Were Mattie and Fiona the colleagues who wanted to sell the formula to a big pharmaceutical company? Fiona worked for a pharmaceutical company. Did Angus know? Suddenly the most important question was that one. What did Angus know?

Eleanor thought back to when Angus began to show an interest in her romantically. Wasn't it about the same time Frieda died? Now that Frieda was gone, Eleanor had the information they wanted. She had the formula and a sample of a drug that might make them all rich. What if Angus knew that? Fiona said he didn't have money. Maybe he needed money. Maybe Fiona wanted the money she felt she deserved and Angus was going to get it for her. Angus could even be a serial killer like the television character, Dexter, who also worked for the police. What if everything Angus had said and done was a lie?

In her mind, she replayed every tender word, each kiss and caress and felt like a total fool. Eleanor felt her heart sink into a hole and a horrible ache replaced it. She did not want to lose Angus. She had to find another explanation, but she could not think clearly, and she knew clear thinking was mandatory.

She went to the kitchen, poured herself a stiff glass of Crown Royal and called Mattie May.

"Hello, Eleanor, what is it that you want?" Mattie had caller ID.

"Mattie, I would like to meet with you to discuss some things that have been on my mind. Are you going to be home?" Eleanor politely inquired.

"Yes, but I'd rather meet you at Roseanna's. I can be there in 10 minutes." Mattie suggested.

"I'll be there," Eleanor agreed and ended the call. Did Mattie suggest a public meeting place because she was afraid?

Eleanor finished her drink, put on a jacket, and began her walk down the hill. When she got to the bottom, there was no sign of the Lincoln Town car at Roseanna's. Eleanor entered and found a seat near the window overlooking the ocean. From this vantage point she could see Mattie when she came in to the restaurant. A waitress brought her a menu and water. She didn't wait long before Mattie arrived and slowly made her way to Eleanor's table.

"Good evening, Mattie." Eleanor felt for some reason that she had the upper hand. Mattie's fear was palpable.

"Eleanor, what is it you want?" Mattie's voice trembled slightly as she repeated her earlier question.

"Have you eaten, Mattie? I'd like to buy you dinner," Eleanor offered and realized she was hungry.

Mattie hesitated at first but then accepted. As they waited for their meals, they seemed to size each other up like boxers getting ready to spar.

"Are you the Maude Squad?" Eleanor blurted.

Mattie's eyes bulged in surprise as she sputtered her reply, "I thought *you* were the Maude Squad!"

Eleanor laughed out loud. It was so clear to her now that Mattie was telling the truth. Her response was as honest as it could be, and her fear made sense. "What exactly do you know about them?" she questioned, "and why do you suspect me?"

"I know they kill old people. The Do Nothings noticed a pattern of deaths among the elderly in our area. Eva found a link online about a group called the Maude Squad and then we found an ad in the newspaper. We saw you and your friends in Silverton that day when Enid Ragsdale was found dead. We figured you were the killers. Mavis was at Twin Oaks the day Jean Scattergoods died waiting for the Maude Squad. She saw several of you there and then Jean died. The evidence was overwhelming. You invited us for tea and we figured you meant to poison us because you had seen us in Silverton and suspected we were onto you. Are you denying it?" Mattie demanded.

"Wow, that does sound incriminating, but that's exactly what we thought about you and your Do Nothings. We also saw a pattern of deaths and noticed the ads with the Maude Squad connection. You have a research scientist, a pharmacist, a geriatric nurse, and a doctor in your group. I saw the book of poisons on your table. We thought you were the perfect suspects to commit mercy killings."

"Oh no, we are all professionals who have taken an oath to do no harm. We would never kill." Mattie was shocked at the thought.

They paused to assess each other once more. Eleanor believed Mattie. "Why did you drive by my house late at night and then again the other day?"

"I couldn't sleep. Sometimes I drive around when I can't sleep. Yesterday, I decided I needed to confront you, but then I saw Fiona McBride at your house and I guess I just freaked."

"That's the other mystery. How are you involved with Frieda and Fiona?" Eleanor continued.

"Fiona is a horrible piece of work. I knew her when we worked for a pharmaceutical company in California. She thought she was so smart. Frieda had developed a formula for skin renewal. It was to be used for burn victims, but Fiona stole it and took it to the company where they patented it as a cosmetic youth serum. Fiona took all the credit and pocketed the profits. Frieda was furious, but she was a brilliant chemist and developed other drugs that eventually were patented and used to help people. Fiona continued to use Frieda and her work to her own advantage. I'm not sure what happened exactly, but Frieda disappeared. I suspect it had to do with a falling out she had with Fiona over one of Frieda's discoveries. I didn't even know Frieda was living here until just after she died. I knew her as Frieda Jansen." Mattie studied Eleanor closely.

"What is your connection to Fiona McBride? I can't tell you how disturbing it was to see her after all this time here in Sand Beach, looking just like she did so many years ago. Has she sold her soul to the devil to keep her ageless?" Mattie wondered.

So it wasn't Angus who startled Mattie when she saw them on the deck, but Fiona.

"Do you know Angus?" Eleanor asked.

"No," Mattie admitted. "Is he the guy that was with you and Fiona?"

"Angus is Fiona's brother. He's an old friend of Walter's." Eleanor didn't think it necessary to tell Mattie more about Angus.

"I see," Mattie said, acting as if she did see more than Eleanor had told.

"Do you think it is possible that Fiona knew Frieda was here?" asked Eleanor.

"I don't know. All that happened so long ago. I doubt Fiona cared much about Frieda, and most likely moved on to other victims when she disappeared. It does seem rather odd that we would all end up here in the same area." Mattie gazed off out the window as if her ponderings could somehow be answered by the sea.

Dinner came and Mattie and Eleanor enjoyed each other's company in a way neither of them could have thought possible. Mattie shared her grief in the loss of her friend, Eva, and Eleanor talked about her children. When the meal was finished, and the conversation lulled they were both reluctant to leave.

"If the Maude Squad isn't either of us, then who?" asked Eleanor.

"I have no idea," answered Mattie. "I have concerns about Eva's death, but I'm positive she had no contact with the Maude Squad."

"What concerns you?" Eleanor asked.

"Her little cat was dead on her lap when she was found. I don't know for a fact if cats die from broken hearts, but I doubt it."

By the time Eleanor returned to her house on the hill, daylight was fading. Her mind was weary with suspicions, plots, and counterplots. She couldn't figure any of it out anymore. The people she trusted were suspect and those she suspected were now found innocent. Where was Angus in all this?

Eleanor decided things would look better in the morning.

When Eleanor woke on Monday morning, her mind was a clean slate for 15 seconds. Then she remembered the mess and befuddlement of the previous day. It was Independence Day. Nancy and Dennis had invited her over for a barbecue later in the afternoon. She knew it would be a big gathering with most of her coffee friends there along with many people from the village. Nancy had called last night to remind her that it would be lovely if she invited Angus and his sister too, but Eleanor had made no effort to do so. She was still questioning Angus' motives and his loyalty to his sister, but she didn't know how to find the truth. Maybe Cleo's way was the best—just ask. Eleanor was afraid of the answers.

As soon as she settled in with her coffee and crossword puzzle, the telephone rang.

"Good morning, Ellie." Angus was all smiles and happiness. Eleanor could hear it in his voice. She did not feel the same.

"Good morning, Angus," she replied coolly.

"Is everything all right?" Angus was suddenly concerned.

"Of course, I just haven't had my coffee yet." Damn him for being so perceptive. Detectives must be the worst in relationships. They analyze every little detail.

"I thought we should take the boat out on the bay tonight and watch the fireworks from there. What do you think? It should be twice as beautiful with the reflection on the water," Angus suggested.

"Sounds like a lot of work, Angus. It would be a late night if we have to take the boat back to the marina and then drive back." Eleanor sounded sour even to herself.

"You aren't turning into a party-pooper, are you?" Angus asked.

"No, never. What about Fiona? Will she be joining us?" Eleanor could feel herself succumbing to his charms.

"I don't know. Don't you want her there?" Angus was testing her.

"Of course, I wouldn't want her staying home alone. Nancy and Dennis have invited us all to their house for an evening barbecue. There will be fireworks here again tonight. Perhaps we could do both." Eleanor didn't know what she was thinking. There were issues that needed to be resolved. If she talked to Angus amid a large group of people, would she get the truth? Was she afraid to be alone with him and his sister out on the water after dark?

"Now that sounds like a plan. What time is the barbecue?" he asked.

"Not until 7:00. It doesn't get dark until 10:00 now. I'm sure Nancy doesn't want company into the wee hours," Eleanor reasoned.

"Okay, I'll meet you there and we'll play it by ear. We can always leave and go out on the water and take Fiona home if she wants an early night. I'll see you later."

Eleanor sighed as she hung up the phone and returned to her puzzle. Why was life so hard? When she was with Angus, she was so sure about him, yet when he was away, she suspected his motives. How did people trust anyone these days?

Eleanor dialed Josephine's number. She was in need of an expert's knowledge.

"Hello," Josephine answered on the first ring.

"Josephine, it's Eleanor. Can you talk?"

"Certainly, what's up?"

"Tell me about serial killers. How do you recognize them?" Eleanor didn't want to waste time chit-chatting.

"What's happened? Does this have to do with the Maude Squad? What was in that letter, Eleanor?" Josephine could hardly contain her curiosity.

Eleanor gave her a brief account of her meeting with Mattie May.

"It is definitely not the Do Nothings, trust me. They were also on the trail of the Maude Squad and they suspected us." Eleanor and Josephine both chuckled at the thought.

"So, you are back to the serial killer angle," Josephine asked. "Do you have a suspect in mind?"

"Yes, but I'd rather not tell you. Just tell me how I can know."

"Well, most serial killers have suffered some kind of trauma, abuse, or neglect as children. Many of them are mentally ill and have average or lower IQs. Some can be quite charming and appear normal. It might be hard to just pick them out of a crowd, Eleanor. Many exhibit antisocial behavior, bed wetting, cruelty to animals. They have various motives as well. Some want control, some suffer from psychotic breaks with reality, some have missions to rid the world of evildoers, and others derive a thrill from killing. Does that sound like any one you know?"

"No, but maybe I really don't know them?" Eleanor was determined to investigate further.

"Are you coming to Nancy's tonight?" Josephine asked.

"Yes," Eleanor replied.

"Are you bringing a serial killer?" Josephine teased.

"I'm bringing deviled eggs."

"Fabulous, I'll see you there."

Eleanor thought a while then went back to her puzzle.

Later that evening, Eleanor walked down to Nancy's with her deviled eggs. After she greeted Nancy and Dennis, she found Cleo, Pearl, and Dede and quietly filled them in on the latest development involving Mattie and the Do Nothings. They laughed uproariously when she told them about being suspects themselves and didn't seem to mind that they were back to square one.

"Hey, Darlin'." Angus' sudden appearance behind her and his breath on the back of her neck made Eleanor nearly jump out of her skin. "I always have that effect on women," he chuckled.

"You startled me!" admitted Eleanor. "Where's Fiona?"

"I introduced her to our hostess and she's chatting with her. Probably wondering who designed the ocean for her." Angus was making fun of his sister. Eleanor liked it. "Can I get you ladies a drink?"

"That would be wonderful, thank you," Dede cooed.

"What a lovely piece of man that is!" Pearl remarked as she watched him walk away.

"I don't know, he looks like a serial killer to me," Josephine whispered.

"When did you get here?" asked Eleanor.

"I've been outside admiring the view." Josephine was also watching Angus walk away.

Eleanor was positive her friends had all contracted a rare form of dementia. "I think I'll help Angus with those drinks," she said as she followed after him.

Later, Eleanor made a point of seeking out Fiona to question her about Angus' childhood. Fiona seemed pleased to reminisce about their past. Eleanor kept her wineglass filled and Fiona talked on and on.

"Angus and I grew up in Los Angeles. He was such a cute little boy. All my friends wanted to date him when he was older. I didn't blame them. He was handsome, smart, athletic, and always charming."

"Did he get along with your parents?" Eleanor pried.

"Not always. Our parents were always busy, but we were both very close to our grandparents. Angus adored our grandfather. He was a police officer, you know. It's why Angus chose that profession. I can't say I wanted to be like my grandmother. She was old and wrinkled. I never wanted to be that. Anyway, our childhood was pretty normal. Our father worked in a bank and our mother was an aspiring actress. She did a lot of local theater, but her career never amounted to much. She was beautiful though, and died young, so she will never be old," Fiona sighed.

"Did he play football?" Eleanor wondered if there had been head trauma.

"Did who play football?" Angus had found them.

"Fiona's telling me all your secrets. It's a shame about the bed wetting," Eleanor teased and watched as a puzzled look came over his face.

"Let's eat," was the only comment he made.

After feasting on Dennis' gourmet burgers with special sauce, Angus suggested a walk on the beach.

Eleanor felt a little self-conscious as Angus took her hand in his and lead her down to the village.
The beach was crowded with visitors waiting for the fireworks to begin. It was just good fortune that the weather was warm and there was no wind. Angus led them north toward the tunnel that passed through the point to a more private beach. Navigating the rocks took all Eleanor's concentration but as soon as they reached the other side, Angus turned to her with a serious look in his eyes.

"What are you playing at, Eleanor? I heard you interrogating, Fiona. Do you think she is the serial killer or do you suspect me?"

"Are you the serial killer?" Eleanor asked bluntly before realizing she was alone with him on a secluded beach. How easy it would be for him to squeeze the life out of her and toss her into the outgoing tide.

"Seriously, don't you know me by now?" He looked more hurt than angry.

"There is a great deal I don't know about you. I didn't know you had a sister who stole Frieda's work and claimed it as her own. I don't know how loyal you are to her and her need to avoid aging. I'm not sure if you aren't playing at something with me to gain something for her." Eleanor was now throwing all caution to the wind. She just wanted to know Angus' real intentions.

"What do you know about Frieda's work? What could I take from you for Fiona's benefit? Did Frieda leave you the secret to the fountain of youth?" he asked.

"I know plenty," she sulked.

Angus shook his head. "This is what comes of trying to do the job that trained experts are supposed to do. Eleanor, you are a terrible detective. If I was the killer you seem to think I am, you would be dead by now. Besides, I was not a bed wetter, I didn't mistreat animals, or suffer sex abuse as a child!"

Eleanor suddenly felt foolish and ashamed.

Angus took Eleanor's face gently in his big hands and looked into her worried eyes. "I'm not the bad guy, Ellie," he said softly, "and it's usually women who use poison to kill their victims. Men are more violent. That's why I didn't eat any of your deviled eggs."

Eleanor smiled. She knew he was teasing, because she had seen him eat three of them. "Am I a suspect too?"

"Not any more. I ruled you out when Frieda died. You were truly frightened."

Eleanor's eyes widened in surprise. Never had she once thought she could be a suspect, and now at least two people claimed they thought she could kill someone.

"I guess you never really know someone," she whispered.

"I forgive you, if you forgive me." Angus offered.

"Okay," and they sealed their truce with a tender kiss.

"Let's go back before your detective friends call out a search party," he teased.

As they walked, Eleanor began to wonder if Angus had actually exonerated himself.

"Are you working this case, Angus? I thought the police had given up on it."

"They called me in as a consultant. I've had a lot of experience working homicide. If I can help, I will."

"Are old people still dying?"

"Of course, but some are being helped along. It might be a case of a serial killer who sees herself as an angel of mercy."

"How do you know the difference?"

"There are patterns that the killer uses. I can't tell you, because I know you can only keep a secret if it involves one of your recipes." Angus tried to lighten the mood.

"How do you feel about mercy killing," Eleanor pried.

"It's homicide, Ellie, and that's against the law. No one has the right to decide for another if they should live or die." Angus was firm in his belief.

"But what if that person wants to die?" Eleanor persisted.

"How would you know that?" Angus asked.

"Angus, I know some things that might help in the case."

"I'm sure you think you do, but I am already aware of the Maude Squad, the ads in the newspaper, and the Do Nothings, who by the way suspect you of being the killer." Angus surprised Eleanor again. "Trained professional," he added.

Eleanor had nothing else to say.

Later that night, Eleanor lay in bed thinking. Angus hadn't answered her questions about Fiona stealing from Frieda. He had simply asked more questions. He didn't answer, because he didn't know. Eleanor felt sorry for Fiona because she knew Angus would make it his business to find out. She began to worry that the recipe for dying that she thought was so valuable that others would steal it or even kill for it, might also be a gift that could put her in prison if someone found it in her possession. Enough worrying she told herself and picked up the novel she needed to read for book club and quickly fell asleep.

It was Wednesday, July 5 and for a moment Eleanor thought it was a day of woe. She dreamed about Walter dead in his favorite chair with Feathers lying lifeless on his lap. Today she would call and check on Walter. Maybe he was ill. There was a good chance the lockdown was over. She needed to know when she could visit again. She missed Bootsy. Today of course was a day of woo and Eleanor had no idea what to cook for Angus, especially if Fiona was coming too. Fiona would be happy with a sprig of mint and a glass of water. She really needed to pay bills, finish the book club selection, and there was Frieda's manuscript to read. Really, what did she do with her time!

After her habitual puzzles were completed and she was getting ready for her walk, Nora appeared. It wasn't like Eleanor to forget that Nora came on Wednesdays, but she had a lot on her mind lately.

"Good morning, Mrs. Penrose." Nora always greeted her with the sweetest smile.

"Good morning, Nora, sorry to dash off, but I've lots to do today. Will you start in the office please? I need to get some work done in there." Eleanor wondered if she had given up on making a friend of Nora.

"Certainly, Mrs. Penrose," Nora responded.

Eleanor started her walk and her mind was full of thoughts about dinner. She didn't want to go into town today. Maybe she had some pasta in the pantry, a little bacon, onion, some parmesan cheese—pasta carbonara. She knew there was nothing fresh for a side. She would stop at the store on her way home and pick up something green. Broccoli was a healthy choice.

Climbing back up the hill with the makings for a green salad, thoughts of old people and their pets came into her mind. She remembered Henry Ott and his dog, the old woman in Silverton and her dog, Eva and her little cat. She wondered how many of the serial killer's victims owned pets and how many of them were killed along with their owners.

When she got to the hidey-hole, she took the love note, put it in her pocket and replaced it with a small heart-shaped agate and went on her way. Let someone else wonder who had left a love note.

Nora had finished cleaning the office and the bathrooms and was vacuuming the living room when Eleanor returned. She put her few groceries away and slipped quietly into the office. Studying the information board, Eleanor focused on the list of victims. She didn't know all of them and she didn't know if they had pets or not, but she did know a few. She began to organize a new list.

| Victim | Pet |
| --- | --- |
| Henry Ott | dog |
| Gertie Frank | parakeet |
| Lidia Garfield | ? |
| Howard Welk | ? |
| Edith Allen | ? |
| Edward Eberlee | ? |
| ~~Frieda VanHorn~~ | ~~cat~~ |
| Claire Dobs | ? |
| Adele Grimes | ? |
| Jackie Anne Heart | ? |
| Mrs. Potts | ? |
| Eva Long | cat |
| Enid Ragsdale | ? |

Eleanor heard Nora turn off the vacuum and left the office to inquire about Mrs. Potts.

"Nora, did your Mrs. Potts have a pet?" Eleanor inquired.

"Funny you should ask, she had a silly little ferret. He was such a loyal little guy. When I found her that day he was curled up beside her. It makes me sad to remember it. I think he died too, probably from sorrow."

"Thanks, Nora," and Eleanor returned to her office to add ferret to the list.

By the time Nora had finished cleaning, Eleanor had made a few calls to friends and the local animal shelter and made several additions to her list.

| Victim | Pet |
| --- | --- |
| Henry Ott | dog (d) |
| Gertie Frank | parakeet (d) |
| Lidia Garfield | 2 cats (d) |
| Howard Welk | dog (d) |
| Edith Allen | ? |
| Edward Eberlee | dog (d) |
| ~~Frieda VanHorn~~ | ~~cat~~ |
| Claire Dobs | cat (d) |
| Adele Grimes | goldfish |
| Jackie Anne Heart | ? |
| Mrs. Potts | ferret (d) |
| Eva Long | cat (d) |
| Enid Ragsdale | ? |

Eleanor noticed a disturbing pattern.

She paced around the office and tidied up, paid her bills, called Rosewood Manor to check on Walter and just as she was settling down to read a few pages in her book, the telephone rang.

"Hello, Ellie, it's Angus. I just wanted to know if we are still on for tonight. I thought you might be tired of me."

"I'm never tired of you. I'm actually looking forward to it," Eleanor admitted.

"Fiona is begging off. She says she ate too much yesterday and needs to fast today," Angus scoffed.

"Awww, that's a shame," Eleanor lied.

"Yeah, that's what I thought too. I'll be there at 6:00."

Eleanor finished the novel and had time to bake brownies before Angus arrived promptly at six.

He greeted her with a big bouquet of lilies and a kiss.

"Thank you, these are so beautiful," she exclaimed and rushed to put them in water. "Dinner is almost ready, Angus, pour yourself a drink."

While Eleanor was busy, Angus wandered into the office with his drink and that was where Eleanor found him studying her chart of victims and their pets.

"What is this, Eleanor?" he demanded. "I take it all back. You are a good detective. Do you know who the killer is, too?"

"Do you?" she parried.

"I have a pretty good idea." He sounded sure, but Eleanor thought he was bluffing.

He looked closely at the pictures on the information board. "This is Fiona. I wouldn't recognize the others. They're young. Frieda and Mattie worked with Fiona at the pharmaceutical lab. She told me what she did. I don't think she has any remorse. Sometimes I don't know her. She's greedy, vain, and selfish, but she can be kind and loyal."

"She's your sister, Angus. You love her," Eleanor responded. "She didn't break any laws."

"Only the laws of human decency," he declared. "I'm sorry she used your friend in that way."

"I'm just glad that you didn't know about her connection to Frieda. I feared you might be after one of Frieda's formulas and not after me. Do you think I'm greedy, vain, and selfish too?" Eleanor teased.

"I'm not sure. What formula did Frieda leave you?" Angus looked at her suspiciously. "Could it make you rich? Fiona told me you are only after my money. By the way I have a check for you. It's for Walter's boat." Angus pulled out his wallet and handed Eleanor a check.

"I'm sure Walter would want you to have it, Angus." She looked at the writing on the check. It was dark, strong and angular. She had seen it somewhere before. "You were his favorite fishing companion."

"No, I'm sure you were his favorite, Ellie." Somehow his words were filled with meaning that made Eleanor feel guilty.

Eleanor's eyes filled with unshed tears and she quickly turned to go to kitchen to check on dinner.

After their feast of pasta and salad, brownies, and ice cream, Angus suggested they take a walk. When they got to Jean Scattergoods' house Angus stopped and pulled a heart-shaped agate out of his pocket.

"Does this mean you love me, too," he asked sweetly.

"What?" Eleanor was confused. Suddenly she made the connection between the writing on the check and the love note she found earlier in the hidey-hole. "How do you know about the hidey-hole?"

"Bootsy told me all about it the day we visited Walter, but that's not all." He took a key from his pocket and unlocked the door to Jean's house. "I bought it. Now I can really keep my eye on you."

Eleanor was speechless. Did she need watching?

"Come on in," he said as he opened the door wide. "I was hoping you could help me decorate this place —in a manly style. I think you have impeccable taste."

Eleanor stepped inside. It was totally empty, but the view of the ocean filled every window and the brilliant orange sky was breathtaking. Eleanor didn't know exactly how she felt about it.

"Are you stalking me?" she asked.

"Are you angry?" he asked. "I understand why you won't marry me, Ellie. This is the closest I can get to you. I just hope you don't think it's too intrusive."

"I don't know. I'm not sure how I feel. You have the right to live wherever you want, Angus. I think you would make a wonderful neighbor. You won't have to drive far to come for dinner."

"I figure I can walk home and the neighbors will never know what time I leave your house." Angus had thought of it all. "You're not mad?"

"No, I'm just surprised," Eleanor admitted.

Angus gave her the grand tour of the kitchen and the downstairs bedrooms. She thought about how she would decorate each room to suit him and then they walked slowly back to her place hand in hand.

Thursday, July 6, Eleanor woke from a deep and restful sleep. She didn't remember any dreams, but she knew she had to go to Rosewood Manor to visit Walter.

Arriving just before lunch, Eleanor could not believe how delighted she was to see Feathers. He had free reign in Walter's wing and flew to her immediately landing on her shoulder and telling her, "I love you, Ellie," over and over again. The patients all loved him and followed him around pointing at him as if they had never seen him before.

Walter and Alice walked hand in hand down the long corridor together, paying little attention to the people around them or each other. They seemed to be in their own worlds. Eleanor ate lunch with them and noted how distant and uncommunicative Walter seemed.

After lunch, Eleanor talked with the nurse on the floor about the recent outbreak of norovirus and how Feathers was working out with the patients. By the end of the afternoon, Eleanor was ready to leave Feathers there for another week. She kissed Walter goodbye and drove home. Instead of her Wednesday of Woe, it was a Terrible Thursday, but at least it was over.

As she drove up the hill to her house, she saw Angus' pickup parked at his new house. She thought about stopping but chose to drive home. She couldn't wait to wash off that institutional smell. Later, when she had showered and put on her pajamas, Angus called from her porch.

"Do you feel like company and some pizza?" he asked.

"Sure."

"I'm at your door. Let me in."

Eleanor did not have the energy to worry about how she might look. They ate pizza and snuggled on the couch until sundown and then Angus went home, and Eleanor went to bed.

Friday, July 7, was coffee day. Eleanor woke with the sun flooding her room. She could hardly wait to get to the Boat House to share everything she knew with her friends.

As she drove there she reviewed the happenings of the previous week. What did they know? What should they know? What was better left unsaid?

The Boat House was busy. Tourists were here for the good weather and the start of an early weekend. Eleanor and Josephine were the first to arrive with Pearl and Cleo following soon after. Dede came last but early for her. They drank their coffee and discussed the barbeque at Nancy's house. The main topic was Fiona and her weird California culture. Eleanor reviewed her frank discussion with Mattie about the Maude Squad. They laughed about being suspects but got quiet when Eleanor disclosed her concerns about Angus being the serial killer.

"You can't really believe that!" countered Josephine.

"No, of course not, but I had doubts when Mattie told me about Fiona's betrayal of Frieda."

"Can you tell us about Frieda's secret then?" prompted Josephine. "It seems that Fiona's betrayal of Frieda doesn't make Angus a serial killer. The two things are not related. You're not being objective, Eleanor."

"He might not be a serial killer, but he could be using me to get something for Fiona—something Frieda left me." Eleanor sighed. "Angus is still working the case as a consultant, so they believe a serial killer is at work here. He can't tell me anything, but I've discovered an interesting pattern. Several of the victims had pets that were also killed."

"Didn't we already know that?" asked Pearl. "Remember the Silverton lady and her dog and Henry Ott and his dog were both found dead."

"Right, Angus didn't say, but I figured it out myself. The MO of the serial killer is to kill the person and their pet. If there is no pet, they call it a natural death. They find the victim sitting in a chair with the pet on their lap. Frieda's was a natural death because her cat was still alive. Eva Long's cat was dead, and Eva had absolutely no connection with the Maude Squad. What do you make of that?"

"The Maude Squad is a red herring," Dede mused.

"The serial killer has a trigger that involves old people and their pets," added Josephine.

"Maybe the killer couldn't catch Frieda's cat," offered Cleo.

"Angus thinks it is a woman, because they are more likely to use poison. He suspects an angel of mercy type of serial killer," reported Eleanor. She wondered if she had overstepped her bounds by revealing too much, but decided knowledge was power and the more her friends knew the more empowered they would be.

"This is giving me chills and goosebumps," Pearl confessed as she shivered.

"Do you think Angus knows who it is?" asked Dede.

"If he does, he isn't telling." Eleanor sighed.

"Even if he suspects someone, he would need proof that would stand up in court. It must be very difficult to catch a serial killer unless you actually catch them in the act," noted Josephine.

"Who do you think it could be?" Cleo asked. "Do we know anyone who is a woman, feels sorry for old people and their pets, and has access to pentobarbital?"

"I would guess a doctor or a nurse who has had a psychotic snap," Josephine offered.

"We kind of thought that when we figured it was the Do Nothings," reminded Cleo.

"I'm sure it isn't them, but Mattie could have been lying. If she was, she's an excellent actress." Eleanor remarked. "Maybe we need to do what Angus suggests and leave it up to the trained professionals."

"Poop, that's no fun!" exclaimed Cleo.

On the drive home, Eleanor realized she had not told her friends about Angus buying Jean Scattergoods' house. She spotted his truck outside the house and stopped to check on him.

"Hello, Angus," she called. The door wasn't locked so she went inside. Angus was sanding down the hardwood floors with a loud sanding machine and wearing ear protection. When he saw her, he turned it off.

"Hi, Ellie, I'm just making a few minor improvements. What are you up to?"

"Absolutely nothing, would you like some help? I'm pretty good with a paintbrush," she offered.

"Hey, I won't refuse."

"Where's Fiona?" Eleanor spoke as she looked around the empty room.

"She's on a time out. It's what happens when someone is very naughty and embarrassed by their bad behavior."

"I see," Eleanor did not believe a word of it. Fiona probably didn't like getting her hands dirty. "I'll go home and change into my grubbies and be right back."

Eleanor was better than her word. Not only did she return with paintbrush in hand, she also brought a picnic hamper filled with delicious treats; ham and cheese sandwiches, fresh Oregon strawberries, chocolate chip cookies, and a chilled bottle of white wine.

Angus worked on sanding the floor while Eleanor painted the downstairs bedroom. It was a beautiful summer day that allowed her to open the windows wide and let in the gentle sea breeze. She knew when Angus finished because she could hear the cry of gulls. Later when her job was done, she washed her brushes and went upstairs to see if Angus was ready for lunch.

The first thing to hit her was the smell of the sealant he had used to cover the floors. Then she noticed that he had painted her in and closed the door. There was no way she could reach the exit without walking on his newly restored floors. He might be a good detective, but he certainly hadn't thought this through.

Eleanor went back downstairs, popped the screen off one of the windows, crawled outside, and used the outside stairs to get to the deck. Angus was in his truck talking on his cell phone. As soon as he saw her, Eleanor could see the surprise register on his face.

"Oh, Ellie, I'm sorry, I can't believe I forgot you were downstairs!" His apology sounded sincere.

"I think you might need a time out," she put on a mock mad face. "Are you ready for lunch, or did you forget about that too?"

"I was totally thinking about getting this equipment back to the rental company. I was just about to drive off. How did you get out?" Angus got out of the truck. "You didn't walk on the floor, did you?"

"Are you trying to kill me?" Eleanor queried. "That sealant is very potent stuff. It might be affecting your brain. I escaped through the window. Now you'll have to put the screen back on."

"I am so sorry!" He exclaimed once again and pulled her into his embrace for a big bear hug before going downstairs to fix the screen. Eleanor remembered leaving the picnic hamper on the counter in the kitchen. There was no way she could get to it now until the floors were dry and that could take days.

"Our lunch is in the kitchen," Eleanor lamented when Angus appeared once more.

"Oh, do you want to ride into town with me and grab some lunch there?" he offered.

"No, I'm tired. I think I'll go home and take a nap," Eleanor felt a little of love's luster growing dull.

That night before Eleanor went to bed, Angus called to apologize once more. He seemed to realize his mistake may have been a costly one.

Eleanor spent her evening making a new list of medical personnel she knew who might have access to pentobarbital.

Eleanor woke with the feeling that something wasn't right. It was Saturday, July 8, she needed to go grocery shopping, maybe pick up some new towels, walk, and work on her list of suspects. She wondered if the others from her coffee group were even thinking of the serial killer. Perhaps she would call them and pick their brains. Angus. Was he going to be working at his beach house today? Would she see him when she went for her walk? He was what didn't feel right. There had been a shift. He was distracted. Eleanor thought it must be Fiona. She'd like to be a fly on the wall at their house. As fond as she was of Angus, she couldn't stop her mind from suspecting him of being something sinister. What if he and Fiona were a team of serial killers? What if they killed old people because of their relationship with their grandparents? Maybe they had abused them. Maybe Angus had been a bed wetter. Maybe he was a liar. Fiona wasn't normal, that was for sure. Angus was charming, but so was Ted Bundy. He might still be after Frieda's formula. Just because he said he didn't know about it didn't mean that was true. Eleanor decided she would take a break from Angus. Too much of a good thing isn't good at all.

Eleanor decided to walk the trail behind her house and not risk seeing Angus. As she breathed in the fresh sea air infused with a hint of pine, her mind began to clear and her heart to soften. What had Angus done to make her suspect him? She knew him. He was kind, smart, and funny. She was being silly.

Later, when she drove by Angus' house, she noticed his truck was not there. The floors needed time to dry. Eleanor could put him out of her mind for today.

After all her errands were done, Eleanor sat on the couch with a light snack and Frieda's manuscript. As interesting as Frieda was, her storytelling left a lot to be desired. It wasn't any wonder Eleanor kept dozing off while she read, but she was determined to finish it and see if there were any other interesting facts to be discovered. She read about her childhood growing up in Singapore, her capture and incarceration by the Japanese during WWII. Frieda returned to Amsterdam and then moved to the United States to study nursing and became a brilliant chemist. She was hired to work for the pharmaceutical company where she met Mattie and Fiona. Her description of the falling out was not detailed, but this is where Eleanor found a sketch of the plant that Frieda had given Eleanor. It had the same ruffled leaves with the pretty pink trumpet flower that grew outside her house—the one that she couldn't kill. The following two pages were filled with numbers, letters, and signs Eleanor could not understand. This must be the secret formula for the poison in the vial. She wondered if the plant had anything to do with it. Maybe that was the secret ingredient. She finished the manuscript with Frieda leaving California for Oregon where she met and married her husband. They raised four children on a dairy farm, and then moved to Waterton where Frieda worked as a nurse—nothing interesting here. Eleanor was wondering how she would finish the final chapter of Frieda's life when the doorbell rang.

Angus stood outside her door, picnic hamper in hand. Eleanor took a deep breath and opened the door.

"Are you still mad?" he asked softly.

When Eleanor did not respond he continued, "I managed to rescue your picnic basket. The sandwiches had to go, but the rest looks good. I found some replacements at Mrs. Kelly's grocery and thought maybe you'd like to share a loaf of bread, some cheese, and wine with me."

Eleanor opened the door wider to welcome him inside. "Let's eat on the deck," she suggested as she led him through the house and out the sliding doors.

Angus opened the hamper and began to set out a lovely picnic.

"I guess we need glasses for the wine and a knife to cut the bread," she noted and went back inside to retrieve them.

Angus followed her. It was clear to him that she was still holding a grudge. As he passed by the open office door, he noted the list of suspects she'd added to her information board. It surprised him to see that it was similar to the one he had at home.

They returned to the deck, Eleanor sliced the bread and cut the cheese while Angus opened the wine and poured generous amounts into their glasses.

"I never thought you were the type to hold on to a hurt," he remarked. "I understand it's a fault I have to get caught up in my work and ignore the women in my life."

Eleanor held her tongue. She knew the value of a pregnant pause. This was getting good.

"It's the reason Margo left me. There just wasn't enough time for her when my work was so intense. I thought I could have a relationship with you now that I'm not working 24/7 on homicide cases, but I'm making the same mistake. Consulting on this case is consuming me and I'm sorry."

"I think I understand the consuming part," Eleanor admitted. "Maybe I can help you solve the case. Then we could continue an ordinary life."

Angus shook his head, "Ellie, it takes a long time to catch a serial killer. Sometimes they're never caught. I don't want you involved. You don't seem to understand how dangerous they can be. This isn't some kind, merciful person acting out of goodness, but a sick, twisted subhuman, killing innocent people. I know how you see the world and I don't want you to see what I see."

"Seriously, you believe I don't think that maybe you are the killer? You think I don't have some dark and sinister suspicions about why you are here. I'm not eating this food or drinking this wine because it might be poisoned."

Angus smiled and his dimples appeared like sunshine on a cloudy day. He took a big sip of wine and bit into a slice of cheese.

"I don't believe you, Ellie, because I didn't see my name on your list of suspects," Angus knew he had won the argument when Eleanor sipped her wine.

"This is my wine, you know," she stated.

"Okay, do you forgive me?" he asked in all seriousness.

"Do you mean for locking me in a house filled with toxic fumes, or forgetting I was even there? Are you going to continue to ignore me because this case may never be solved? Will you be distracted until it is?"

"You're going to have to forgive me for all of it. It takes a great deal of patience to solve a case like this, but I think we are getting close. It's a matter of getting sufficient proof. I promise to devote myself to you entirely when it's closed." Angus raised his hand as if taking an oath.

"Fine," Eleanor responded. "I don't need your entire devotion. I need my space too. Just be present when you *are* with me."

"So can we kiss and make up?" Angus prodded.

When Angus left, Eleanor's lips felt raw from kissing. When she went into her office for lip balm, she was surprised to see three new names added to her list of suspects.

Eleanor woke early Sunday morning with an idea. It was July 9, she had nothing to do other than read the Sunday paper and lounge around in her bathrobe all day. It was the perfect day for a stakeout. She called Cleo, Pearl, and Josephine and told them of her plan. Dede would be in church. Eleanor was excited as she brewed coffee for her thermos and drove into town where she rented a van with tinted windows. She left her car at the rental agency and met the others in the parking lot of Fred Meyers. They piled into the van and drove to Dede's house hoping her Sunday service was over. Pearl raced in and moments later came out with Dede and a bag of speculaas cookies.

"Oh my goodness, this is so exciting!" Dede exclaimed.

"What do you know about stakeouts?" asked Josephine.

"I Googled it," said Eleanor. "The most important thing is to be unnoticed. Then we need to conduct a spot check of our location by driving by once and getting a perspective before we set up our position."

"Who are we staking out?" asked Cleo.

"There's a list in my bag," directed Eleanor.

"There are so many suspects!" exclaimed Pearl. "Where do we start?"

"Look at the last three names," Eleanor said.

"Of course," Josephine looked at the others and they all nodded in agreement. "It makes perfect sense that the killer would be a veterinarian."

"Why didn't we think of that before?" asked Dede.

"There are more than three vets in town," Pearl noted.

"Yes, but only three women," added Cleo. "Eleanor, you are a genius!"

"Not really, Angus gave me a hint. It might not even be them. It could be someone who works in the office of a vet—anyone with access to pentobarbital." Eleanor admitted.

"So where do we start?" asked Dede.

"I've never liked Dr. Bledslow," offered Cleo. "She asked Steve once why I was looking at our dog's underside."

Pearl began to giggle.

"He had a growth there. I thought she was very unprofessional," Cleo explained.

"I know where she lives, and it isn't far." Eleanor didn't like her either.

Dr. Bledslow lived in town. Eleanor drove by, scoped out the house, turned around, and parked on the opposite side of the street.

"What now?" asked Pearl.

"Now we wait and watch for suspicious activity." Eleanor turned off the motor.

They ate cookies and drank coffee. It wasn't long before they all had to go to the bathroom, so Eleanor drove to the nearest gas station.

"This isn't very exciting. I don't even think Dr. Bledslow was home," Pearl remarked as they climbed back into the van.

"You'd think veterinarians would stay home on Sunday," offered Eleanor.

"Let's check out Dr. Johnson," Josephine suggested.

"I really like her. I can't imagine her being a serial killer," Cleo whined.

"That's the point." Josephine schooled them on the finer points of the sick and twisted minds of serial killers and how normal they could appear.

"Okay, where does she live?" asked Eleanor.

Cleo gave directions that proved wrong. Pearl Googled her address and they finally wound up driving down a long private driveway east of town.

"I think we have been noticed," Dede said a little sarcastically.

"I'll turn around and go back out," Eleanor responded. "At least I can see her looking out the window, so we know she is home."

"Thank goodness for the tinted windows," Dede moaned. "I can see the headlines already: **Mayor Arrested for Stalking Local Vet.**"

"I'll park over here behind this hedge," Eleanor explained. "We can see her if she leaves her house."

"No one drink any more coffee," ordered Cleo.

"Good idea," said Pearl who already had to go again but was determined to hold it.

It wasn't long before Pearl couldn't hold it any longer and got out of the van to relieve herself.

Unfortunately, that was when Dr. Johnson drove by in her station wagon. She stopped at the end of the driveway and continued on toward town.

"I tried to hurry. I hope she didn't notice us," Pearl was breathing hard from her run back to the van.

"It's okay, Pearl. We don't want to follow too close behind her. This road only goes back to town anyway," Eleanor reassured her.

They followed a safe distance behind her until she turned into the Fred Meyer parking lot.

"I'm going in," said Dede.

When she came out she had a bag of steaks. "What's a stakeout without steak?" she joked. "Let's go back to my house and I'll cook dinner."

No one disagreed.

Eleanor tossed and turned all night and dreamed of car chases and pink flowers. When she fed the flowers to Walter he was cured, but when Alice ate them she died. Fiona appeared in the dream eating the seeds and grew younger, and when Angus ate the leaves he turned to light and disappeared. When she finally opened her eyes, she had a hard time remembering what day of the week it was. Monday, July 10, wasn't she supposed to visit Walter yesterday? What must Bootsy think? Who was distracted now? She hadn't even read the Sunday paper, but had wasted the entire day chasing wild geese. Oh well, it had been fun. What was that quote from John Lennon? Something about the time you enjoy wasting isn't time wasted. She would just go with that. She would read the Sunday paper today, and there was book club tonight at Mercedes' house. Maybe she would visit Walter tomorrow. That would really shake things up at Rosewood Manor. She'd never been there before on a Tuesday.

Eleanor took her walk down to the beach, passing Angus' house without even thinking about him. When she climbed back up the hill she realized she hadn't even noticed if his truck had been there or not. It was not. She wondered what he was doing and how he spent his time when he wasn't with her. She wondered if living so near to him would be a problem and felt just a little territorial in her tiny village. Nancy came out to greet her and they made plans to have lunch later.

The day whizzed by and before Eleanor noticed, it was time for book club.

Mercedes lived alone in a small house in town. It was cozy and welcoming. The members gathered in the front room and began to chat while they waited for everyone to arrive. Several cats roamed through the room and Eleanor could hear birds singing from another room. She wondered how Mercedes kept them from killing each other.

When everyone was there, they began their discussion of the book. It was a simple book, and everyone had enjoyed it.

"The main character was so sad when her pet died," Mercedes observed. "The world is full of such suffering. It breaks my heart. If you could end suffering, would you?"

"That kind of suffering is part of life. Because our pets have such short life spans, they teach us about growing old and ultimately about death," Kimberley suggested.

"It isn't exactly the same kind of suffering as physical pain. You know the kind brought on by diseases or horrendous accidents. I would consider ending that kind of suffering, because there seems to be no purpose for that other than suffering itself." Wren rarely spoke but tonight she freely expressed her opinion.

"Emotional suffering is just as real as the physical kind and often worse because the person doing the suffering is often alone and not medicated." Josephine always sounded like the expert she was.

"Yes, and animals feel emotional pain just as humans do, suffering grief when their owners die and separation anxiety when they are left alone. Just imagine the suffering they must go through when their owners are angry with them. They don't have other friends to turn to as many of us do." Dolly was an advocate for those in the animal world.

"But pain and suffering often do teach us something," argued Dede. "Sometimes when we wrong someone and they make us suffer, we never do it again. The same thing applies to animals."

"Animals may not understand death. They only feel the ache of loss. People don't always take that into consideration when they get puppies late in life. Who would adopt a child late in life when they know the chances of dying before that child is grown is almost a certainty?" Mercedes asked.

"There are rules about adoption. It's difficult to adopt a child after the age of 40," Kimberley informed the group.

"Sadly, that's not the case for pets," sighed Mercedes.

"I know I would not get a puppy at my age," said Pearl. "I just don't have the energy anymore."

"Me either," admitted Cleo. "There are so many older pets that need homes."

"But kittens are so cute," Josephine almost purred, "and no one knows how long they or their pets are going to live. I say get a pet and love it until you can't."

"So selfish," whispered Mercedes so only Eleanor could hear. "I wonder if animals had the power, would they put their suffering owners down?"

"So self-righteous and judgmental," Eleanor thought but said nothing.

Several times Dede tried to bring the discussion back to the book and its theme of racial inequality and every time Mercedes managed to bring it back to the topic of suffering. It was getting late when finally, Wren asked if she could help with the dessert and she and Mercedes went into the kitchen. Eleanor looked at her friends sitting across the room and saw Dede roll her eyes while Cleo just shook her head. When they returned with coffee and cake, Eleanor noticed that Josephine and Pearl both abstained. The others drank the coffee and ate the cake, and no one died. Was Eleanor being paranoid or was something strange happening here? She had always liked Mercedes and never noticed how strongly she felt about old people and their pets. Was it because her name had been the last one on the list of suspects?

Pearl finally announced her choice for the next book, and everyone rose to leave, thanking Mercedes for her hospitality.

238

It had grown dark outside and the members of the coffee group walked to the corner and began to whisper together.

"Do you think she is okay?" asked Dede.

"That was really strange," Cleo agreed.

"Her name was on your list, Eleanor," Pearl whispered. "Do you think we are in danger?"

"There is no proof whatsoever that she has done anything. You are all hysterical," Josephine said sounding brave, but she looked over her shoulder at Mercedes' window and then hurried to her car.

The others shrugged their shoulders, got in their cars, and drove away.

Eleanor had parked around the corner and as she walked to her car she noticed a van that had been parked across the street turn and slowly follow her without turning on its lights. The hair on her neck stood up and all her instincts told her to run. Instead, she grabbed her car key as if it were a weapon and picked up the pace.

When the van pulled up beside her she heard a familiar voice call out to her softly, "Eleanor, get in." The door opened, and Eleanor obeyed.

Angus sat in the driver's seat. He silently rolled down the street, turned around and resumed his position where he could observer Mercedes house. Eleanor realized he was on a stakeout.

"What are you doing here?" he asked.

"It's book club," she answered innocently.

"I see."

"How long have you been out here?" she asked.

"You mean tonight?" he asked. "Just a couple of hours, but I've been watching her off and on for a week."

"Do you think she is the serial killer?" she asked but knew the answer before he could say.

"Maybe," he wasn't giving anything away. "What do you know about her?"

Eleanor took her time, "She's smart, kind, lives alone with lots of cats and birds. I don't think she has ever been married. She's younger than most of the rest of us in book club, maybe early sixties. I really don't know much more about her personal life, but she is an excellent vet. She takes care of all my friend's small animals, including Feathers. Oh, last month she went to Mexico to pick up supplies for her clinic and tonight she acted very strange."

"What do you mean by strange?" He was very calm, and Eleanor realized he must have a great deal more patience than she and her coffee friends had to keep vigil for a week.

"She just kept talking about animals and pets and how old people shouldn't have puppies or kittens since they die and can't take care of them. She wanted to rid the world of suffering. It wasn't even on topic with our book, but she wouldn't let it go." Eleanor could hear how incriminating it sounded as she said it.

"She must relate to those poor lost animals," Angus said, "she was raised by her grandparents who died when she was 10. After that she spent eight years in nine different foster homes where she was most likely molested and abused. It's unclear how she came to be so kind to animals, but she clearly fits the profile. She is an angel of mercy, even her name means mercy."

"What are you going to do?" Eleanor asked.

"I'm going to watch her until she makes a mistake and then I'm going to catch her." He seemed very confident.

They sat quietly for several minutes watching Mercedes' house. When her lights went off, Eleanor decided it was time for her to go home. Just as she was opening the car door, Angus reached over to stop her. Mercedes was leaving her house. She got in her car and pulled away. Angus followed a safe distance behind with Eleanor an unwilling passenger.

The small town of Waterton was rolled up tight for the night. Even the traffic lights were blinking reds because there weren't any cars on the main street. Angus was very careful to remain unnoticed. They followed her to the veterinary clinic where she slipped inside, turned on the lights, and from what they could see from across the street, checked on some animals that were there for the night. After about 20 minutes, she came out carrying a small package. She got in her car and drove back to her house. The only suspicious thing was the package and the fact that she drove by Dede's house on her way home which was out of her way. She actually drove around Dede's block two times. Angus pulled over, turned off his lights and waited for Mercedes' bedroom light to come on and then go off before he declared it safe for Eleanor to get in her car and go home.

The entire evening had creeped Eleanor out. All the way home, she kept her eyes on the rearview mirror, afraid that Mercedes had seen her and was following her. Only one car came up behind her and it turned off at Bayside. She was never so glad to get into her house and lock her doors, checking each one not only twice but three times. When she finally got into her bed, she was wide awake and imagining a dozen ways Mercedes could kill her and her friends along with their pets. She worried that Dede had said something to set her off but couldn't think of anything. Josephine would be the most likely victim. Mercedes had said she was selfish for wanting to have kittens, but Josephine lived miles up the river. Eleanor was the oldest of her group and the only one who lived alone. What if Mercedes thought she was suffering because of Walter and decided she needed to be put down. The telephone ringing caused Eleanor to jump.

"Are you okay?" It was Angus.

"Yes," she answered but it was a lie. "I'm home, the doors are locked and I'm in bed, but I don't think I can sleep."

"Do you want company?" The question held a hint of innuendo.

"No, yes, no, I don't want you driving out here late at night leaving Fiona all alone. What if Mercedes saw you and tries to take you out? Do you have a pet?"

"You are the only pet I have," he murmured in an attempt to take her mind off scary thoughts.

"Are you flirting with me?" Eleanor accused.

"Maybe, do you like it?" he asked.

"Yes, I think I can go to sleep now. Thanks for calling Angus. Now I can dream about my flirty new neighbor instead of a serial killer."

"Good night, Ellie, I'll call you in the morning."

Eleanor turned off her bedroom light, but her mind didn't turn off and her eyes didn't close for a long time.

When day broke, Eleanor was still asleep. She didn't know that another person in Waterton had died during the night, along with her little dog. Evidently it wasn't Dede's house that Mercedes had been scoping out, but her friend and neighbor Nellie Arnest whose husband had died recently. Nobody would know about Nellie for almost two days. On Wednesday Dede and Nellie had planned to go shopping together in the valley. Dede would find her friend sitting in her favorite chair with her little poodle curled in her lap.

Eleanor woke late. It was Tuesday, July 11. Today she would visit Walter, but first she planned to pay a call on Bootsy. Maybe she would like to go shopping with Eleanor or visit the zoo. Eleanor didn't want to spend too much time with Walter. She planned to pop in and bring Feathers home with her. She really missed that bird.

It was just what Eleanor needed to get her mind off the ugly that kept creeping in all night. She picked Bootsy up and whisked her off to the zoo where they totally enjoyed all the animals, especially the otters. They rode the zoo train, and then ate a lunch of hot dogs and elephant ears while they watched a show starring the birds of prey out on the grass.

"So how is your summer going?" Eleanor asked.

"Pretty boring really, mom and dad are both busy all the time. I really miss Granny Scattergoods and the beach. I wish she hadn't died," Bootsy lamented.

Eleanor wanted to invite Bootsy to come stay with her in the worst way but didn't want her anywhere near Waterton or Sand Beach until this murder business was put to rest. She was afraid to even mention the idea because who knew how long it would take to actually catch the killer. Today Eleanor just wanted to think about happy things.

"You know Angus bought your granny's house," Eleanor mentioned.

"He told me it was a secret." Bootsy seemed relieved that Eleanor knew. "I told him about the hidey-hole. I hope you don't mind."

"No, it really belongs to him now. He left a note in it for me, of course it isn't as fun as the stuff we put in there, but Angus is a good guy." Eleanor felt a tinge of sadness. "Let's take one of those elephant ears to Walter. I bet he'd enjoy it."

Rosewood Manor was just the same as always. Eleanor didn't notice anything amiss even though no one knew she was coming. Walter looked clean and well groomed. Bootsy gave Alice a big hug and took her outside while Eleanor and Walter walked the long hall to his room. She noticed he shuffled his feet as he walked. It was something she hadn't noticed before. When they got to his room, he lay on his bed exhausted and fell into a deep sleep. Eleanor told him all about Angus, the coffee group stakeout, and the scary night of following Mercedes. Walter began to snore. She kissed him gently and left the elephant ear on his bedside table before she went looking for Feathers.

Bootsy had left Alice watching television. Together they packed up Feathers, promising to bring him back for a visit soon. Then Eleanor took Bootsy home.

The drive to Sand Beach was long and quiet even with Feathers in the backseat. Eleanor revisited her day with Bootsy and felt renewed even though she was tired beyond words. She couldn't wait to soak in the tub, drink a big glass of red wine, and sleep without dreams.

It's Wednesday, July 12, Eleanor thought as she opened her eyes and stretched. It's wonderful what a good night's sleep can do for a person. Today Eleanor would prepare a grand and glorious meal for Angus and maybe Fiona. It was the day of woo and she felt like grilling something fabulous like marinated Mongolian pork chops. Angus would love it.

She reached for her phone to check the caller list. Angus said he would call yesterday, but he had not called in the morning or last night. Could he still be watching Mercedes? Maybe Fiona was done with time out and they were spending time together. She thought about calling him but didn't feel comfortable doing that even in this day and age when women called men all the time. She was still old school.

Eleanor remembered Nora and quickly got out of bed. Feathers greeted her warmly and it was as if he had never been gone. They spent several minutes in deep conversation, she stroked and fed him, and then readied herself for a long meditative walk on the beach. Before she left the house, she picked up a few things she had left lying around. Nora didn't clean up clutter. As she tidied up she remembered Frieda's manuscript. Wasn't she reading it on the couch? Where was it? She didn't remember seeing it lately. Maybe she had put it in the office. She checked the office—nothing. It was not in the safe or by her bed. Eleanor was disturbed. She looked under the couch, between the cushions, and even under her bed. It just wasn't there. She tried hard to remember when she was reading it. She remembered the pink flowers and the pages of detailed formulae. She remembered thinking about writing the final chapter. The doorbell rang and even though Eleanor knew it was Nora, Angus came to mind. He had interrupted her plans for the final chapter too. She had left the manuscript on the couch when Angus had arrived and now it was missing. Eleanor felt her heart chip just a little and then it began to crack.

If having a cracked heart wasn't enough, when Eleanor returned from her supposedly peaceful walk on the beach, Dede called to inform her of Nellie's death. Eleanor got in her car and drove to Dede's house.

Pearl and Cleo were already there offering comfort and sympathy in the form of cake and Lemoncello. Josephine arrived shortly after Eleanor and together the coffee friends shared what they knew and developed a plan to catch a killer.

"Let's just ask Mercedes if she is the killer," suggested Cleo. "It worked with Mattie."

Everyone ignored her.

"Do you think it could be Angus?" asked Pearl who hated to see a good man go to waste.

"The manuscript is missing. It has a formula in it for a drug that can kill and leave no trace. Fiona knew about it and possibly told Angus who had an opportunity and motive to take it if he is the killer." It hurt Eleanor to think she had been used, but she needed to know the truth. "He also added the names of the three women vets on my chart of suspects, possibly to throw us off."

"If what you think is true, Eleanor, now that he has the formula, there is no reason to continue to romance you," Josephine surmised.

"Right, so why not accept his marriage proposal and see what he says?" Cleo suggested with delight. "If he agrees, he's not the killer, but if he hesitates, then we know he's guilty."

"Yes, but guilty of what?" Pearl wanted to know, "Killing people is different than using someone to get what you want."

"He has been cooler lately. He said he would call and then he didn't. He claims he's distracted by the case." Eleanor didn't want Angus to be the killer. "How could he live here so long and not be suspected if he's a murderer?"

"It's who he kills. Remember old people die and it's natural. No one thinks murder," Josephine reminded them.

"We don't want to put Eleanor in danger," warned Dede. "She's the only one who lives alone and far out of town too."

"Now that he has a home there, it would be easy for him to get to her house on foot without possible witnesses," Pearl noted.

"Maybe you should move into town for a while, or visit your daughter," suggested Cleo.

"You could stay with me, I have an extra bedroom," offered Josephine.

"No, no, that's not going to help. What if the killer is Mercedes? We can't forget her odd behavior the other night. She has access to the drug. She fits the profile, and I really don't want it to be Angus." Eleanor put her head in her hands.

"We can't give him a pass," Josephine cautioned. "He fits the profile too. It's not uncommon for serial killers to be part of the law enforcement community, and if he has what he wants, he may be ready to be rid of you, Eleanor."

Eleanor had come to comfort Dede in the loss of her friend, but now she was afraid.

"He's coming for dinner tonight," she said. "Maybe I should kill him before he kills me."

"Maybe you should invite Mercedes," Cleo suggested. "That way we could get them both."

"Yeah, but what if it's someone else?" Dede wondered aloud.

"What if it's Fiona!" Pearl exclaimed. "I don't like her at all."

"Has anyone seen Fiona lately?" asked Eleanor. "Maybe they're a team and he killed her because she did something he didn't like."

"I haven't seen Fiona since Nancy's party," Dede said.

"Does anyone know if his ex-wife is still alive?" Pearl inquired. "Maybe he did her in too."

"Do we even know for sure if Fiona is his sister?" Cleo speculated, "Maybe she's another one of his wives."

"Well, so far we have a lot of theories but no plan," moaned Josephine. "If catching a serial killer was easy, the police would have done it already."

"Let's all go to Nancy Wilson's house tonight and do a stakeout from there. If Eleanor gets into trouble, we can rush over and save the day." Cleo felt inspired.

"How will we know she's in trouble?" asked Pearl.

"She'll signal us by calling us on her phone, or by putting that American flag out on the deck," suggested Cleo.

"What if I just scream? Do you think you could hear me?" asked Eleanor.

"Leave the windows open or stay on the deck. Can we see your deck from Nancy's?" asked Dede.

"I don't know," Eleanor admitted.

"Go get your groceries, Eleanor," ordered Josephine. "We'll check with Nancy. If we don't like what we see, we'll show up."

"Be sure to get enough to feed us all," Cleo said.

Angus was punctual as always. He brought yellow daisies and a bag that held a bottle of Crown Royal to restock Eleanor's liquor cabinet. He gave her a sweet peck on the cheek and made his own drink.

"Can I make one of these for you?" he asked.

"I don't know, *can* you?" Eleanor knew she was being a brat but couldn't help it.

"*May* I make one of these for you?" He didn't seem bothered by her correction.

"Yes, please." Eleanor went to get a vase for the flowers.

"I'm sorry I didn't call you yesterday. I got caught up in more projects at the house and noticed that you weren't home. Did you visit Walter?" Angus eyed Eleanor from under his bushy brows.

As if on cue, Feathers flew into the room protesting Angus' appearance by landing on his head and flapping his wings while squawking, "Intruder, intruder."

"You don't need to answer that," Angus said, ducking and covering his eyes in a protective gesture.

Eleanor couldn't help but laugh at the big gray bird's antics. She had missed his silliness.

"It's all right that you didn't call. I'm not some love-sick teeny bopper waiting by the phone, and surely neither of us wants to feel obligated to account for our every minute." Eleanor took the marinating pork chops out of the refrigerator and Angus, freeing himself from the unruly Feathers, took them from her and placed them on the counter.

"I want to feel obligated to you, and when I don't know where you are, I worry about you."

Eleanor ignored his tender comments, picked up the pork chops and walked out to the grill. Angus was familiar with the barbecue and took over while she returned to work on the sugar snap peas. When she came back outside, she brought their drinks which they sipped in an uncomfortable silence. Eleanor walked around trying to see Nancy's deck.

"If you're trying to see if your friends are at Nancy's I can tell you. I followed them all the way from town and watched them get out of the car. Are you missing some kind of party?"

Eleanor should have known her friends' sleuthing was no match for Angus' powers of observation.

"I don't know what you are talking about," she lied. "You must know that this morning Dede found her neighbor, Nettie Arnest, dead in her chair with her dog on her lap."

"Is that what's upset you?" he asked.

"Doesn't it upset you?" she snapped.

"Of course it does. I just don't want you to be upset with me."

In that moment Eleanor saw Angus, not as a strong, confident older man, but as an insecure little boy hungry for approval. She felt a tenderness for him that made all thoughts of serial killers melt away. This was her friend of several years, who had eaten at her table hundreds of times, befriended her husband, laughed with her, and wiped away her tears.

Eleanor wrapped her arms around him and simply held him until the pork chops began to burn.

After they feasted on the charred pork, sugar snap peas, and chocolate cake, a cool breeze drove them inside to snuggle on the couch. Angus shifted his weight to get comfortable as Eleanor watched the fog roll in.

"What's this?" he asked as he pulled Frieda's manuscript folder out from under the couch cushion.

"Where did that come from?" Eleanor couldn't hide her surprise. "I swear I looked under every cushion for that!"

"Well it must have slipped down along the side here. It gave me a nasty poke," Angus said, rubbing his hip.

"Sorry," Eleanor apologized as she took the file into her office, quickly checked to see that it was all there, and slipped it into a drawer.

"Do you need ice?" she asked when she returned.

"Only in my drink," he responded.

They sat companionably and sipped their drinks. Neither of them wanted to talk about serial killers. Angus put his arm around her and held her close.

"I'm so tired, Ellie," he murmured in her hair. "I'm tired of all the darkness in my life. I don't want to do this work anymore. I'd like this moment to go on forever—just the two of us together."

"I love you, Angus." Eleanor snuggled closer.

It wasn't long before she nodded off with her head on Angus' chest.

Meanwhile at Nancy's house, the group of friends had come up with a plan.

"We can set a trap and see who comes to take the bait," Cleo said.

"Let's go over this once again," Dede insisted. "This could be very dangerous."

"Okay, Eleanor has to be the bait. She takes Feathers to Mercedes for a check-up and laments about Walter and how sad she is, yadda, yadda, yadda. Then we watch Mercedes 24/7 and follow her when she comes for Eleanor," Cleo recapped.

"Maybe one of us should be with Eleanor so she isn't alone," suggested Pearl.

"What if she doesn't come right away?" Dede wondered. We could be on a stakeout for weeks.

"What is it that will trigger her need to kill?" Nancy was now in on the plan.

"Hopefully, the visit with Eleanor and Feathers will trigger it. Eleanor is elderly, she lives alone and has a pet. We'll make sure she says all the right things. Let's write a script for her." Josephine got out her pen.

"Does anyone know what's going on at Eleanor's with Angus?" asked Pearl.

"We can't really trust Eleanor to be objective," cautioned Josephine. "She's in love."

"It's too foggy to see anything. The lights are on and there hasn't been any screaming or phone calls," Nancy noted. "I'll send Dennis over to see if everything is okay. He can go borrow a cup of sugar."

"Very original," smiled Cleo. "I'm sure Angus is too dumb to see through that one."

"How are we baiting Angus?" Pearl asked.

"If he is indeed watching Mercedes, he should follow her to Eleanor's," Josephine explained.

"We should investigate his activities too," Dede suggested. "He isn't on a stakeout tonight."

"Let's follow him tomorrow, before Eleanor goes to Mercedes and see what he does all day," Josephine said.

"Maybe Eleanor should take Feathers to all three vets and see if any one of them takes the bait," Cleo ventured.

"We can't be everywhere. Let's just stick to one at a time. Remember, this is a dangerous person," Josephine reminded them.

"I'd like to interview Fiona and see what she thinks Angus is doing," Pearl offered, "maybe she'll let something slip."

Eleanor woke up screaming, jumped off the couch, and began to hobble wildly through the house.

"What's wrong?" Angus called after her.

"Charley horse," was all she could get out. She began to moan.

"I know! Mustard is the remedy!" Angus hurried to the kitchen to get some mustard.

Dennis was just walking by when he heard the screaming and began frantically banging on the door. Feathers who was also startled out of a deep parrot sleep flew through the house squawking, "Murder, murder, most foul!"

Finally, after administering the mustard, Angus answered the door.

"Is everything allright here? It sounded like someone was being murdered." Dennis didn't wait for an invitation but barged right in looking for Eleanor.

Eleanor limped in with her hair askew, a teaspoon in her mouth, and a puckered look on her face. She did not love mustard on a spoon, but it did relieve the cramp.

"Charley horse," Eleanor explained. "Sorry if I disturbed the peace."

Eleanor woke to a dim, foggy morning. It's Thursday, July 13. She sighed and could think of nothing except that she had told Angus that she loved him. Something wasn't right. She got up and walked to the kitchen. She had not cleaned up after dinner. Feathers had not been put in his cage and flew freely through the house uttering words she could not understand. She fed him and cleaned the kitchen.

As she worked something troubled her as she played back the previous evening. She knew she had searched the couch for Frieda's manuscript. There was no way she would have missed it where Angus found it. Besides, it was out on the couch when Angus had interrupted her that day, and last night it was neatly in the folder. Somehow, Angus had taken it and returned it, hoping to fool her. There was no other explanation. Then she remembered he wasn't on the couch when she woke up with the cramp.

He had come out of the office.

Eleanor went into her office and took the manuscript out of the drawer. She flipped through the pages until she came to the sketch of the pink flowers and the pages that contained the formula. They were all there. Everything was as it should be, except where was Frieda's letter? Hadn't she left it inside the manuscript folder? Then she noticed the picture covering the wall safe was off. The safe was not locked and when Eleanor opened it, she found the vial was gone. There was an envelope addressed to Ellie. Eleanor opened it with dread and read:

*Dear Ellie,*

*Please forgive me. I had no right to invade your space or your life. I believe I could have been happy with you, but I don't think you could be happy with me. There is something dark and broken in me that pulled me into what I do, and as hard as I try, I cannot stop. Bringing you into my troubled world would never be acceptable to me, so I must leave yours. I'm so tired and sorry if I have caused you pain, but I know you, and you are better off without me. I love you, Ellie. —Angus*

Her mind raced. If Angus had read Frieda's letter and taken the vial, what did that mean? A cold chill ran over her from head to toe. She picked up the phone and dialed Angus' number. It rang several times, but no one answered. She fumbled through the telephone book and dialed the police.

"Hello, this is Eleanor Penrose. I need to speak to Officer McGraw. It's urgent."

"Mrs. Penrose, how can I help you?" Officer McGraw asked calmly.

"I've been trying to reach Angus McBride and he doesn't answer his phone. I'm worried that he may have had an accident. He was supposed to call me. Could you check on him?" Eleanor hoped she didn't sound like a possessive lover.

"No need, Mrs. Penrose. I talked to Angus this morning. He took his sister to the airport. He probably just forgot to tell you." Officer McGraw was very kind.

"Well, that's a relief." Eleanor felt foolish. "Thank you."

Eleanor hung up the phone and called Josephine. They made plans to meet at Dede's immediately.

By the time Eleanor arrived at Dede's house, the entire coffee group had assembled there. Eleanor decided it was time to tell them about the vial of poison and illicit their help in finding it.

"What do you think this means?" asked Eleanor who was relieved to know that Angus had not killed himself as she imagined. She let them see the farewell letter.

"Did you tell him you would marry him?" pried Josephine.

"No, but he got what he wanted and left. What I thought was a suicide note was just a breakup letter," Eleanor's voice cracked a little.

"Does this prove he is the serial killer or not?" asked Pearl.

"I'm not sure it proves anything. We still don't know where he went or if he'll be back." Dede reasoned.

"You could file a report with the police, Eleanor. He did break into your safe and steal the vial of poison," Cleo said in defense of her friend.

"He may have done me a favor," Eleanor said blinking back her unshed tears. "If someone found that vial in my house, they may have reasoned that I was the serial killer. There's no way I can go to the police and tell them my vial of traceless poison has been stolen by a consultant who is investigating homicide by poison."

"It's brilliant really," Josephine commented. "What do you suppose he'll do with it?"

"I think he and Fiona have gone to California. He told me she had friends that were like her and loyal to her. She's an intelligent woman who made her living developing drugs. She would understand the formula Frieda left and perhaps they can reproduce it, sell it, and make a fortune." Eleanor speculated.

"Great, he's not home. Let's go to his place and see if we can find the vial!" suggested Cleo. "There may be other clues there."

They all looked at each other and without words piled into Cleo's car and sped off to Angus' house.

"We may never know. He might not return, but he has so many ties here. The police don't seem to suspect him of being the serial killer. I think he'll be back," Dede said.

"Then we'd better hurry. How will we get inside?" asked Pearl as they parked around the corner.

"Pearl, you stay in the car. If he comes back, call Dede's cell phone," Josephine said.

The others got out of the car and quickly opened the gate and let themselves into the backyard where prying eyes could not see them.

They checked the back door, but it was locked. Cleo found the guest bedroom's window open. Fiona most likely suffered from hot flashes, too. It was quite a feat, but after several attempts, they managed to climb through the window with the help of a bench from the patio.

"Where would he put the vial?" wondered Josephine. "Have you ever been in his house, Eleanor?"

"Not recently," she whispered as if he might hear her.

"Come in here!" cried Dede.

They followed her voice to what appeared to be an office. On the desk were several files, but the most disturbing thing Dede had discovered was a list of suspects. The surprising name on it was Eleanor Penrose. Once they saw that they didn't notice the other name that should have given them a real clue to the identity of the killer, a name they all knew but which did not appear on Eleanor's list.

All of them looked at Eleanor as if waiting for an explanation. She didn't have one. For an instant she could see suspicion in their eyes, but then they moved on to investigate the files on the desk. There were several, including a dossier on every vet in the county. There was no way they could read them all.

Cleo began to open the desk drawers searching for the vial. Josephine checked behind every picture for a safe but found nothing. Dede had moved into the kitchen.

"Look at this," she laughed. "There is absolutely nothing in his refrigerator! As soon as he finds out you're not the serial killer, Eleanor, he'll be back for dinner."

Dede's phone began to ring at the same time they heard the garage door opening.

They hurried out the back sliding-glass door, slinked under every window, opened the yard gate and slowly walked down the sidewalk and around the corner. When they got in the car they were all shaking with adrenaline overload. Cleo quickly started the car and drove away.

"Oh my God!" Pearl prayed, "Let's never do that again. Did you find anything?"

"Oh yes," said Dede, "He thinks Eleanor is the serial killer. She was on his list of suspects."

"What about the vial?" Pearl persisted.

"Nothing," sighed Eleanor. "I can't believe Angus suspects me of murder."

"You suspect him," Josephine reminded her.

"I suspected him of using me to get the formula for Fiona. I never really believed he was the killer. Why would he suspect me? What have I done?" Eleanor was truly in distress.

"Gee, let's take a look at the facts," suggested Josephine. "First of all, you love Angus, you have a demented husband you think has cheated on you, and you have a vial of poison in your possession that can kill and leave no trace. I'm beginning to think he may be on to something."

"You think Angus thought I was planning to kill Walter?" Eleanor was shocked.

"If Angus knew about this poison, maybe he took it to kill Walter, because he wants you for himself," offered Cleo.

"We know neither Angus nor Eleanor is the killer," Pearl announced. "Angus knows how dangerous this poison is and must have taken it to protect you, Eleanor."

"Did he take Frieda's letter too?" asked Cleo.

"Yes, so now the only proof I have that it ever existed is the manuscript Frieda left, so why would he return that?" Eleanor was puzzled.

"It's just someone's memoirs. Maybe Angus never saw the formula and just thought it was Frieda's story and didn't want to destroy it," offered Dede.

"I'm positive Fiona told Angus about the poison. It was the reason Frieda left California. I told him about Fiona's betrayal. He must have confronted her and then needed to know what was in the memoir that might incriminate Fiona. When he didn't find anything, he returned it. Maybe he sent the vial with Fiona to have the formula verified," Eleanor said, repeating her earlier theory.

"However, this doesn't get us any closer to finding who is killing old people, and we aren't getting any younger," Cleo complained as they arrived at Dede's house.

"Let's have our coffee at my house tomorrow," suggested Eleanor. "We can look over the clues we have and try to see this with fresh eyes in the morning."

"I'd like to see Angus' note again too," said Josephine. "It may look different now that we know he suspects you, Eleanor."

The ladies got in their cars and drove their separate ways. None of them noticed the little green car parked across the street— watching.

Friday, July 14, Eleanor woke and remembered that Angus had taken the vial of poison. He knew about Frieda's formula and he suspected Eleanor of wanting to kill Walter. Fiona was in California possibly with the vial, Angus was done with her and she didn't blame him if he believed she was capable of murder. The coffee group was coming to her house this morning, so they could review what they knew about the serial killer, which wasn't much. Eleanor got up and got busy.

She made a big fruit salad and put on a pot of coffee. Dede was bringing an eggless casserole, Cleo offered to bring a bottle of Prosecco, Pearl was making her walnut walk-a-ways, and Josephine was squeezing fresh orange juice.

While she waited for her friends, she set the table and worked on the crossword puzzle while she cooed to Feathers who hovered over her watching her every move.

Eleanor was surprised when the doorbell rang early and even more surprised to see who stood on her doorstep.

"What a surprise, Nora! It isn't even Wednesday. Come in." Eleanor looked outside and saw Nora's little green car, but nothing else. She knew her friends would arrive soon. She thought about asking her to stay for breakfast but remembered what they planned to discuss and scrapped that idea.

"I baked these muffins and thought of you on my way to work," Nora said, looking around taking in the smell of freshly brewed coffee and the table set for company.

"That's very sweet. I don't know when you find the time to bake." Eleanor reached for the muffins. "I didn't start cooking until I retired. There was always so much to do. Really good cooking takes time and energy."

"Don't you want to sample them?" Nora seemed uneasy. "I really value your opinion."

Eleanor broke off a piece of muffin and put it in her mouth. It tasted off, but Eleanor didn't want to hurt Nora's feelings.

"Very tasty," she lied. "You're not thinking of opening up a bakery I hope. I don't know what I'd do without you. Would you like a cup of coffee?"

"That would be lovely," Nora said. She smiled and waited while Eleanor went to the kitchen for the coffee. "It's about time you did something for me. I'm sick and tired of slaving for you, you old bitch. All I do is clean up your filth and if that's not enough, I have to clean up after your dirty animals too. You're all the same—old, lazy, and good for nothing."

Eleanor returned with the coffee, but she didn't feel right. Her eyes wouldn't focus, and her legs could no longer hold her up. She tried to stay upright and not spill the coffee, but everything faded to dark and down.

That was when Nora went to work. She quickly cleaned up the spilled coffee and pulled Eleanor up off the floor and onto the couch. She posed her carefully so that she looked as though she were sitting naturally in her favorite spot. Just as she took out the syringe with the fatal dose of pentobarbital, Feathers swooped into the room squawking, "Murder, murder!" He landed on her head and dug in with his claws. The pain and surprise caused Nora to cry out and drop the syringe. In all the mayhem, she did not hear the coffee group open the door and she didn't see them take in the scene with horror on their faces, but she did feel the bottle of Prosecco land soundly on her head.

"Call 911," ordered Dede as she rushed to Eleanor to see if she was still breathing.

Pearl and Cleo literally sat on Nora who was out for the count. Josephine was on the phone with the 911 dispatch giving a detailed account of what to expect.

"We need an ambulance at 303 Sunset Avenue in Sand Beach. There is a 72-year-old woman with an overdose of pentobarbital and we also need the police. We think we have a serial killer unconscious due to a blow to the head." Josephine sounded so professional. "Hurry, please hurry."

Eleanor woke up later that day in the hospital. She did not know where she was but saw several familiar faces around her. She didn't feel bad but actually felt rested and refreshed.

"What happened?" she asked.

The familiar faces rushed to her bedside.

"She's awake!" Josephine cried.

"Thank, God," said Dede.

"How do you feel?" asked Cleo.

"I'll go get the doctor," Pearl offered.

"I feel fine. I just am a little disoriented. Why am I in the hospital?" Eleanor's memory was fuzzy.

"We'll tell you all about it after the doctor sees you," Dede promised.

They all gathered in the waiting room to tell Angus that Eleanor was awake. He was afraid he had let her down and didn't want to be the face she saw when she woke up.

"I don't deserve her," he murmured, "but I can't stay away."

"You two definitely have some issues to work out," Josephine noted, "but I think you do deserve each other."

"What happened to Nora?" asked Pearl.

"Did I kill her with that bottle?" Cleo was eager to know if she too was a killer.

"They took her to the emergency room and checked her out. Evidently there were some nasty claw marks as well as a concussion, but she'll live," Angus reported.

"Was she on your list of suspects?" Dede wanted to know just how good Angus was.

"Yes, she was one of many. We became suspicious of her after Mrs. Potts died. Most of her victims were people she cleaned for, some on a regular basis, others hit and miss. That was what threw us off. Then we found out she also cleaned for Mercedes and had access to her clinic where she helped herself to the pentobarbital.

Officer McGraw found a supply of it in her house along with some very hateful journals. Nora was an angry woman. She documented most of her kills. It won't be difficult to convict her."

"Wow, and I was always so envious of people with housekeepers." Cleo felt as though she had dodged a bullet. "I wonder if Eleanor will hire someone else or just clean her own house after this."

"You can be sure when Eleanor hires a housekeeper, they will be thoroughly vetted before they are allowed inside her home again." Josephine had no doubt Angus would take care of that.

"Nora was always so sweet," Pearl remarked, "I never would have guessed. What happened?"

"She's been at work for some time, probably killing old people for years without anyone ever suspecting her. Killing their pets was something that started recently and pretty much caused law enforcement to look at the deaths differently. She'll undergo an intensive evaluation. After that we'll know what triggered it, but right now I wouldn't want to speculate," Angus commented.

"I wonder how she knew about the Maude Squad. Do you think she was responsible for the personal ads in the newspaper?" questioned Cleo.

"Nora cleaned for Eva Long and probably overheard her talking about it with her friends, then used the ads to throw suspicion on to the mysterious Maude Squad. It will all come out in time," Angus reassured them.

"I suppose she was able to get into their houses because they trusted her with their hidden keys," guessed Pearl.

"Yes, unlike some who just climb through the window." Angus pointed his remark directly at Pearl.

"I have no idea what you are talking about," Pearl responded innocently. She had not climbed through any windows. She had been the lookout inside the car.

"You left the bench under the open window. Your fingerprints were all over the refrigerator. Were you hungry?" Angus tried to look stern but there was a twinkle in his eyes as he looked at each of them in turn. How could he be angry with friends who had saved the woman he loved?

Dede looked especially guilty. She knew it would be her prints on the refrigerator and could see the headlines, **Waterton Mayor Found Guilty of Breaking and Entering.** She quickly turned away and began looking at some magazines.

"I'm hungry now," Cleo said, thinking about her missed breakfast. "We should go back to Eleanor's and make sure Feathers is okay. Then we can eat."

"Why don't you ladies go get dinner? Don't go to Eleanor's. It's a crime scene. We still don't know what Eleanor ate that was drugged." Angus spoke with authority. "I'll take care of Feathers. Eleanor will need to give a statement now that she's awake. I believe you have already given your account of the events."

Eleanor's doctor appeared, and the group gathered to hear his assessment.

"She's very lucky. She ingested just enough pentobarbital to knock her out. There doesn't seem to be any negative side effects other than some bruising from the fall. We'll keep her overnight for observation and most likely send her home tomorrow."

"Thank you," Angus said, "May I talk to her now?"

"Of course, she was a little confused upon waking but that won't last long," the doctor reassured them and walked away.

"Will she be able to get into her house by tomorrow, Angus? Or will she need to make other arrangements?" Pearl questioned.

"Forensics should be finished tomorrow, but she shouldn't be there alone. Are you ladies up for a sleepover?" Angus seemed amused by the thought.

"Angus, tell Eleanor we'll be back soon," said Josephine, and with that they left Angus to deal with an uncomfortable situation.

"Hi Ellie," Angus spoke softly as he entered her room. She looked small and fragile in the hospital bed.

"Is this an official visit, Detective McBride?" Eleanor was no longer confused. "If it is, I'd like to file a complaint. Someone broke into my house and took something irreplaceable from my safe."

Angus flinched inwardly, "What was taken?" he asked dreading her response.

My heart, she thought, but what she said was, "A gift from a dear friend."

Angus crossed the room to her side and took her hand, "I'm sorry, Ellie, once I knew what you had, I couldn't ignore the risk to you. If that vial or Frieda's letter was ever found in your possession, you could be implicated in a multitude of crimes. Just having that substance was a crime."

"Did you seriously think I would use it on Walter?" Eleanor was indignant.

He paused, "Maybe not Walter, but Alice for sure."

Eleanor's surprised expression said it all. Killing Walter was never an option. The thought of killing Alice had never occurred to her although she might have wished her dead. Eleanor wondered if he could be right. Perhaps in time she could have been tempted to use the drug for evil. It wasn't just Angus, but everyone had a dark side. Josephine often referred to it as the shadow self.

"I warned you about the dark inside of me. It's what made me a good detective and probably a bad friend. I've tried to stay away from you, Ellie, because I didn't want that darkness infecting the way you see things, but I can't. I'm drawn to you like a moth to a flame."

Eleanor was touched. He was poetic even though a little corny. She squeezed his hand in response because she didn't trust her voice.

"If you don't file a complaint against me, I won't file one against your friends for breaking and entering. I'm fairly certain I've got the mayor's fingerprints on my refrigerator."

When Eleanor smiled, Angus knew he had a shot.

Officer McGraw poked his head into the room, "I hate to interrupt, but are you feeling up to making a statement, Mrs. Penrose?"

Eleanor nodded.

"If you have no objections I'll go get the hero who saved the day," Angus said as he left.

Eleanor had no idea what he meant and looked to Officer McGraw with a puzzled expression, "What happened? Who is the hero he's talking about?"

"Just tell me what you remember." Officer McGraw didn't want to influence her in any way.

Eleanor told him what she remembered and then dozed off again. When she woke, Dede, Josephine, Cleo, and Pearl filled her in on the events she missed while being the victim of a serial killer. Needless to say, they came out looking very brave and heroic in their dramatic recap.

Eleanor opened her eyes. It was Friday, July 21. She was home. There was no threat of a serial killer. It was coffee day. This afternoon she would get her hair done and pack for her trip to France. She felt good. She was alive, and she was happy.

She got out of bed and immediately greeted Feathers who was now her personal hero.

"I love you, Ellie," he parroted Walter's voice.

"I love you too."

On her way to the Boat House, Eleanor wondered what the group would talk about this week. Without a serial killer to catch, it might be a very boring conversation.

She drove into the parking lot at the same time as Pearl and Cleo. Josephine was already inside.

"You look great," Cleo told Eleanor. "Maybe there's something to be said for getting some extra sleep. How do you feel?"

"Good, lucky, grateful to have friends to save my life now and again." Eleanor reiterated her gratitude.

"We were all lucky Angus didn't turn us in for breaking and entering. You know he's going to hold that over my head for a long time." Dede had arrived in time to hear the last part of Eleanor's thank you. "I'll probably have to cook for him while you're gone."

"You have no idea. I think he plans to have all of you decorating his beach house while I'm away as well," Eleanor predicted.

"Have you worked things out then?" Josephine pried.

"Absolutely, I can't blame him for being who he is, and we were both equally suspicious of each other. It might take a little time to earn back the trust we've lost, but I think he's worth it. He's offered to keep Feathers and take him to visit Walter while we're in France," Eleanor explained.

"How long will you be away?" Pearl asked.

"I have to be back to testify against Nora, and Bootsy has school, so about four weeks. It's a long time for Bootsy to be away from her parents but they think it's the gift of a lifetime, and she's absolutely over the moon. There are only a couple of years between her and my youngest grandchild, so hopefully they'll all get along. We plan to stay with them at a French villa and travel from there. I'm looking forward to seeing those rascals and experiencing everything through their young eyes."

"That sounds wonderful," Josephine remarked.

"Feathers may have a new vocabulary when you get back," Dede warned. "I can already hear him saying, 'I love you, Ellie,' in Angus' voice."

"What happened to Frieda's recipe for dying?" Cleo queried.

"Angus claims Fiona destroyed it." Eleanor rolled her eyes. "Don't worry, Cleo, I think I know what the secret ingredient is, and I know where to get it."

A mysterious silence settled over the table.

"Not to change the subject, but have I ever told you about my first husband?" asked Josephine.

Eyebrows went up and each of them leaned in to listen.

"Do you need him killed?" whispered Cleo. "I'm pretty good with a bottle of Prosecco."

If you enjoyed
**A RECIPE for DYING,**
you'll want to follow Eleanor,
Feathers, and the rest of the gang
in the Coastal Coffee Club series,
Coming Soon from GladEye Press
Fiction.

- Visit www.gladeyepress.com for fantastic deals on these and other GladEye Press titles.
- Follow us on Facebook: https://www.facebook.com/ GladEyePress/
- All GladEye titles can also be ordered online or from your local book store.

## About the Author

Patricia Brown was born in Oregon City, Oregon, and was educated at Oregon State University, graduating with a degree in elementary education, a career she pursued for 28 years. She lives in a small town on the Oregon coast with her husband where she dabbles in the arts and enjoys the company of family and friends. This is her first novel.

# Acknowledgments

Of course, my thanks go out to every literary teacher I ever had, my friends and family who endured my endless chatter about the book and provided fodder for my pen, especially Suzanne Weber, Kathryn Christensen, and April Petersen, my first readers who inspired and encouraged me.

A special thank you to my publishers, J.V. Bolkan and Sharleen Nelson at GladEye Press, who took a chance on me. And my husband, David, whose clever quotes appear without end as the voice of lovers and parrot.

# ALSO FROM GLADEYE PRESS

Available for purchase at: www.gladeyepress.com and wherever fine books are sold.

### The Time Tourists, A Novel
Sharleen Nelson
DANGER. ROMANCE. TIME TRAVEL . . .
Step into time with Imogen Oliver in this first book in the Dead Relatives, Inc. series as she investigates a young girl who ran away from home with her boyfriend in 1967 and never returned, and then travels back to the turn of the 20th century to locate a set of missing stereoscopic glass plates with a mysterious connection to her own life.

### Teaching in Alaska
### What I Learned in the Bush
Julie Bolkan
Among the first outsiders to live and work with the Yup'ik in their small villages, this book tells Julie's story of how she survived the culture clashes, isolation, weather, and her struggles with honey buckets—a candid and often funny account of one *gussock* woman's 12 years in the Alaskan bush.

### 10 Takes: Pacific Northwest Writers
### Perspectives on Writing
Jennifer Roland
From novelists to poets to playwrights, Jennifer Roland interviews a variety of authors who have one thing in common—they have all chosen to make the Pacific Northwest their home.

### Washington's Festivals, Fairs & Celebrations
Janaya Watne
Northwest native and fierce outdoorswoman, Janaya Watne has written an information-packed exploration of Washington's vibrant festival calendar. Tourists as well as the well-established who are looking to find the perfect week, weekend, or one-day trip will enjoy this handy guide.

GladEye
Press

CPSIA information can be obtained
at www.ICGtesting.com
Printed in the USA
FFHW01n1555300618
47251244-50114FF